Natio   :e

Comedic retrospectives from the national service years

Jim Green

Contents

Message from Number 10

Having been deemed unfit to undertake training for any of the various trades on offer to national servicemen conscripted during the nineteen fifties, Aircraftsmen Second Class Harrison and Albright had been stuck in the pool flight of their square-bashing camp in Shropshire for some weeks.

They met up for the first time at the appraisal interview two days prior to being allocated a permanent posting.

'Useless, shiftless, idle and unemployable,' was the curt assessment of the perspiring, grossly overweight warrant officer in charge of pool flight. 'You're a shower of bollocks, fit only for latrine duties. Even then I'd think hard before using any crapper you'd worked on because I'd probably catch a dose of something very unpleasant up my rear end'.

And with one that size, thought AC2 Harrison, he could do himself a right mischief.

*

On their first day at RAF Padgate, and with an unconcealed lack of enthusiasm, 'Ginger' Harrison and his new oppo 'Sticky' Albright were sluicing out the lavatories adjacent to Hut 29.

Ginger was a beefy, thickset youth with an unruly crop of bright carrot red hair. His companion was tall, lean, angular, and carried himself in an awkward, loping self-conscious gait.

'Crap job this,' said Ginger as he carelessly threw half a bucket of ice cold water over the walls of an empty cubicle, drenching both seat and toilet paper; for the occupants, for the use of.

'I'm a tradesman, me'

'Oh aye, what's yer trade then?'

'Joiner, brickie, sparks. Whatever's on offer like,' replied Ginger who was set to attack another unsuspecting cubicle with the remains of his bucket. He stopped in mid motion and looked quizzically at his workmate. 'Why do they call you Sticky?'

'I was apprentice to a plasterer'

'Proves me point then, two qualified tradesmen stuck in a stinking bog when –

Sticky interrupted him to point out, 'Ah weren't qualified like'

'Well, as near as like it,' Ginger continued brightly. 'Never mind, it's Friday, early closing. Wonder what the grub's like over the weekend in this dump? Diabolic most likely; it always is over weekends'

'Ah'm not bothered. Going home to me mam's fer some decent chuck'

'Good cook is she?'

'Great. For Sunday dinner she'll 'ave roast beef, Yorkshire pudden, 'horseradish, baked spuds, sprouts, carrots, and for afters, spotted dick, custard, and –'

'Don't. I'll be stuck here with cold greasy bacon sannies'

'Come home with me if ye like'

'Would that be okay?' enthused Ginger. 'I mean, what about your mam?'

'She loves having visitors. She'll be over the moon ah've brought a mate home.' Sticky reflected for a moment then enquired for confirmation, 'We are mates, aren't we?'

'Course we are'

'You'll come with me then?'

'You're on pal. Where do you live?'

'Skelmeresdale'

'How long is the train journey?'

'Can't afford the rail fare, ah'm hitching''

'Hitching be bolloxed; takes too long over a weekend, there and back. How much brass have you got?'

Sticky fumbled around in his hip pocket and produced a single crumpled note and some assorted coinage. 'Seventeen an' a tanner'

'Right, we'll find out where the orderly room is'

'You what?'

'The orderly room, 'explained Ginger patiently, 'where we'll find the fixer; ten bob should do it. You'll have some left over for us beer and fags'

Sticky looked perplexed, scratched the top of his head nervously and replied, 'Ah don't rightly know what you mean'

'Leave it all to me. Every camp has a fixer, usually a bent clerk in the orderly room who can get you anything at a price' He opened a window and bellowed loudly to a passing airman, 'Hey sprog, where's the orderly room in this gaff?'

Ginger's outburst startled the airman who pointed to the insignia on his sleeve and riposted huffily, 'Look here, can't you see, I'm a senior aircraftsman'

'SAC, oh yeah? We all know what that means; soft and cuddly. Just tell us where the chuffing orderly room is at, pillock'

Acting Corporal Leonard 'Smudger' Jacobi was seated at his desk taking a telephone call when there was a rattle on the window facing him. He looked up to observe two airmen, the burlier of whom was beckoning his attention. Smudger ignored them and continued with his call until another more abrasive rattle caused him to take heed and end his conversation abruptly.

He opened the window and said, 'Where's the fire?'

'Are you the clerk what deals with travel warrants?' enquired Ginger.

'I'm Corporal Jacobi what deals with travel warrants'

'I'm Ginger Harrison and my mate Sticky 'ere wants one, from the bottom of the pile like'

Smudger looked around cautiously from left, right and behind him.

'Cost you two quid with a leave pass thrown in'

'Ah've only got but ten bob,' pleaded Sticky.

'Then you won't be getting a travel warrant, AC2 Plonk'

Ginger leant forward, grabbed Smudger by his battledress lapels and pulled the astonished face up close to his own. 'Give him it for ten bob or I'll smash your lights in'

'All right already, alright. Enough with the violence; put me down.' Ginger released his grip and although Smudger was shaken, he contrived to conceal his apprehension by smoothing out imaginary creases in his uniform and straightening the lapels. 'Okay, okay,' he continued as he was regaining his composure, 'I'll do him a deal. Ten bob for the warrant and he can owe me for the leave pass'

'He'll owe you nowt,' replied Ginger. 'You'll give him both for ten bob'

Smudger considered the lesser of the two evils; being shafted for a few shillings or beaten up. 'Right, ten bob it is.' He went back to his desk, sat down, unlocked and opened the bottom right hand drawer from which he withdrew two pads.

As he was doing this, Sticky whispered to Ginger, 'What about your warrant?'

'Name, rank, serial number,' asked Smudger who rapidly committed to paper the details provided, tore off the top copy from each of the pads, stuffed them loosely in an envelope which he slung through the window in Sticky's direction. He was returning the pads to his desk drawer when Ginger announced,

'I'll have one and all'

Smudger was rattled. 'Why didn't you say that before? Look we're closing in an hour or so and I've still got lots to do. Name, rank and serial number'

As even more rapidly he completed the transaction, he complained, 'I don't know why I bother. I'm up for demob next week and I've got a debtors list as long as the camp barber's pole. Now I'm being forced to give the stuff away –

'Hold up,' interrupted Ginger. 'Do you mean blokes around here owe you?'

'Over one hundred pounds; it's like drawing teeth. They're quick on the draw with promises but slow on coughing up when I ask for the cash'

'And you're getting demobbed next week?

'I've just told you haven't I?'

'You'll need to get your cash in then'

'Fat chance, I'll have to write it off'

'No you won't. Give us a list and I'll get your brass in, first thing Monday. I used to be a part time debt collector for a bookie and he never had no complaints'

'I wouldn't want any violence,' cautioned Smudger.

'There'll be no punch-ups. I'll just lean on them, gentle like. Go on, get your list out'

Smudger went back to the bottom drawer, withdrew a piece of paper, studied the contents and passed the list to Ginger. 'Don't flash this around the camp,' he warned.

'Don't worry mate. Oh, by the way, I'll have my warrant for nowt. You can deduct it from all commission you'll be paying me when I bring your brass in'

Monday morning arrived all too soon, and in its coming, brought with it Ginger and Sticky disconsolately trudging their way back to base from Padgate railway station. As they approached the brow of a rather tiresome hill, Ginger aimed a venomous kick at an empty can lying in the pavement. It flew into the air, fell back down like a dead duck and ricocheted off the freshly painted front door of a nearby house.

Seconds later a Panama hatted head followed by gloved hands clutching a set of trimmers popped up from behind a hedge top. The head had a dog collar around its neck.

'What on earth do you think you're playing at?' enquired the dog collar sternly.

'Sorry padre; didn't know it was your house,' apologised Ginger cheerfully and without contrition.

'That's quite bedside the point, you might have injured someone. I'm going to report you to your commanding officer, Wing Commander Barclay. He is a member of my flock. What's your name, airman?'

'Arbuthnot Fishporter'

'And the name of your accomplice,' added the vicar unreasonably.

'Bernard Billingsgate'

'Right, I'll make a note of that when I get indoors. You'll find yourself in deep waters over this outrage'

'Suit yourself your reverence,' replied Ginger unconcerned as he indicated to the open-mouthed Sticky to follow him on and over the hill.

'Dozy old pillock'

'That's not nice, Ginge, him being a holy man an' all'

As they commenced their descent, Ginger announced, 'We should get ourselves a bit of a racket like Smudger'

'Eh?'

'At the latrines like'

'Doin' what?'

'Charging the sprogs for use of the usual offices; penny a

piss, tuppence a dump'

Sticky regarded Ginger with a look of horror.

'Relax. I'm pulling your leg mate'

They were silent for a few minutes and then Sticky stopped, put down his tattered weekend case and speculated, 'What about we fix up one o' the showers a bit an' charge' them to use it? Me dad's got an old shower rail and curtain in the shed and me mam'd borrow us some of her scented soap'

Ginger considered the suggestion for a moment and then dismissed it.

'Naw, showers are too fancy for them scruffs. A zinc tub at the fire, a big bar o' carbolic and a wire arse scrubber is what they'd reckon as luxury'

This was the first day of the last week of Smudger Jacobi's eighteen months of national service. It had been good fun by and large and he didn't regret a minute of it but now as discharge day loomed closer, he couldn't wait for his release.

He had some business to get out of the way first though, and in the main that centred around the induction of his replacement, Senior Aircraftsman Simpkins, a laconic young man who had a shifty Uriah Heep look about him. Smudger's initial priority of the day was as ever the issuing, copying and distribution of station orders, on completion of which task he spent the rest of the morning running through the required procedures for running an efficient orderly room. It was just going on noon when his immediate superior, Flight Sergeant Quirk, visited the office.

'Getting set for the off then corporal?'

'Yes flight,' replied Smudger.

'Got your piss-up organised?'

'The biggest this camp will ever see'

'Records up to date, no shite lying around for me to fall arse over tits into after you've shoved off for Civvy Street?'

'No flight, everything shipshape and bristol fashion'

'Good. And your man here,' Quirk nodded in the direction of Simpkins without affording the newcomer as much as a glance. 'Is he genned up?'

'About half way through his induction, flight; we'll be finished by four-thirty'

'By the way corporal, have you seen my bike lying around anywhere?'

'No, no I haven't'

'Damn thing seems to have disappeared. I'm almost sure I rode it back from the mess last night. Better make sure you lock up everything before you leave this afternoon. There's been a spate of thefts around the camp lately and we don't want no sticky fingered tea leafs helping themselves to His Majesty's stationery, do we?'

'No chance. You know me flight'

'Yes, I'll give you that lad. Twelve months in charge here and not so much as a sheet of bum paper unaccounted for. Pay heed SAC Simpkins and do likewise'

When the flight sergeant had departed Simpkins observed icily, 'Sarky old sod'

'Flight S'r'nt Quirk? Naw, he's okay when you get to know him. Went out with a bird last night, spent half a week's wages on her, and came back home without as much as a goodnight kiss. Now, to sum up,' Smudger gestured to the mounds of neatly stacked pads that all but filled the three steel filing cabinets facing them. 'This is your empire, your stock-in-trade, your Aladdin's Cave, your Gussie -'

'You what, what did you say?'

'Gussie, Great Universal Stores'

'Oh...'

'Every conceivable type of official form for RAF personnel, for the use of; requisition order pads for Form treble O, for wiping the arse or the wanking of; Form 1250 for the identification of; Form 250 for the charging of; Form 295 for taking the leave of; Form 121 for service records, for the falsifying of. Excused duty chits and sick notes for the skiving of, officer commissions for the wangling of, postings for the arranging of at a price, passionate leave dispensations for the randy of –'

'Don't you mean compassionate leave?'

'No, I don't mate. But we got those too'

'Oh'

'Every form every conscript ever needs to get his time in. And now,' Smudger unlocked the bottom right hand drawer of his desk, opened it, and gazed lovingly at the contents. 'Here is where it's at mate, here is where you'll make your fortune; ration books, clothing coupons, sweet coupons, commendations, discharge papers - and your biggest profit centre; travel warrants. Guard them with your life mate, show them to no one, always keep them under lock and key, and give out no freebies to no fucker. If you do, you're in dead lumber. Look after these little darlings and they'll look after you'

'About the black market side -'

'Never ever refer to the business in those terms cock,' interrupted Smudger forcefully, 'or some tosser of an officer will catch on and fry your bollocks for breakfast. Convenience store, that's what you're buying. That's what the bods call it. When someone's making plans to nip back home for a bit of nookie, they tell their mates 'I'm off up the convenience store'. They all know what that means. He's coming to see you for a travel warrant and some pussy bait'

'What?'

'Clothing coupons'

'Why do you call it a convenience store?

'Because you'll be open for business twenty-four hours a day, every day'

'Should I be taking notes?'

'No, write nothing down, no time, never. Keep it all in your head. Anyway, I can give you the entire marketing strategy in a few brief words. Service His Majesty's requirements from the top,' Smudger pointed to the piles of pads in the filing cabinets and then indicating the contents of the drawer, he added, 'Service your private customers from the bottom. That's all there is to it'

'Eh?'

'It's simple. When I took charge here twelve months ago I discovered that there's no backtracking system at HMSO where all this stuff comes from. So, for all those forms I knew I could sell under the counter, I requisitioned sufficient quantities to last beyond the time you and I are picking up the old age pension. On His Majesty's requirements drawn from the top, any discrepancies can be spotted within hours. On your personal customer requirements drawn from the bottom, nothing irregular will come to light until the year two thousand and frozen stiff. Savvy? Pads start with serial number 00001950 for official authorisations and 00002000 for unofficial'

'Fancy...'

'Got your two hundred and fifty oncers handy mate?'

Simpkins produced a wad of ten-pound notes, which Smudger snatched from him, and then one by one, he held several of the notes up to the light for closer inspection.

'What are you doing?'

'Checking for fakes; you'll get a lot of Mickey Mouse money coming your way in this business. It's okay; they're kosher - so far.' He regarded Simpkins suspiciously and said, 'How did you come by the geld?'

'Got it from my dad; he was a quartermaster in the RAMC during the war'

'Ah well then, he would know better than anyone what a good investment you're making'

'That's what he reckoned.' Simpkins walked over to the desk and looked into the bottom right hand drawer. 'What do I charge for the under-the-counter stuff?'

'Up to you mate- but don't get too greedy. On travel warrants, if you're talking a return journey of say six hundred miles, thirty bob to two quid is the going rate, depending on how you grade the schmuck. You got no overheads, so settle for what you can get'

'Doesn't Quirk ever get suspicious?'

'Naw, he pisses up big time, day and night; gets through a case of Glenmorange every week. He signed up for thirty years after some old tart walked out on him and he's been commiserating with himself ever since'

'How can he afford a case of whisky every week?'

'He can't. I give it him to keep his eyes closed and his trap shut'

'How do you manage that?'

'Easy. I have a deal with a sergeant in the stores section,

I'll introduce you to him later and you can keep the arrangement going so as to keep Quirk soft and sweet. It works like this, he gives me booze in bulk, and I give him travel warrants in bulk. Good, eh?'

'Isn't that all a bit risky?' Simpkins was having second thoughts about the deal they had just sealed and Smudger sensed his anxiety. He moved in quickly to allay the buyer's fears.

'You want to be in business to make big bunce on the side, easy money - right?

'Well…yeah'

'Okay then, to be successful in a business where the profit is high, like up the wall and through the roof, you have to take the odd risk or two. But look at it this way. Who'll be taking the bigger risk, the stores sergeant or you? The SIB can count all his cases of booze but how can they count travel warrants that don't officially exist? Savvy?'

*

At four thirty-five Smudger and Simpkins were walking back to their respective billets when a bicycle approached from the direction facing them. The rider was Ginger and his control of the machine was erratic in the extreme. He stopped and, still seated on the saddle with one foot on the ground for support, pulled out from a pocket of his battledress top a bundle of notes, which he handed to Smudger.

'Here's your wedge then mate. Have a count of it and then you can settle up with me'

Smudger counted the notes with the rapidity of someone used to handling cash, and remarked appreciatively, 'Ninety-four quid. I'd never have believed it possible'

'Three on your list are on leave. I'll nobble them when they get back'

'Keep whatever you can screw out of them,' offered Smudger gratuitously. 'I won't be here to collect'

'Ta muchly. Well then, me usual rate is fifteen per cent but what with this and the free warrant, I'll cut it back to ten'

'Five'

'Seven and a half'

'Done'

Smudger paid off Ginger, put the rest of the cash away and enquired, 'Where did you get the bike Ginger?'

'Borrowed it from behind the Sergeants Mess'

'The old bugger must have been really pissed last night'

'You what?'

'It belongs to my flight sergeant. You'd better ditch it smartish'

'Like fuck I will. I sold it to one of your debtors this morning'

'So how come you're still riding it?'

'Borrowed it back like'

*

The dawn of Thursday broke in a heavy downpour and the inclemency increased in tandem with the passing hours and progressively darkening skies; everyone venturing outdoors in RAF Padgate that day wore a groundsheet and had the lugs of their forage caps pulled out to avert the cold rain dripping into ears and down the neck.

Thursday was also demob day minus one for Smudger but he was impervious to the weather conditions, warm and snug as he was in his final bout of duty in the orderly room. He was also making good use of his replacement SAC Simpkins whom he dispatched at regular intervals on numerous assignments around the camp, assignments he would normally have undertaken himself as they would have afforded opportunities to indulge in a variety of unofficial but rewarding bits of business. Now all of that was at an end and Simpkins was too thick to be entrusted with what Smudger knew about how to make really big money in any RAF base, anywhere in the world.

The door burst open and ushered in a blast of icy cold air and a rain sodden Simpkins dripping pools of water on the floor from his groundsheet.

'It's pissing down out there,' he announced unnecessarily.

'Really, I hadn't noticed,' replied Smudger without looking up from his desk. 'I wouldn't stand there flooding out the room if I were you. Better dry it up with the mop in the cupboard. Quirk will be here in a few minutes on his morning skive'

'Met that bloke Ginger and his mate; they heard about your demob piss-up and asked if it would be okay if they came along'

'What did you say?'

'I said it'd probably be okay'

'And so it is, the more the merrier. Now get mopping'

*

Going on nine-thirty, Smudger, Ginger and Sticky linked arms as they staggered back to camp on the short journey from The Farmers Arms.

'Stand by your beds,' sang out Ginger lustily.

'Here comes the Air Vice Marshal,' contributed Sticky.

'He's got lots of rings,' added Smudger.

'But he's only got one arsehole,' concluded Ginger.

As they went through the main gates and past the guardhouse, they were called to a halt by the duty sergeant. Fortunately for the unruly threesome, he was a long time beneficiary of Smudger's extramural activities.

'What have we here then, the three caballeros?'

'Aw, c'mon sarge,' protested Smudger, 'it's my last night here'

'I know it is lad, and if it were anyone else, you and your mates would be spending it in the cells. Now, get on with you and keep the noise down'

'Come with me,' said Smudger after they'd walked on a dozen or so yards, 'and we'll have a night cap with my charges in Hut 47. I promised them all a drink before I turn in'

'Where'll you get booze at this time of night?' enquired Ginger.

'I've got some stashed away in my locker'

'Do you bunk up with the lads then?' enquired Sticky.

'Naw, I've got my own little room at the head of the billet'

'Don't you know owt Sticky,' said Ginger with a playfully sarcastic edge to his voice. 'Who do you think lives in the little room at the top of our billet, Santa Claus?'

'Me dad says, never sup at home,' cautioned Sticky.

'Miserable old git,' assessed Smudger.

'Aye,' added Ginger. 'That's why his missus never lets him have no how's-your-father'

'You what?'

They were hardly in the door of Hut 47 when one of the inmates announced,

'Have you heard the news corp?'

'It can wait until I get the booze out'

Smudger departed and Sticky whispered to Ginger, 'Isn't that the bloke you asked directions of to the orderly room?'

Ginger looked to where Sticky was indicating and recognised the SAC who had taken exception to his abrasive request for directions.

'Yeah, that's him, sniffy sod'

'Right then, what's this news you can't wait to tell me?' asked Smudger as he came back into the billet laden with assorted bottles of beer and spirits.

'Clement Atlee's coming on the wireless in a few minutes,' volunteered the aforementioned SAC, 'with an announcement regarding the Korean War and national service'

'Well, good fucking luck to him mate, it don't affect me no more, I'm off out of it first thing in the morning'

'Don't be too sure. It might still affect you Corporal Jacobi,' sniffed the SAC.

'No fucking way. My kitbag is packed and – '

'Shush, here he comes now,' said another airman.

Someone turned up the volume on the tannoy system just in time to hear a plummy BBC accent enunciate, 'We are going over now to Number Ten Downing Street for a special announcement from the Prime Minister, Mr

Clement Atlee...

"*I am speaking to you from the cabinet room at Number Ten Downing Street on a matter of grave national importance. Due to escalating hostilities in the Korean War, His Majesty's Government has decided that as from midnight tonight, all national servicemen in the Army, the Royal Air Force, the Royal Navy and the Fleet Air Arm, will have a further six months added to their period of conscription...*"

'Fucking hell!' shouted an astonished airman.

'Bastard,' reckoned another.

'What did he say?' asked Sticky

'Belt up,' replied Ginger.

'Does it mean more pay?' enquired someone else hopefully.

'Fuck off,' snarled his mate.

'Did you get that Smudger?' Ginger asked. 'Your demob is up the kyber'

'Doesn't affect me mate, it's only for sprogs coming in'

'It's chuffing not. It's for everyone,' contradicted Ginger.

'Not for me, it isn't, my discharge papers are in my pocket'

'Yeah, but they don't get signed until tomorrow, do they?'

'So what?'

'So, they won't be getting bloody signed now, that's what'

'Gerroff, hey sarge,' pleaded Smudger to the patrol watch sergeant who'd just entered the room. 'That's bollocks, isn't it? I'm still okay for demob aren't I'

'Sorry corporal, Clem Atlee's got you by the short and curlies. It applies to everyone. You're gonna be with us for another six months and there's nowt you can do about it'

Smudger departed to his lonely little room in despair and Ginger went outdoors to relieve himself. When he returned he handed the SAC a glass announcing,

'No hard feelings mate, have a cocktail on me'

'Oh,' said the SAC, taken aback by Ginger's unexpected generosity.

'Thing is, I never drink strong liquor'

'You're all right, it's mainly mineral water'

'Oh well, thanks awfully'

As the SAC delicately sipped his free drink, Sticky turned to Ginger and remarked, 'That were right nice of you'

'What?'

'Giving him a cocktail like'

'Oh, it's cocktail okay, I slashed in the glass while I was in the bog'

Witness for the defence

Ginger and Sticky were swabbing the latrine floors when Corporal Tilley arrived to enquire, 'Which one of you pricks locked up the stores hut last night?'

'Me,' volunteered Sticky. 'It were me'

'Well you couldn't have because some thieving sods   . cleared it out overnight'

'Maybe they broke in' suggested Ginger.

'They didn't have to; it was unlocked. They just walked straight in and helped themselves to the entire bleeding contents. I'll have to put you on a fizzer Albright and you'll be up before the flight commander tomorrow. You'll get fourteen days jankers for sure'

'But corp,' protested Ginger, 'Sticky goes on leave at the end of the week'

'No he don't; not now he don't. He'll be too busy clearing out the cookhouse shit for the next fortnight'

*

Back at the billet that evening Sticky was bemoaning his misfortune when Ginger came up with an idea. 'I'll be your witness. I'll say I saw you lock the door'

Sticky brightened up but had his hopes dashed just as quickly when Spider Greenhalgh cautioned, 'I'd think twice about that Ginger. They'll ask you to swear an oath on the bible and if Sticky is found guilty, you'll go down as well – but for much longer'

'How come?' asked Ginger.

'Because swearing on the bible when you're lying gets you twelve months in the glasshouse guaranteed'

'Maybe you could say you was Jewish,' suggested Sticky.

'Do I look like Jewish?' replied Ginger indignantly.

'Wouldn't make any difference,' said the knowledgeable Spider, 'they'd just hand you a Jewish bible to take the oath on'

Ginger thought for a moment or two and pondered, 'What about them sects you read about in the newspapers? They're for nutters I reckon, so one of them would do me. Do you know any Spider?'

Spider also reflected before replying, 'The Rosicrucians'

'You what?'

'Rosicrucians. They're a closed sect'

'And they don't have to swear on the bible?'

'I wouldn't think so'

'That's it then. I'm a Rosicrucian'

'If you say that, they'll just find a Book of Common Prayer and ask you to take the oath on that,' advised the unrelenting Spider.

'But us Rosicrucians don't go in for common prayer books'

'Makes no odds mate, they'll still shove one up your nose'

'What's that book lying on your bed Spider?'

Spider picked up the paper-front manual in question, flicked through the pages, and replied, 'Old Moore's Almanac. Why d'you ask?'

'Because I'd swear on one of them'

Spider laughed as he threw the book back on top of his bed. 'You're losing it Ginger. Almanacs only contain predictions, most of which are a load of bollocks'

'That's okay then, I'll swear on a load o' bollocks.

*

Occupying most of the rickety stacking chairs in the Spartan waiting room, disparate doleful airmen comprised the supporting cast for the day's courtroom drama. Ginger nudged one of them roughly and instructed, 'Bunch up sprog'

'Ouch, that hurt,' protested the startled recruit who was up on a charge for a sloppy kit turnout, and that after only three days service. He was feeling sorry for himself but Ginger was in no mood for dishing out sympathy.

'Would you like another?'

'No'

'Then shove up'

The door opened and in walked a sight to terrify the already highly-strung Sticky Albright. It was Sergeant Jordan, the NCO in charge of station orderlies. As ever, the peak of his cheese cutter cap was pulled down in line with his bushy eyebrows, his waxed moustache bristled, his boots and brasses gleamed, and the creases in his uniform were razor sharp. The very appearance of Sergeant Jordan even at a range of one hundred yards across the drill square was enough to send beads of cold sweat trickling down Sticky's spine. Now he was petrified.

With hands clasped behind his back and swagger stick clenched between upper right arm and torso, Jordan strutted back and forth scanning the day's miscreants. 'What a sorry shower. I've seen more effervescence in a glass of Andrews Liver Salts.' He stopped in his tracks and regarded Ginger and Sticky sternly. 'You lad,' as he pointed his stick at a startled Sticky, 'Come with me'

Shaking in his boots, Sticky stumbled to his feet and followed the marching steps of Jordan along the short corridor and into an anteroom. Sticky endeavoured to stand rigidly to attention but the shaking intensified.

'Stop wobbling like a bleeding jellyfish,' barked the sergeant.

'Yes sarge'

'Yes sergeant!'

'Yes sergeant'

'You are as guilty as the cookhouse custard you great

long streak of piss. When the officer arsks you how you plead, you speaks up loud and clear and you replies 'guilty as charged sir'. Do you understand me you shiftless airman, do you follow my meaning?'

Terrified and flummoxed, Sticky croaked,

'Yes sergeant, ah mean, no sergeant'

A disturbing thought struck Jordan and he enquired,

'What's Harrison doing here?'

'He's me witness sergeant'

'Witness, what do you need a bleeding witness for?'

Sticky's mouth had all but dried up but he managed to squeak, 'Ah'm pleading not guilty sergeant'

'Not fucking guilty?

'Yes sergeant'

'Not fucking guilty! And that fat barstard is here as your lying barstard witness?'

'Yes sergeant, ah mean, no sergeant'

The door swung open and one hand on the knob, the other on the jamb, Corporal Tilley announced, 'That's us Sarge, we've been called'

Sergeant Jordan marched back out into the corridor where Ginger was already standing to attention and shouted at the pitch of his voice, 'Escort, witness and accused. Qu-i-ck march'

Presiding officer for that day's court proceedings was Squadron-Leader Aljonquin Phartingail ffoulkes-Knight who was feeling particularly fragile after an excessively boisterous session at the mess the previous evening. He spoke to the clerk to the court in a husky voice, 'All right, wheel in the next lot'

In marched escort, witness and accused followed by Sergeant Jordan.

'Acc-used,' he barked, 'two steps forward, mar-ch!'

'I say sergeant, intervened Phartingail ffoulkes-Knight, 'would you mind awfully turning down the volume a smidgen? I have a frightful head this morning'

'Sir!' replied Jordan just as loudly.

The presiding officer winced and began to study the notes in front of him.

'This is a fearfully serious charge Airman Albright. Dereliction of duty inasmuch as you failed in your responsibility as the prescribed orderly on the day of the alleged offence; failed to secure and make lock fast the door to the latrine stores hut. Damn poor show. How do you plead?'

'Not g-guilty sir,' stammered Sticky.

'Do you have representation?'

'Eh?'

Sergeant Jordan leant forward and whispered in Sticky's ear, 'He means do you have a witness, you bleeding pillock'

'Yes sir'

'Are you prepared to accept my award or will you elect to have your case deferred to appear before the station commander?'

'Eh?'

Rather more forcefully, the sergeant whispered, 'Just fucking say 'yes' '

'Yes sir'

'Very well, let the witness take the oath and give evidence'

'Acc-used, two steps backwards, mar-ch! Witness for the defence AC2 Harrison, two steps forward, mar-ch!'

The squadron leader groaned and regarded Ginger icily.

'What evidence do you submit in defence of the accused?'

'He's innocent of the charge sir'

'Yes, I rather surmise that is why you are gracing us with your presence here today, but what proof are you offering?'

'I saw him lock the door of the hut sir'

'You were a witness to this?'

'Yes sir'

'And you are prepared to take an oath on that?'

'Yes sir'

'Very well, clerk to the court, hand the witness the bible'

'Sorry sir,' said Ginger. 'I'll take the oath but not on the bible'

'What?'

'I said – '

'I know what you said but why can't you swear an oath on the bible?'

'It would be hipo-hypo-. Well, it wouldn't right sir. It's against me religion'

'Are you Jewish?'

'No sir'

'You're hardly Sikh, Hindu, Mohammedan or a member of any other known eastern faith, are you?'

'No sir'

'What then is your persuasion?'

'I'm a Rosicrucian sir'

'Rosy what?'

'Crucian sir, Rosicrucian'

'Are you making this up airman?'

'No sir. I attend their services in the tent hall regular like when I'm back home'

'And this is a recognised form of worship?'

'Yes sir'

'What is your book of prayer?'

'The almanac sir'

'You are taking liberties, aren't you airman?'

'No sir'

'The almanac is your book of prayer?'

'Yes sir, we do all our readings from it like'

Squadron-leader Phartingail ffoulkes-Knight considered the matter and conferred with the clerk to the court, 'Have a shufti at the supplement to King's regulations and see if there's anything on Rosicrucians'

The clerk referred to a volume on his desk, thumbed through the pages, read to himself for a few moments and reported, 'Rosicrucians, Humanist sect, founded six thousand years BC. Sun worshippers; still active, and still practised by devotees'

'Hm,' murmured Phartingail ffoulkes-Knight, and then returning to Ginger, asked, 'would you be prepared to take a solemn oath on the - almanac?'

'Yes sir'

The presiding officer did not believe him of course but he was in urgent need of a strong alcoholic restorative and so he decided to press on.

'Well, it takes all sorts I suppose. Sergeant, do we have an almanac?'

'Sir!' barked out Sergeant Jordan. 'Corporal Tilley has one, for reference, for the use of, sir'

Phartingail ffoulkes-Knight shuddered as he replied, 'Then get it man, procure a copy straightaway, and let's put an end to this farce'

Sergeant Jordan sprang to attention, saluted, and left the court on his appointed mission. When he returned a few moments later he glowered at Ginger as he thrust the dusty tome in front of him.

'Place your right hand on top of the book Harrison' commanded the squadron leader.

'Sir'

'Do you swear by the – almanac - to tell the truth, the whole truth, and nothing but the truth?

'Yes sir'

'Did you witness AC2 Albright insert a key into the door

lock of the latrine stores hut and close it securely?'

'Yes sir'

'Case dismissed'

'Escort, witness and accused,' screeched Sergeant Jordan. 'E-bout turn!

'E'ft, right, 'eft right…'

They left the courtroom and marched along the corridor towards the exit.

'I'm not finished with yet you fat, lying barstard,' Sergeant Jordan admonished Ginger. 'Rosey fucking crucians. I'll have your bollocks out to dry on a flagpole before long, mark my words'

'Are you threatening me sarge?'

'No lad, not threatening, promising'

'Oh well, that's okay then, just as well to know, like'

*

Ginger and Sticky were enjoying a celebratory ale or two in the Farmers Arms later that evening when Sticky nudged his mate and said, 'Look over there Ginge. It's Sergeant Jordan, pissed as a fart'

'Right then, let's go over and join him. We'll have us some fun'

'No Ginge, he'll have me up on a charge again'

Ginger got up and walked towards Sergeant Jordan's table, followed reluctantly by his fearful mate.

'Hullo sarge, enjoying yourself?'

'Eh?' Sergeant Jordan was heavily inebriated and had difficulty in focusing on the intruder. 'Oh, it's you, the fat barstard, fat lying barstard, rosey fucking crucians'

'No hard feelings now sarge, what's done is done, have a drink with us'

The sergeant gave some consideration to this unexpected offer and mellowed. 'All right lad. Just a half-pint though. I've supped enough for tonight'

Ginger went to the bar and ordered a bottle of Fowlers Wee Heavy, an extremely strong and highly concentrated beer extract that he knew would flatten Jordan after a few sips.

'There you go sarge, get that down you'

'Cheers,' said the sergeant as with a flourish he downed the contents of his glass in a few rapid slurps, after which he talked gobblygook for a few minutes before crashing out in his seat.

'Okay, give us a hand. Let's get the old git out of here'

Between them Ginger and Sticky supported their unconscious superior outdoors and after they'd staggered a dozen or so yards, Ginger said, 'Leave him to me.' He picked up the fourteen stone dead weight and slung it over his shoulder as though it were a feather.

'We'll never get him on a bus the state he's in,' said Sticky.

'We're not going on no bus'

'Are ye gonna carry him back to camp like?'

'No I'm chuffing not'

At that, Ginger veered off the road into some thickset, clambering over gorse and overgrown weeds until he reached a clearing beside a little bridge that had a stream trickling underneath it.

Ginger dropped Jordan like a sack of potatoes onto the ground, laid him out flat on his back and then systematically divested him of his overcoat, jacket, trousers, shirt, tie and everything else all the way down to his underpants. When he'd finished stripping his adversary, he bundled the clothes together, walked to the centre of the bridge and hurled them into the murky waters below.

'That's the King's uniform you threw away Ginge,' whined Sticky. 'We'll get six months for this'

'No we won't. The old soak won't report us because he'll look a big enough arse walking back to camp in the buff. He won't want none of this appearing on no charge sheet because he'd never live it down. They'd be pissing themselves in the sergeants mess for years'

Several hours later Sergeant Jordan opened his eyes and gazed in disbelief at the stars above. He had a blinding headache, his throat was parched, and he was cold, very cold. He staggered to his feet to discover his semi-nakedness. Frantically he searched around for his clothes but to no avail.

Dressed only in his underpants, socks and boots, Sergeant Jordan eventually ventured out onto the main road in a vain attempt to hail down a passing car but those motorists who caught his appearance in their headlights just honked the horn and sped on.

Half an hour later he walked through the camp gates where the corporal of the guard reflected, 'Bit nippy out tonight for PT, sarge'

'Mind your own,' replied Jordan as he marched on purposefully but unsteadily towards his quarters.

Get fell in

On the eve of Corporal Tilley's release from national service, he and Sergeant Jordan got drunk together. Both woke up the next morning with severe hangovers, one of them went home for good, the other on fourteen days furlough.

'What have we done about Tilley's replacement?' enquired Flight Lieutenant Ashford of his next in command, Pilot Officer Dawkins.

'Nothing yet, Sergeant Jordan said to wait until after he returned from leave'

'He said what? Who's running this section, you, Sergeant Jordan, or me?

'Well, I suppose he just wanted to be in on the selection process, sir'

'In that case he should not have gone on leave. Let's get on with it now. Can't have that shower spending the next fortnight looking around for fresh skives. Let me have a list of the orderlies'

Pilot Officer Dawkins opened a desk drawer, withdrew a sheet of paper, got up and walked across the room to where Flight Lieutenant Ashford stood drinking his morning coffee. Ashford was gazing out of the window, harbouring lustful thoughts about what he'd like to be doing right then to several members of the group of WAAFs who were drilling in the square.

He studied the list for a moment or two and said, 'I'll

make my choice from one of these wasters'

'Wouldn't we be safer having someone transferred in to replace Tilley? There's no evidence of intelligence among this mob'

'Who said anything about intelligence? The only way to keep a bunch of shiftless orderlies in order is to appoint the most disorderly of them as leader. Tilley was useless, little more than Jordan's bum boy, and we don't want another of those'

'Who then?'

'Harrison'

'But he's a lout, sir'

'Indeed he is Dawkins; idle, insolent, obnoxious and argumentative. He's our man. Get him in here this afternoon for interview. I'll make him up to corporal and we'll announce it in station orders tomorrow'

'But sir, if you do that you'll be leapfrogging three ranks and breaking the regulations. Airman Harrison only an AC2'

'Screw the regulations. Just do as I say. I've got the mother of all hangovers and I do not need further aggravation'

Hands in pockets and forage cap pushed back, Ginger was casually shuffling along on the way back to his place of work after an unscheduled NAFFI break when he was hailed from behind. He looked over his shoulder to observe an airman in overalls leaning on the handle of an extra wide yard brush. It was SAC Bainbridge who was technically in charge of the orderlies in the absence of Sergeant Jordan and Corporal Tilley, and who was also officially next in line for promotion. SAC Bainbridge and Ginger Harrison shared a mutual disregard for one another

'Pilot Officer Dawkins was up the latrines looking for you,' said Bainbridge, getting off his brush handle and making a leisurely stab at sweeping the tarmac. 'And he was none too pleased you wasn't there'

'What did you tell him?'

'I said you was on a skive,' replied Bainbridge maliciously.

'Ta mate, I'll do the same for you sometime. Did he say what he wanted?'

'You're up before Flight Lieutenant Ashford at two o'clock this afternoon'

'What for?'

'Dunno, but you'd better get yourself an alibi'

'But I've done nowt'

'No? Well, that's all right then, you've nothing to worry about.' When Ginger was out of sight he added, 'You never do fuck all around here anyway'

*

'Maybe Ashford's found out about the pots of paint I nicked that time we was working at the officers mess shining up their bogs like,' mused Ginger.

'You'd best get shot of them tins Ginge,' advised Sticky.

'What, and lose out on some easy brass? Mad Taffy down the village pays half a knicker a tin. That's thirty bob I'd be throwing away'

'Better than going to jail'

'Naw,' reflected Ginger. 'Maybe Ashford knows nowt about it'

Ginger arrived several minutes early for his interview and was escorted into a small waiting room by the duty clerk. As he had no intention of brooding over what lay ahead, he settled down comfortably to devour the contents of the latest edition of 'Bright & Breezy', a pocket size soft porn magazine of the time. After a while he glanced up at the wall clock. It read quarter past two. He wasn't bothered. Good little skive this, he thought.

'Sorry to have kept you Harrison'

'Sir'

'Ladies Day Luncheon at the mess, don't you know' said Flight Lieutenant Ashford by way of explanation.

'Sir'

'Now, why do you think you're appearing before me today?'

'Dunno sir'

Ashford opened a file on the desk in front of him, flicked rapidly through the pages with a thumb, and said,

'Dismal'

'Sir?'

'Your service record, you've been in the RAF for twelve months and you have absolutely nothing to show for it – apart from a clean sheet on discipline'

If you only knew sir, thought Ginger.

'Couldn't even get yourself on a training course'

'Sir'

'Well, I'm going to give you an opportunity to change all that'

'Sir?'

'Now that Tilley's gone, I'm making you up to corporal in his stead'

'Sir?'

'Don't keep repeating yourself like a bloody parrot, man,' the flight lieutenant snapped. 'Do you understand what I'm saying?'

'Yes sir'

'Then tell me how you feel about that'

'Well - I dunno sir - I mean, I'm just one of the lads'

'Think on airman,' said Ashford meaningfully. 'If you refuse this promotion, you'll be turning down four pounds fifteen shillings a week'

The one pound ten shillings Ginger picked up on pay parade each week rarely lasted more than three days. He did an immediate about-turn.

'Sir, thank you sir, I'll be honoured to accept the promotion, sir'

'Very well, here's a chit to take to the stores for your stripes. You'll need three sets; dress, battledress, overalls. Sew them on tonight because your first duty as the new section corporal will be to lead your men out on parade tomorrow morning. All clear so far?'

'Yes sir'

'Here also is a letter of authority to hand to the duty NCO on your first visit to the corporals' mess of which you may avail yourself as of tomorrow. Ah, you may also move into Tilley's old quarters tonight. He had a room in your billet, didn't he?'

'Yes sir'

'Well, that should cut down on the flitting, what?'

Ashford chortled as he seemed to think he'd made a funny.

'Now, let's move on to more serious matters.' Ashford frowned, folded his beefy arms, and leant back in his chair. 'Your responsibilities; you will of course be working closely with Sergeant Jordan on the formulation and implementation of these responsibilities'

Like fuck I will, thought Ginger.

'There's far too much loafing and skiving among the men – and you should know all about that, being among the worst offenders. You'll start at once on earning your four pounds fifteen shillings a week. I want the loafing and the skiving to cease and I want it to cease straightaway. I want a higher output of work from the men and when I do my daily inspections from now on, I want to see those piss stones virgin white and gleaming like an old maid's teapot. I've only been in post here for a month but I know what's going on. You chaps are a shower, an absolute shower. See to it Corporal Harrison, see to it'

'Sir!'

*

'Ah've never had a room all to meself'

Sticky was inspecting the newly promoted Corporal Harrison's quarters.

'What?'

'Always had to share with me four brothers'

'Separate beds like?'

'No, all in the same bed'

'Bloody hell'

'They used to fart a lot'

'Give over Sticky,' Ginger grimaced. 'You're putting me off me fag'

Later in the day, having collected his stripes, having had Sticky sew them on, having had his first pint at the corporals mess ahead of schedule, and having cajoled a reluctant airman to move his kit into the new quarters, Ginger called a meeting of his charges. They were lounging around in one of the latrines when Ginger made his first announcement.

'Right now, my policy is this. Don't mess me about and I won't mess you about. Okay? Now, Ashy wants two things. Less skiving and more work'

A groan rose up from the assembly.

'He'll get what he wants and he'll get it this way. Controlled skiving''

'What's that when it's at home?' enquired a puzzled airman

'Controlled skiving',' explained Ginger,' means getting more work done in less time, equals more free time for everybody. What's happening right now is that everyone's pissing off at the same time and nothing gets done on time. Do you follow me?'

His charges said nothing but looked at each other doubtfully.

'Okay, okay. Who can read and write?'

A solitary hand was raised.

'Right, Specky Watkins, you're volunteered. You and Sticky'll go round everyone and draw up a rota for skives. No time never from now on will more than two of you be away on a skive at the same time. Get this right and you'll have more time for skiving and spend less time working. That's me target and I'll make bleeding sure we reach it. Are you with me?'

'Yes corp,' sang out the chorus of enlightened airmen.

The lone voice of SAC Bainbridge added a note of discouragement,

'What'll you be doing?'

Ginger looked at him and replied, 'I'll be keeping a close eye on you mate'

*

With the bright new corporal's insignia gleaming on the sleeves of his grubby denim top, Ginger led his men out onto the square for the morning parade.

'Right lads, get fell in'

The reviewing officer of the day was Squadron Leader Phartingail ffoulkes-Knight but this did not become evident to Ginger until several sections behind him had been inspected, and the officer and his entourage emerged at the front of his row.

'Bloody hell,' murmured Ginger.

Phartingail ffoulkes-Knight moved along the line issuing

compliments and reprimands as he saw fit until he reached Ginger when he stopped, gaped at the section NCO and exclaimed, 'Good God'

'Sir,' acknowledged Ginger, saluting enthusiastically.

'Who made you up to corporal?'

'Flight Lieutenant Ashford, sir'

'Really?'

The parade over, Ginger dismissed his charges, and Squadron Leader Phartingail ffoulkes-Knight walked back across the square followed by his entourage.

*

During the next fourteen days Ginger's strategy for controlled skiving bore its first fruits. His charges performed their duties swiftly and efficiently while at the same time enjoying increased leisure time. On his daily inspections of the latrines Flight Lieutenant Ashford could find no fault and was in fact of the opinion that the standard of hygiene had increased significantly. Ginger was also enjoying his new status. At four thirty every afternoon on cessation of duties, he headed straight for the corporals mess where he took full advantage of the various facilities on offer; food, drink, snooker, darts, dominoes, and participation in the four-card brag school.

Contentment reigned among everyone connected with the orderlies section until the fifteenth day when Sergeant Jordan returned from leave.

'He's done what?' barked Jordan.

'Promoted AC2 Harrison to corporal,' repeated Pilot Officer Dawkins.

'Has he gone mad?' Sergeant Jordan refused to address as 'sir' any officer under the rank of Flight Lieutenant as he looked upon them as little more than jumped up, wet behind the ears, public school educated, poncified pouffters. 'Harrison is an idle lout, a conniving barstard, useless git, bleeding criminal, a disgrace to the – '

'Yes indeed,' interrupted the Pilot Officer cheerfully. 'I agree wholeheartedly but the qualities you've just listed identify precisely with those that Flight Lieutenant Ashford sought in a replacement for Corporal Tilley'

'Was they? Well we'll soon see about that'

He stormed off but decided he would bypass the flight lieutenant and go straight to Squadron Leader Phartingail ffoulkes-Knight.

'It's not right sir. The man's a menace. He was up before you as a crooked witness and lied on the holy book'

'The almanac?' questioned the squadron leader.

'Well, what he called his holy book, sir'

'Indeed'

'But he still lied'

'Yes, yes, yes,' snapped Phartingail ffoulkes-Knight. 'I'll have a word with Flight Lieutenant Ashford. Now please push off. I have a heavy schedule ahead of me today'

Jordan's next port of call was the latrines.

'Where's Harrison?' he shouted to one of the orderlies.

'The corp, you mean sarge?'

'Where is he?' Jordan screamed.

'Up the corporals mess on his break, sarge'

'Get on with your work you idle airman,' he instructed brusquely.

Clenching his swagger stick, he purposefully marched the short distance from the latrines to the corporals' mess, striding past the duty corporal and into the dining quarters. He looked around and espied Ginger in a corner slurping from a large steaming mug.

'Harrison!'

'Corporal Harrison,' replied Ginger without looking up.

'Outside, I want a word with you'

Ginger took a few more few sips, placed the mug down slowly on the tabletop, got up and ambled outdoors.

'Good leave, sarge?'

'Don't cheek me up, airman'

'Like I said, sarge,' he replied, pointing to the stripes on his sleeve,' it's Corporal Harrison now'

'Corporal, my arse, I'll have them stripes off you faster than you sewed them on'

'I didn't sew them on. I had it done for me'

'You had one of my men sew them on?' Jordan barked.

'No sarge, I had a mate do it'

The sergeant glared at Ginger. He turned on his heels and departed hurriedly while Ginger strolled back into the mess to finish his beverage.

An idea struck Jordan. He changed direction and headed back towards the latrines.

'Right, get outside all of you, apart from SAC Bainbridge.' The orderlies laid down their buckets, sponges, mops and the like, and departed hurriedly.

'SAC Bainbridge, I need your assistance'

'Sergeant?'

'I need you to help me fix that fat barstard Harrison once and for all. Can I rely on you?'

'Yes, sergeant,' responded Bainbridge gleefully.

'I wanted a regular to replace Tilley but if it had to be another national serviceman, by rights then it should have been you. Now, you do as I say and I'll make sure Harrison's out and you're in'

'Sir'

'Now, here is what we do…'

*

'And you say there's been an all-round improvement since Harrison was promoted?'

Phartingail ffoulkes-Knight was addressing Flight Lieutenant Ashford whose presence before him he had earlier requested.

'Yes sir, remarkable. Improved timekeeping, higher productivity, enhanced standards of hygiene – and, dare I say it, a better atmosphere among the men. Harrison really has got that shower of idlers pulling together'

'Hmm,' pondered the squadron leader. 'Maybe I've misjudged the blighter. Maybe some responsibility was all that was needed to straighten him out'

*

Sticky was waiting for Ginger on his return from the mess.

'The sarge has got it in for you Ginge'

'Tell me something I don't know'

'No, ye don't understand. Sergeant Jordan came into the bogs, ordered us all outside like and kept Bainbridge back. The sarge is having Bainbridge stick some dodgy gear in your room and then he's goin' to call in for a kit inspection at five o'clock - when you're up the mess - and find it'

'The sneaky sod,' replied Ginger. He thought for a moment and then continued, 'Wait a minute; wait a minute. If he'd ordered you all out, how do you know what was said?'

'Ah was in a cubicle having a crap'

'That must have been nice for them while they was discussing how to shaft me'

*

The front entrance to Hut 29 led directly to the corporal's quarters, and some fifty yards away stood a grimy coal bunker beside a group of outhouses. Sticky and Ginger were secreted behind the bunker keeping a close lookout.

'I've just thought of something Sticky,' said Ginger. 'He won't be able to get in. I lock the door of a morning before going on parade'

'Sarge give him a key'

'Did he now'

'Shush,' cautioned Sticky. 'Here he comes '

They crouched low as SAC Bainbridge emerged from between two huts pushing a wheelbarrow laden with cardboard boxes. He pulled up at the entrance, looked all around him, then unlocked the door and began to rapidly stack the boxes in the narrow hallway. As he was about to close the door Ginger and Sticky rushed him.

'Gotcha,' said Ginger to the intruder. 'Right mush, you help Sticky and me load them boxes into your locker'

'Like fuck I will,' replied a hostile Bainbridge.

'Yes, you will, or I'll smash your lights in'

While they were debating the point, Sticky had himself moved most of the boxes onto SAC Bainbridge's bed.

'Right, open your locker,' ordered Ginger.

'I've lost the key,' said Bainbridge who was beginning to feel scared by now.

'Open it!' shouted Ginger as he shoved the SAC roughly.

Bainbridge complied reluctantly and Ginger and Sticky between them began filling the locker with the boxes. Just as Ginger was loading the final box, the back door to the billet burst open and in marched an SP sergeant and two corporals attired in white caps, belts and gaiters.

'This him, corporal?' asked the sergeant indicating SAC Bainbridge.

'Yes, sergeant,' answered Ginger.

'Good work'

'But sergeant - , 'blustered Bainbridge.

'But me no buts you miserable little tealeaf, you'll spend the rest of your time in the glasshouse for this'

'But – '

Just then Sergeant Jordan walked in through the front entrance with a look of utter astonishment on his face.

'What's going on here?' He was just in time to see his prodigy, head bowed and handcuffed, being led away by the two SPs.

'Your corporal just apprehended that scroat nicking from His Majesty's Stores,' the SP sergeant informed him.

*

'Capital show, Corporal Harrison,' said Flight Lieutenant Ashford enthusiastically. 'Well done'

'Well sir, I thought it was me duty to report to the SPs as soon as I saw him nicking the stuff like'

'I say, why aren't you wearing your insignia?'

Ginger placed three sets of stripes on the desk in front of the officer and said,

'Best I give you these back now sir than have you take them from me for decking Sergeant Jordan'

'Have you?' enquired Ashford anxiously.

'No sir, not yet sir'

Camping it up for Christmas

Occasional instruction on matters of general knowledge was compulsory for national servicemen, and Sergeant 'Bunny' Hare was conducting such a class in the hut set aside for educational purposes. Draped over the blackboard hung a large-scale map of South America and Bunny used his pointer to indicate the south-eastern coastal area.

'Can anyone tell me what kind of fish is to be found here?'

'Kippers,' suggested Ginger amid a burst of ribald laughter from his fellow students.

'No, it sodding well isn't,' sniffed Bunny. 'Does anyone else have a sensible suggestion to offer me?'

'Barracuda?' speculated LAC Emerson

'Not quite, but closer'

'Hey sarge,' another classmate piped up.

'Yes?'

'Are we having a panto in camp again this year?'

'I'm glad someone here is showing a modicum of interest in community activities. Yes, as a matter of fact, we are. There will be another panto in the camp theatre staged over two nights prior to Christmas leave, and shortly after you lot have stopped taking liberties, Sergeant Withinshawe and I will be having a discussion about the arrangements'

Ginger leant over and, cupping a hand to his mouth, whispered to Sticky, 'That'll be after they've had a cuddle in the bog'

'What did you say AC2 Harrison?'

'I said we should have a Christmas log on the stage this time sarge'

'What a super idea,' enthused Bunny. 'I'll make a note of that'

*

Education Sergeant Stan Withinshawe was boiling the kettle and laying out cups and saucers on a trestle table when Bunny returned to his office minutes after the class members had dispersed.

'Honestly,' said Bunny, 'I don't know why I bother. Thickos, sickos and weirdoes; they get worse every week'

'Oh, I know, I know,' agreed Stan, hands on hips as he waited for the kettle to come to the boil. 'My lot is just the same. Hopeless'

'Now, panto,' continued Bunny as he sat down at table producing a bulky folder from his bulging briefcase. 'I've had a think, I've had a scribble, and I have an idea'

'Let's have it then. Don't keep me in suspense'

'What if instead of going the traditional route doing the standard stuff they've be staging here for years and years and years, long before our time ducky, what if we threw caution to the wind, what – '

'Oh, do get on with it Bunny. Not another interminable soliloquy, please'

'Bitch'

'Well, you're always on you are, always doing your actual thespian'

What if,' continued Bunny, ignoring Stan's sarcasm, 'what if we were to devise our own panto, write our own script, and include in it every pantomime character you've ever heard of. Mother Goose, Baron Hardup, Widow Twankey, Sinbad, Robinson Crusoe, Man Friday, Aladdin, Cinderella, The Ugly Sisters, Prince Charming, Puss in Boots, Goody Two Shoes, Babes in the Wood, Wishee Washee, Simple Simon, Dick Whittington - '

'Bona!' squealed Stan.

'We could let our imagination run riot. There'd be something for everyone'

'Bunny, it's inspired'

'Thought you'd like it,' minced Bunny.

But there's a problemo or two'

'Problemo? Explain'

'Casting, dear; it would be impossible'

'No it wouldn't'

'What about the sets, the costumes, the script'

'Now who's being theatrical, you sound like Ethel Merman. Do you think I've not thought it all out?'

'Who'd be your Widow Twankey for example?' countered Stan.

'Glad you asked that because I see Twankey as the star of the show'

'Do you have someone in mind?'

'Yes, I do'

'Who for gawd's sake?'

'That obnoxious lout Harrison'

'Harrison?' gasped Stan in disbelief.

'Perfect for the role, he was born to play the fat old trout'

Stan paused for a second or two to consider the suggestion and said,
'Ye-es, I can see the sense of it. But would he agree?'

'Not at first he won't, but I'll think of something to sweeten him up'

'And the costumes, the sets, what about those? Quite an undertaking Bunny, quite an undertaking you have to agree.' Stan folded his arms and pouted. 'We could always ask the Warrington Rep for assistance like we did last year, but I doubt they could help us on this production. It's too much Bunny, it's too ambitious'

'Where there' a will, there's a way,' replied Bunny confidently. 'We girls will all have get our thinking caps on, our patterns and sewing kits out – and as for the sets and the scenery – there's enough raw butch labour around the camp to build a battleship. We just have to provide the motivation ducky. 'Build the sets, paint the scenery, hump the props – and get a starring role'. That'll be our platform. The lure of the greasepaint, it never fails. Oh, I feel a hot flush coming on'

'Ah,' countered Stan in his role of devil's advocate, 'but what about the script?'

Bunny stooped to pick up his briefcase and handed Stan a large manila folder.

'I told you I've had a scribble. Have a peek-a-boo at this, petal'

Stan opened the folder, pulled out the handwritten pages it contained, and began to read. He got as far as page four and stopped.

'I don't need to read any more. Bunny, You're a genius, you stand alone. Right, let's get this show rolling. Casting call, set designers, seamstresses, wardrobe, music, routines, chippies, painters, sparks, scripts, posters, programmes, tickets...'

*

'You want me to dress up as a fat tart?' exploded Ginger indignantly.

'Not as such,' explained Bunny delicately. 'Widow Twankey is a pantomime dame, an artiste, a lady of quality'

'That's as maybe but she's still a fat tart'

'Will you do it?'

'Gerroff'

'I'd also like to cast your oppo as Simple Simon'

'Sticky could do that okay. Look sarge, I'll paint your scenery, I'll even hump it, but fat tarts is out'

'You don't much like working at the latrines, do you?' intimated Bunny, moving in for the kill.

'Of course I don't. They're nowt but shite houses'

'What if I could fix up you and your mate with a cushy little number instead?

'Like what?' asked Ginger suspiciously.

'Like being appointed as official orderlies to look after the camp church and its environs – oh, hark at me – 'camp church' – I must remember to write that down'

'What's environs?' asked Ginger, ignoring the unintentional pun.

'The vestry, recreation hall, that sort of thing'

'Any shite houses?'

'No'

'Good skive is it?'

'Superb'

'And you could fix it up like?'

'I've already done so. The present incumbents have just been demobilised and I've spoken to the various padres who use the place for services and counselling. They're all in agreement. You and your oppo can take up the vacated positions immediately after you return from Christmas leave'

'Like after we've put ourselves about as a couple of prats in your panto'

'In a manner of speaking, yes'

'Okay sarge, you're on'

'Good, that's settled then. You'll be a smash. Who knows, you might even be tempted to take it up professionally when you leave the RAF. Good pantomime dames are in great demand and the pay is excellent, as much as two hundred pounds a week'

'Two hundred quid a week for dressing up as a fat tart?'

'Sometimes more'

'Bloody Nora!'

*

The turnout for the casting call exceeded even Bunny's high expectations. Word had travelled around camp like wildfire that Ginger was to appear as a fat tart in the pantomime and almost everyone else it seemed wanted to get in on the act.

'Settle down please, settle down,' called Bunny to the assembled aspirants. Sitting beside him at the makeshift producer's table was the panto's stage director, Stan Withinshawe. 'Now, let's have some decorum here, a bit of organisation. Featured artistes to the left, dancers and chorus to the right, and all the rest of you stagehands, chippies, sparks, painters et cetera - to the rear'

'Typical,' complained a volunteer carpenter as he trudged to the back of the hall, scuffing his hob nailed boots across the floor. 'Fuck the workers'

'You, airman,' rebuked Stan. 'Have a care. Them's genuine parquets you're clumping all over with your great clodhoppers. Honestly, some people have no consideration'

'Now,' announced Bunny authoritatively, 'the casting of featured artistes. As you probably all know already, the star of the show is to be Widow Twankey, and that part will be played by AC2 Harrison.' This evoked a cacophony of catcalls and wolf whistles at which Ginger shook a belligerent fist at his oppressors. 'The only other part to be cast so far is that of Simple Simon and that has been awarded to AC2 Albright'

'Playing himself is he?' shouted someone.

Bunny waited until his charges had settled down, then he continued, 'However, that still leaves lots and lots of super roles, and Sergeant Withinshawe and I will now confer as to how we can best share them out. After that, we'll deal with the dancers, the chorus, and the backstage hands'

As Bunny and Stan went into a huddle, the aspiring thespians clustered around in little groups, chatting among themselves; smoking, yawning, arguing, and occasionally breaking wind.

'Okay,' said Bunny after ten minutes or so, 'choosy-choosy time'

'Corporal Jacobi,' called Stan.

'Yeah'

'You are to play the part of Baron Hardup'

'Oy, muzhik already,' replied Jacobi.

'Baron Hard-on, more like,' said his mate.

'Messrs Bradshaw, Beale and Wise, are you all here?'

'Yes,' chorused the trio.

'You are to be our Ugly Sisters'

'But sarge, we did them last year,' complained one of the sisters.

'Yes, and quite charmingly so, may I say,' gushed Bunny. 'That's why you've been selected again this year'

'LAC Gropethorpe?'

A tall, slim fair-haired youth put up his hand and timidly replied in a high pitched voice, 'Here'

'Fairy Queen for you dear,' said Stan meaningfully.

'Nice lallies,' whispered Bunny.

'And a tight little bum as well,' added Stan from a corner of his mouth.

And so the selection process continued until every featured role had been cast, the dancers and chorus chosen, and the backstage staff briefed on their respective duties. At close of play Bunny and Stan provided their guests with several urns of tea and plates piled high with pork pies and vol au vents.

'Here,' Ginger instructed Sticky. 'Leave them shitey little things. Stuff the inside of your jerkin with the pork pies before them other greedy sprogs scoff the lot. We'll have them for us snatch tomorrow'

'Ginger'

'What?'

'Ah can't do Simple Simon'

'How d'you mean?'

'Ah can't read writing like'

'Now he tells us,' sighed Ginger.

He looked around and saw the producer and director chatting in a corner with the tall fair-haired youth. 'Hey, Sergeant Hare,' he called out.

Bunny pranced towards them and enquired,

'Problem?'

'Sticky can't read'

'Oh, don't worry about that. He's only got but three words to say'

'Three words, how many have I got?'

'Oh, oodles and oodles'

'Stroll on'

*

The weeks rolled away and Bunny's innovative production began to take shape. Costumes were created with tender loving care, sets were constructed with much gusto and even more blasphemy, scenery was painted and humped, music was scored with passion, and all manner of other things clicked magically into place.

Came the evening of the dress rehearsal and Bunny was well pleased.

Onstage waddled his Widow Twankey housed in a huge girdle over which was draped an ankle length, multi-coloured chequered cotton dress. The exaggerated dairymaid cap had its peak turned up at a rakish angel and a broad ribbon was doubled knotted under Ginger's ample chin. He was of course heavily made up with rouged cheeks and magenta cupid bow lips.

'Oh, you look divine' gasped Bunny. 'I could wee myself'

'I feel like a prick,' opined Ginger.

Bunny turned to his stage director and said, 'Now Stan, be honest, be bold. Do not try to spare my feelings. What do you think?'

Stan put manicured fingers to his chin and pursed his lips as he took in the full majesty of Bunny's creation before giving out his verdict.

'I've not seen a better turned out pantomime dame anywhere. Not even at the London Palladium; exceptional, beyond comparison, right up there in your actual pinnacle of creative design. A veritable theatrical triumph'

'What about the boots? On the large side do you think?' fussed Bunny.

'Not a bit of it'

'And the mascara, eye shadow?'

'Do justice to Marlene Dietrich, that would,' complimented Stan.

'Here, what about me?' intervened Ginger. 'I'm chuffing freezing standing around here dressed like a fat tart. I ain't got no drawers on'

'Oh, don't worry about that,' replied Bunny, dismissing Ginger's protestations with a wave of a hand. 'Let's get on with the rehearsal'

'Robinson Crusoe, Man Friday, positions please,' called

Stan.

From the prompt side on strutted Crusoe in a Robin Hood costume. He was wearing green tights and his outrageous high-heeled ankle boots had their tasselled flaps pulled out. His companion Friday was blacked up, wore a pink leotard and had a blonde wig perched on its head.

'Right now children,' said Bunny. 'This is the scene where Robin sings his little song to Friday.' He hummed a few bars and continued, 'Just as he hits the final note, in walks Simple Simon bearing a silver salver upon which is a telegram.' Bunny indicated to Friday to pick up on the line.

'Oh Robin,' lisped Friday in a contrived falsetto, 'it's wonderful to be alone with you on this desert island. I wish we could be together here forever'

'So do I Friday, so do I,' replied Robin in deep masculine tones.

'Oh look,' screeched Friday. 'It's Simple Simon. Whatever can he be doing here?'

'Cue Simple Simon,' called out Stan matter-of-factly, as in loped Simple Simon complete with silver salver.

'What on earth...'

'Me costume's too small,' complained Sticky. He was wearing a pageboy suit with pillbox hat and the sleeves of his jacket and trousers were halfway up their respective limbs.

'Just speak your lines, dear,' instructed Bunny softly.

'Telegram for Friday,' enunciated Sticky in a loud voice.

'Excellent,' appraised Stan.

'Now Widow Twankey, this is your big scene and it will bring down the house. I positively guarantee it'

'Not on top of me fucking head I hope,' countered Ginger sarcastically.

'The telegram states,' continued Bunny, 'that you will be arriving shortly to spend a week or so with Robin and Friday on their dinky little desert island. Have you studied the script? Do you know your lines?'

'Yeah, but I never was no use at telling long jokes. Short and smutty suits me best'

'Nonsense, there's nothing to it. Hang on a jiffy while I get into character...' Bunny ruffled his hair and took a deep breath. 'Now, watch, listen and learn'

'Oh Robin, oh Friday, what a day, what a day; I've come straight from my own panto just to be with you. The chorus girls and I got on a train at Liverpool Lime Street. You know the one, the Whores Special. What a journey! Just as we were leaving the station, the carriage door opened and in jumped this GI holding a large paper bag full of sweetmeats. He said, 'Are you all working girls?' 'Oh yes,' we replied, 'we're all in panto', 'Which panto?' he asked. 'Dick Whittington,' we said. Then he asked, 'Would any of you ladies like a yum-yum?' So we all had a yum-yum, then another, and another, all the way to Padgate. As we left the carriage and made our way along the platform, the Yank opened the carriage door and yelled, 'I forgot to ask, which one of you ladies takes Dick?' So we yelled back, 'Oh, we all do, but not for yum-yums'

There was a stunned silence but Bunny persisted, 'Knock them for six that will. They'll be putty in your hands Widow Twankey'

'Or not, as the case may be,' reckoned Stan.

'And just what do you mean by that?' protested Bunny.

'I've heard that joke die the death in Blackpool, Manchester, Stockport, Burnley –

'Well, it won't this time,' interrupted Bunny haughtily. 'It's the way you put it across that matters, not the gag itself. Now, let's press on…'

*

On the opening night Bunny and Stan took it upon themselves to welcome the distinguished guests whom in the main comprised officers and wives. Prior to the start of the performance refreshments were served and the guests preened, posed, and generally set about flaunting rank and status.

'Did you hear that?' whispered Bunny.

'No, what?' asked Stan quietly.

'That fop Squadron Leader Phartingail ffoulkes-Knight just told Wing Commander Barclay that he doesn't agree with men dressing up as women. Bad for morale, he says'

'Cheek'

'He should talk, what with what he gets up to in town'

'What does he get up to?'

'Domination'

'You don't mean…'

'Oh yes, Wing Commander Barclay and all'

'Never'

'Oh yes, at Madame Golightly's'

'How do you know that?'

'Well, you know my friend Julian, Sergeant Wetherby?'

'Uh huh'

'Well he also goes to Madame Golightly for a certain service – not domination, you understand'

'Course not; Julian wouldn't go in for that'

'Well, Julian reckons he saw the two of them in schoolgirl uniforms tied up to bed ends being whipped by Madame herself no less. Julian says they had dummy teats in their mouths and goodness know what up their derrieres'

*

'Overture and beginners please,' called acting stage manager LAC Barry Emerson, at which command a flurry of discordant notes cascaded from the trio of musicians in the orchestra pit; an ensemble comprising piano, drums and rusty violin.

Backstage the activity was intense. Costumes fell apart, lines were forgotten, nerves were frazzled, the atmosphere was electric, and the language was appalling.

There was a drum roll, the orchestra broke into the overture, the lights went down, and the curtain rose.

Throughout the performance Bunny and Stan stood beside each other in the wings and marvelled at how well the show was going, thrilled at the audience participation, and almost cried at the rapturous reception afforded to Widow Twankey every time she made an entrance. Bunny's prediction had materialised. Ginger was indeed the star of the show.

But it was all going too well, something had to happen to burst the bubble, and it did.

Simple Simon slouched off the stage with his silver salver, and to yet another roar of approval Widow Twankey waddled on carrying two hefty suitcases.

'Widow Twankey, how good to see you again,' squealed Friday.

'Oh Robin, oh Friday, what a day, what a day – '

That was as many words as Ginger managed to speak before a bundle of wet clothes hit him smack in the mouth, putting an abrupt end to his delivery and smudging his painstakingly applied make up.

'Get on with it you fat barstard, you idle fucking layabout,' shouted a drunken voice from the middle of the stalls. Ginger recognised instantly that his arch-enemy Sergeant Jordan was providing the insults.

He hitched his girdle and skirts, jumped off the stage, and ran up the aisle to where Sergeant Jordan and his companion Corporal Crabtree were sitting together at the end of a row. Ginger made to head butt Jordan but missed his footing and instead crashed into Crabtree's nose at which there was a loud crack as blood sprouted all over the corporal's dress jacket.

Ginger once again hitched up his girdle and skirts and dashed back onto the stage to the loudest applause of the evening.

Despite repeated raucous demands from Sergeant Jordan to have the curtain down, the pantomime picked up again where it had left off and proceeded to the finish without further interruption.

Jordan was waiting in the wings and when the curtain came down for the last time after a dozen or so encores, he accosted Ginger.

'Knew I'd get you one day you fat barstard, poncified up like a fucking tart. Threw my clobber in a stinking fucking canal, eh? I'll have you put away in the glasshouse and when you come out I'll be looking for you, to put you right fucking back in again'

Bunny and Stan had observed Jordan standing in the wings and rushed over immediately they heard threats being issued against their precious pantomime star.

'You have no right to be backstage Sergeant Jordan,' said Bunny. 'Now, remove your presence'

'Fuck off, you poncified poufter'

'Well, really,' rebuked Stan.

'You too, you little fart'

'I'll have you put in charge,' screamed Bunny.

'Don't get yourself all upset Bunny. Look, there's Squadron Leader Phartingail ffoulkes-Knight at the other side of the stage. Let's have him deal with this outrage'

They rushed across the stage, advised the officer of Jordan's threats, and demanded that he take appropriate action.

'Wouldn't do any good, my dear chaps,' responded the squadron leader disinterestedly. 'If I were to block Sergeant Jordan charging that imbecile, he'd go straight to the station commander first thing tomorrow morning'

'So he'd go to straight to Wing Commander Barclay, would he?' said Bunny.

'Absolutely, mark my words'

'Well, listen to me Goody Two Shoes. If you allow my Widow Twankey to be charged by that despicable cretin, I'll have it spread around the officers mess faster than you can wipe your bum about what you, Wing Commander Barclay, and Madame Golightly get up to of an evening'

'Ah'

'My friend Sergeant Wetherby is your chef'

'Ah…'

'So?'

'Ah, Sergeant Jordan, may I have a word…'

'Sir'

'Look here sergeant, about the little mishap earlier between your corporal and the, ah, pantomime dame chappie'

'Little mishap sir?' Jordan could hardly believe he was hearing this.

'Yes, minor altercation'

'Minor-fucking-altercation, sir?' he barked out.

'What are your intentions?'

'My intentions sir?' spluttered Jordan with incredulity. 'My intentions, I'll tell you what my intentions is. I'm having the barstard assailant arrested and up before you in the morning. Then I'm looking to you to put the fat barstard down for the glasshouse for three fucking years. Them's my intentions, sir'

'And I'm instructing you not to proceed with the charge.' He added ingratiatingly, 'Christmas spirit, eh,

Yuletide frolics, what?'

'Christmas spirit, yuletide bleeding' frolics? He's busted Corporal Crabtree's fucking nose!'

'Most distressing, yes, all things considered though, unwise to proceed, bad for morale after such a jolly fine show'

'Them your final words on the matter, sir?'

'Yes'

'Then I'll go straight to the station commander'

'Wouldn't do that if I were you, old boy,' concluded Phartingail ffoulkes-Knight suavely. 'Not unless you harbour a secret craving for an early posting to the Outer Hebrides'

Thieving sod

'Right you idle layabouts,' barked Sergeant Jordan. 'This hut is like a doss house. Get it cleaned up'

It was Saturday morning and he was addressing his remarks to the handful of the residents left in Hut 29; the majority who lived within striking distance of the camp having gone home on weekend leave. Accompanying Jordan was a slim, fair complexioned corporal bedecked in full kit.

'This here is Corporal Carson,' he continued. 'He'll be billeting with you shower of wasters for a few days until we get him fixed up with quarters. Now look lively, get this shit hole habitable for a non-commissioned officer.' He then indicated to Ginger with his swagger stick. 'You, go up the stores for fresh bedding'

'Why me, sarge?' muttered Ginger.

'What did you say airman?'

'Why should I have to go, sergeant?'

'Because I'm telling you to, you insolent idle airman; the rest of you, move yourselves, move yourselves'

Ginger returned to the billet half an hour later carrying a bale of bedding on his broad shoulders. He threw it down roughly on top of the bed where Corporal Carson was laying out his small kit, some items of which fell to the floor.

'Hey, look out there,' Carson gently reprimanded. 'Those are my personal belongings'

'Yeah?' snarled Ginger. 'So is this frigging bedding. Don't see why I should have to hump it '

'I didn't ask you to,' replied the corporal mildly.

'Maybe not, but by rights it's you that should've gone up the stores'

'I agree, but I could hardly have countermanded Sergeant Jordan's instructions. I've only just met the man'

'Yeah, well.' Ginger was still miffed.

'Cherry Blossom,' said Sticky who was helping the corporal retrieve the items that had fallen to the ground.

'You what?' snapped Ginger.

'Cherry Blossom polish; says so on this tin here'

'So?'

'We just got but standard issue boot black'

'Help yourself to it any time you want,' offered Corporal Carson.

'Ta, ah will'

'No you chuffing won't,' objected Ginger. 'You know the rule in this billet. If you don't have it yourself, you don't use no other bugger's'

'Right, well, I'll see you both later,' said the corporal, sensing that Ginger's irascibility was rapidly mounting. 'I've got to report in at the orderly room before they close. I need to cash in some of my credits'

As he was leaving the billet in walked LAC Barry Emerson.

'Who's he?' asked Barry

'Some tosser Jordan's lumbered us with for a few days,' grunted Ginger.

*

Come eight o'clock Monday morning the billet was full again, and during the course of the day Corporal Carson went out of his way to become acquainted with each one of his temporary boarders. Most of them were wary of him at first and kept their distance because having a NCO around the billet was prohibitive. By Tuesday evening though Carson was gradually winning them over with his infectious grin, his easy going manner and his obvious charm; he was also displaying little acts of generosity that went down well with the inmates; a hairbrush here, shaving soap there, and a seemingly endless supply of cigarettes, which he freely dispensed to all and sundry.

'That Corporal Carson give me five bob 'til pay day,' announced Scrounger Harris to Barry.

'Wish he'd give me five bob. I've just lost half a bar'

'Where?'

'Don't know. Must have dropped it outside somewhere'

Ginger dusted haphazardly around the altar and accoutrements of the communal camp church, collected the missals and hymnals left over from the Anglican Sunday service and tossed them all willy-nilly into a large tea chest located in the vestry. Chores over for the day, he headed back to the rest room for a brew, a fag, and another dozen or so games of snooker before lunch. As he walked along the corridor he heard the strains of a familiar tune.

'Victor Sil-bloody-vester,' he said on entering the room. 'Can't you play owt else?'

'There is nowt else,' replied Sticky who was dancing around the floor with a mop for a partner. 'They've only got but the one record'

'Who listens to Victor Silvester apart from you?'

'Me mam, she always has Victor Silvester on the record player of an evening'

'No wonder she never gets no visitors'

'He's good is Victor Silvester. Ah learned to dance to his records at the Skelmeresdale Youth Club'

'I like a bit o' swing myself. Benny Goodman, Woody Herman, Tommy Dorsey'

The door opened to reveal a tall lean toothy padre who enquired, 'I say, have either of you chaps come across my brief case this morning? I think I left it behind after the service yesterday'

'Aye, vicar,' replied Sticky. 'Ye did and all. Ah put it in vestry cupboard'

'Ah, good man, go fetch it for me please'

As Ginger started to polish around the rest room in a show of industrious dedication, the padre continued, 'Do you chaps have enough to do around here to keep you fully occupied?'

'Oh aye, padre, plenty to keep us on the go like; dusting, polishing, cleaning, we're at it all day'

'I see you're a fan of Victor Silvester'

'Eh?'

'You've got one of his records playing'

'Oh right,' and then Ginger added, 'it's the only one we got'

'Really, well, as you're a fan, I can let you have some more. I've got another dozen or so lying around in my quarters. I'll pop them in later today'

'That'll be right neighbourly of you padre,' replied Ginger, grimacing.

There was an air of doom hovering over Hut 29 when Ginger and Sticky returned in the late afternoon. Most of the occupants sat glumly on their bunks while the remaining few appeared to be searching through the contents of their lockers.

'Someone died then?' asked Ginger.

'We've had a visit from a sneak thief,' volunteered Barry Emerson.

'How do you know like?'

The enquiry came from Sticky and it elicited a growled response from an airman. 'Because, you pillock, we've all had something or other stolen from our kit'

'Better check yours out Ginger,' advised Barry.

'No point, I've got nowt worth nicking'

'Me neither,' added Sticky.

'Who was billet orderly today?' asked Ginger pointedly.

'Scrounger Harris,' answered someone.

'Don't pick on me,' flared Scrounger. 'I didn't nick nothing from no one'

'No one is accusing you,' Barry assured him. 'But are you certain you were here all day – or did you skive off to the NAFFI for half an hour?'

'No I didn't. I was here all the time and nobody came anywhere near the billet'

'There you go then, it weren't no sneak thief,' concluded Ginger.

'You saying it was one of us then?' asked Tiny Loftus, all six foot four inches of him towering over Ginger with intimidatory intent.

'No, it wasn't one of us,' countered Ginger calmly, 'but it was an inside job.' He looked around the room before adding, 'Where's Carson?'

'He said he wouldn't be back 'til going on five,' said Scrounger.

'Coming up for five o'clock now,' pointed out Tiny.

'When did he leave the billet this morning Scrounger?' persisted Ginger.

Scrounger hesitated and then proceeded cautiously, 'He give me two bob to go up the NAFFI for his fags and when I came back he went out. It was ten o'clock'

'You're a lying git, Scrounger,' accused Barry. 'He doesn't need to buy fags. He's been spreading them about the billet like confetti since he got here. You skived off and left him on his own'

'Here he comes now,' announced an airman who was looking out of the window. 'He's about a hundred yards away'

'Right, this is what we do,' instructed Barry urgently. 'We'll tell him what's happened and ask him to search his kit. If he say's nothing's missing, we've got him. Then we –

'Won't work,' interrupted Ginger.

'What?'

'If you do that, I'll tell you what he'll do. He'll check his kit and say 'Oh dear, I've lost my camera and some money', and bollocks like that. Crappy sneak thieves like him always cover their tracks. They nick from themselves so as no bugger can point the finger at them. Then he'll go straight up the SPs screaming blue murder and next thing we're all under suspicion. What happens then? I'll tell you what happens then. We get screwed, he gets new quarters, and all your chuffing gear goes with him. He's one of them remember, he's an NCO'

'Where did you learn all this stuff?' enquired an airman.

'Borstal'

Ginger's predictions were right on the button. Corporal Carson checked his kit, claimed he had property stolen and sped off to the guardroom to report the loss.

'What do we do now?' Barry appealed to his roommates. 'We can't just sit around here and let him get away with it'

'I'm gonna thump the thieving sod when he comes back,' answered Tiny.

'That won't get us anywhere,' objected Ginger. 'We'd all like to thump him but what we need now is to find is a way to nail him. I'll go see Smudger. He'll know what to do'

*

With hands clasped behind his neck and lying fully outstretched on his bunk staring up at the ceiling, Smudger listened silently and intently as Ginger unfolded the details of the dilemma facing the inmates of Hut 29.

'He's got you snookered good and proper,' was

Smudger's summation.

'We was hoping you could think of something to help us out like'

'As it happens, I can. First off though, let's look at matters as they stand. The SPs will have called in the Special Investigation Branch by now and that's where your troubles really start. The SIB wallahs are sadistic sods who don't give a toss who they pin the blame on as long as they can get in and out fast. They'll screw each of you individually in the hope that one of you cracks; any chance of that happening?'

'No chance. Not even Sticky, thick and all as he is'

'Any possibility that Carson is in fact innocent'

'No chance, no way' exploded Ginger.

'Okay, okay, just checking. Listen, I'm a thief. I don't mind admitting it but I only steal from the Government and faceless institutions because they're fair game. But like all professional thieves, I can't stand anyone who steals from his own; let's pin Carson to the ground where he belongs'

'But how?'

'There's a special powder used in forensics that leaves an indelible stain on the fingers of anyone making contact with it. The CID use it in crime detection but the SIB won't touch it because they're too lazy'

'How does that help us?'

'The SIB might not use the powder but they know that it stands up as irrefutable evidence in any court of law. We'll nobble Carson and have the stuff daubbed all over his thieving mitts. He'll be manacled and banged away before the SIB have time to interview any of you'

'Smudger,' said Ginger patiently, 'you're not telling me how'

'Who's billet orderly tomorrow?'

'Me'

'Good, now listen. We need a decoy and I suggest Barry because he's a bit of an actor. Oh, one more thing. Does Carson leave the billet at ten o'clock every weekday morning?'

'Yeah, he reports into pool flight at ten, and it's just around the corner from us'

'What does he normally do in the time between everyone leaving the billet and ten o'clock?'

'How do you mean?

'Does he fidget, move around, or what?'

'Naw, he just lies on top of his bunk reading dirty books'

'Right, here's the plan. Barry gets news tonight of a family bereavement and he has to go home on compassionate leave tomorrow morning. He's catching a train at say, half past ten from Padgate Station. Let everyone else in on the deal so that no one stays behind to screw it all up. Tonight I will doctor a five pound note with some of this powder and – '

'Hold up, where is the powder and the fiver coming from?'

'The powder I get from a hooky CID officer who used to buy travel warrants from me when I was running my scams at the orderly office. The five quid is my contribution to the scheme. It's the least I can do after all the business you boys have put my way over the past two years. Anyway, I'll get it back when they feel Carson's collar'

'Thanks mate'

'Whereabouts in the billet is Carson's bunk situated?'

'First on the left as you enter the billet'

'And Barry's?'

'Right up at the other end of the hut'

'Couldn't be better, now, Barry's in a rush to get away, you're helping him pack, and you offer to walk with him to the main gates. As you're both leaving the billet Barry drops an envelope on the floor right in front of Carson. Inside the envelope is the doctored five-pound note, which he'll pocket, leaving indelible stains on his thieving fingers; we'll let the SIB finish the job'

'What if he goes for a slash before we leave?'

'He'll be back'

'What if he don't open the envelope?'

'He will'

'What if he opens the envelope smells a rat, and leaves the money be?'

'Then you're completely fucked'

*

'Well done you chaps. Wizard show,' said Squadron Leader Phartingail ffoulkes-Knight who was visiting the billet in the company of Sergeant Jordan. 'Pity we had to thrust such a scoundrel upon you, and pity about your stolen property. Not a trace of it anywhere, I'm afraid. The SIB bods searched his kit but could find neither hide nor hair of the loot. Fenced it off somewhere, don't you know'

'I say sir,' interjected a well-spoken bespectacled airman. 'Isn't there a corporate insurance policy to cover us for such losses?'

'You are on His Majesty's service Pilbeam, not back at boarding school'

'Shut your impertinence airman,' barked Sergeant Jordan, 'or I'll have you on a fizzer'

'You will do no such thing sergeant. AC2 Pilbeam has every right to ask the question, and while we're on the subject, didn't you know that Corporal Carson was a confirmed kleptomaniac?'

'No sir,' replied Jordan, but it was clear from the expression on his face that he had no idea of the meaning of the term.

'Didn't he produce a letter from the administrator of the medical block from which he had just been released?'

'He give me a envelope sir, but I passed it over to the orderly clerk for filing like I always do'

'You failed to read the letter inside the envelope then?'

Sergeant Jordan did not reply, and the Squadron Leader excused himself and left the billet. Jordan though stayed behind to have words with Ginger.

'Why didn't you come to me first instead of the SIB?'

'Because you wouldn't have believed me,' replied Ginger sullenly.

'I'll have you out of that cushy number and back cleaning shite houses before – '

'Sergeant Jordan,' called Phartingail ffoulkes-Knight brusquely. 'You're keeping me waiting'

'Sir'

*

A few days later Sticky was rummaging through the tea chests in the vestry when he stumbled across some articles of interest.

'Hey Ginge, look what ah've found'

'What?'

'Have a look for yourself'

What Sticky had discovered was the stolen property.

'Well, bugger me. He stashed it here so's we'd get the blame'

'No, Ginge, so's *you'd* get the blame'

'Why me?'

Because you moaned about carrying his bedding like'

Back to basics

'How much do you want for this pile of old junk then Taff?'

Ginger was rummaging through the record collection in Mad Taffy's second hand store down Padgate village. From the hundreds of 33s on sale he had chosen selected works by Sy Oliver, Buddy Berrigan, Tommy Dorsey, Glenn Miller and Artie Shaw.

'Junk, you'll find no junk in this store, boyo,' replied Taffy with mounting indignation. 'Them is valuable family heirlooms, them is. Cared for, look you. Dusted, polished, nurtured. Neither a scratch nor a blemish on any of them, see; only yesterday I was offered fifteen whole pounds by an Englishman for those priceless records you're holding but I turned it down boyo. Told the fellow I wouldn't let them go for a penny under twenty guineas'

'I'll give you five bob for the lot'

'Fifteen shillings and not a farthing less'

'Ten bob'

'Eight'

'Seven and a tartan banner'

'Done'

*

Sticky tentatively split the reds on the snooker table in the rest room while Ginger lay sprawled out on the tattered sofa listening to the fruits of his purchase from Mad Taffy. Tinny music coursed from the ancient hand-cranked record player.

'Why's there's more reds than colours?' speculated Sticky.

Ginger turned philosopher for the benefit of his dim mate. 'What do you see more of in camp than officers and NCOs?'

Sticky chalked the tip of his cue as he struggled to find an answer to the conundrum.

'Sprogs?'

'Correct. Right then, your reds are the other ranks, the black is the CO, the pink is Farty Night; the blue is Flight Lieutenant Ashford, and so on, all the way down to the brown. That's old bandy Jordan'

'Why's sarge the brown?'

'Because his nose is brown from sniffing around other people's arses, especially mine'

Sticky considered the explanation and replied, 'Good that, Ginge, what about the white though?'

'That's me. I spend my time potting all the colours'

The door of the rest room opened to admit the toothy padre, The Right Reverend Flying Officer Alphonsus St. John Willoughby-Goddard.

'Ah, caught you in the course of your break chaps,

what?'

Ginger eased his bulk from the couch and stood up.

'Just having' a quick breather, your reverence. It's been all go in here today'

'Quite, yes, excellent, good show, capital'

Ginger broke the awkward silence that ensued by enquiring, 'Can we help you?'

'Ah, yes, thing is, tricky situation. Don't quite know how to break the news gently to you'

'Do you want us to clean out the priests bog like, padre?' prompted Sticky.

'Pillock,' chastised Ginger.

'Not exactly, not as such, no; fact of the matter is, I'm obliged to release both of you forthwith from your duties as camp church orderlies'

'Fuck me sideways'

'Beg pardon?'

'Sorry padre, slip of the tongue,' apologised Ginger, 'something up with our work then?'

'No, no. Au contraire; quite excellent, exemplary, first class'

'What then?'

'Thing is, I've been landed with a couple of chaps from pool flight. Back from sick leave, what? Only fit for light duties, what? I'm having to replace you with them, what?'

'Usual two weeks notice is it then?' enquired Ginger.

'Eh?'

'We worked us two weeks notice at the bogs before we came here'

'Ah, not possible, I've made arrangements. You're to report to Sergeant Jordan tomorrow morning'

'You don't mean,' said Ginger, hoping against hope he was in error, 'you don't mean we're going back to the bogs, you don't mean that, do you padre?'

'Regrettably so chaps; back to basics, what?'

*

The redundant church orderlies stood rigidly to attention before the desk of Sergeant Jordan behind whom, standing at ease with arms folded behind his back, lurked a tall fierce looking moustachioed corporal.

'Right then, you idle miscreant airmen,' thundered Sergeant Jordan. 'I've got you back, back where you belong, back where I intend to keep you. Show me up in front of the camp at the fucking pantomime, would you? Hide behind them fairyfied education sergeants' backs, would you? Bung my clobber in a dirty stinking stream, would you? Leave me stranded half-naked in the middle of a fucking dingle, would you? Well, you're not traipsing around now as poncified tarts; you're back working at the bogs. Do I make myself clear?'

'Yes sergeant,' replied the alleged miscreants in unison.

'This here is my new second in command, Corporal Butterfly'

Sticky tried in vain to suppress a snigger.

'Have I said something to amuse you airman?'

'No sergeant'

'Watch it, you great long streak of piss. Now then, you'll be reporting to Corporal Butterfly and he's a stickler for detail. One bog brush out of kilter and he'll be down on like a ton of porcelain. Do you understand what I'm saying?'

'Yes sergeant,' chorused the doleful duo.

'Then get out of my sight and make a start on the latrines for Huts 20 to 28. They haven't been serviced for nigh on a month and they reek to the rafters. Get them cleaned, get them polished, get them spotless'

*

Ginger and Sticky visited the first of the prescribed ablution houses and on surveying the hygienically challenged premises they realised that Jordan had in no way exaggerated the extent of the task ahead of them.

'Shows you what a pisser life can be,' said Ginger. 'Only a few hours ago we was living in the lap of luxury and look at us now. Knee deep in sprog shit'

'Could be worse Ginge'

'Worse? How could it be worse than this?'

'We could be in the glasshouse for nicking all that lead off the camp church roof'

'Yeah, well. Look Sticky mate, nip up the NAFFI and get me some fags before we make a start on this bomb site'

Sticky had gone but a few minutes when Corporal Butterfly made an appearance.

'Look lively, look lively, you won't get far faffing about like this.' He looked around, then asked, 'Where's your mate?'

'Gone on an errand'

'Errand, what errand?'

'To get me some fags'

'Right, you fat bastard, you're off to a bad start - '

Ginger squared up to him menacingly. 'Listen Butterballs, don't ever call me a fat bastard again or I'll chin you. Jordan gets away with it because he and me understand each other but as far as I'm concerned, you're a slimebag, so keep your distance'

Butterballs took two steps back and protested haltingly, 'You're – do you know what you're saying? You are threatening to strike a non-commissioned officer'

'You've got it prick head. Don't ever call me by that

name again and never try to pull any kind of stroke on me or I'll deck you – and you won't be coming back up'

Corporal Butterfly fled the premises without a word of farewell.

*

'Aircraftsman Second class Harrison, you appear before once again, this time as the accused'

Squadron Leader Phartingail ffoulkes-Knight was conducting a hastily convened court of inquiry as a result of a complaint from Corporal Butterfly regarding threats and menaces uttered by the accused with intent of assault on the corporal's person.

'You are facing a very serious charge airman; that of threatening assault on a non-commissioned officer in the course of his duty. How do you plead?'

'Guilty sir'

Eyebrows were raised around the courtroom as the squadron leader requested confirmation of the plea.

'Are you quite sure about that?'

'Yes sir'

'Why did you make these threats?'

'He provoked me sir'

'In what way?'

'He called me a fat bastard sir'

'No swearing in front of the officer,' shouted Sergeant Jordan.

'That will do sergeant,' rebuked the presiding officer. 'The accused is within his rights to employ the terminology in the context of his evidence'

'Sir'

'Well then Airman Second Class Harrison, in the light of your admission of guilt you leave me no alternative other than to award you fourteen days confinement to camp with loss of privileges. You will report to the guard commander in full kit three times daily and you will undertake such sundry duties in and around the camp environs as the commander prescribes. Do you accept my award?'

'Yes sir'

'Now before we clear the courtroom, I have a statement to make on this charge. I take grave exception to the offensive remark issued by Corporal Butterfly to the accused and in the circumstances– '

'Corporal Butterfly denies he made the remark sir,' interrupted Jordan with ill-advised judgement.

'I have yet to complete my statement,' snapped the squadron leader. 'I am minded to reprimand Corporal Butterfly and warn him against any repetition of such unacceptable conduct. Clear the courtroom'

'Sir, e-bout turn, 'eft right, 'eft right…'

Sticky had tears streaming down his face as he frantically scrubbed at the latrine floor with a toothbrush.

'That's fuck all use to me you walking shite house. You're not working fast enough, you idle fucking layabout,' snarled Corporal Butterfly.

'I'm doing me best corp,' sobbed Sticky.

'Well, your best is bollocks'

He dragged Sticky to his feet, shoved him against a wall, and drove a multi-ringed fist straight into his face. Sticky slithered back onto the floor and lay there quite still.

Ginger returned to the billet in full kit after his second guardroom inspection of the day. He looked at the empty bed space and said, 'Where's Sticky?'

'He's up the hospital,' replied an airman.

'Why, what's wrong? Did he have an accident?'

'Not exactly,' advised Barry Emerson. 'Butterballs beat him up'

'What?'

'Take your kit off Ginge and sit down'

Ginger quickly removed his packs and webbing and sat down. 'Well, I'm waiting'

'Butterballs made Sticky clean the bog floor with a

toothbrush and then beat him up because he claimed he wasn't working fast enough'

'I should have guessed this would happen,' said Ginger angrily. 'The bastard couldn't get to me, so he picked on me mate because he knows he's simple. Right, what time is it?'

'Ten past six'

'Perfect. He'll be making his last inspection of the bogs for tonight'

'Don't do anything rash Ginge, this is a job for the SPs'

'Rash did you say? I'm gonna kick fuck out of him. Anyway, the SPs would do nowt. Butterballs is one of their own'

It was dark now and that was good because he wouldn't be spotted as he made his way to where he knew Butterballs would be concluding activities for the day. As Ginger stood in the shadows beside a latrine door Butterballs came towards him, creating as he walked a moving circle of light on the ground from the beam of his service issue torch.

As Butterballs approached, Ginger slammed the door into his face, placed one hand over his victim's mouth and put an arm lock on him with the other. Dragging the struggling body into the latrine and across the newly polished floor, he kicked open a cubicle door and shoved Butterballs' head down the toilet pan, keeping it there for a few seconds before bringing it back up for air.

'How do like that prick head?

The terrified Butterballs gasped and pleaded for mercy. Down went his head again and this time Ginger heard a dull thud as it crashed against the porcelain. Up again dripping with blood and down again for a final cleansing followed by a tug on the chain to complete the ducking.

Ginger hauled the crumpled distressed Butterballs out of the cubicle and threw him roughly in a heap on the floor.

He stood over his terrified victim and said,

'Report this and I'll come back and finish the job'

Ginger left the latrine with Butterballs groaning on the floor. He needed a stiff drink but daren't go near the NAFFI while on jankers. Instead he proceeded to the back perimeter of the camp, climbed through a hole in the fence, and walked the half mile to the Farmers Arms where he gulped down a double whisky purchased with his last few shillings. He knew he wouldn't be back in time for the final guardroom inspection but he didn't care.

*

'Bloody hell, what have we got here?' exclaimed the SP as he and his mates dragged the man away from the burning bed.

*

'So what do you think to it then?'

Ginger had just completed his outline of the circumstances surrounding the damage inflicted on Corporal Butterfly.

'Doesn't look good Ginge,' replied Barry Emerson softly.

'I'll get six to nine months in Colchester,' reckoned Ginger resignedly.

The door burst open and in rushed Scrounger Harris in a state of excitement. He had been visiting Sticky in hospital.

'You'll never guess what's happened up the hospital'

'Has Sticky taken a turn for the worse?' asked Barry anxiously

'No, no it's not that. The SPs admitted Butterballs to casualty in a straitjacket. Claimed he'd had a breakdown'

'What?'

'Yeah, they found him trashing Jordan's quarters. Threw petrol all over the place and set fire to the old man's bedding'

'Fucking hell'

'Did he say owt about me?' Ginger enquired nervously.

'Naw, he just sat there with a blanket round his shoulders, head down, sobbing'

'Serves the cruel bastard right,' said Barry.

'They'll keep him in dock for a week or so,' reckoned an airman who appeared to know about such matters. 'Then he'll be sent home on compassionate leave and when he comes back, they'll post him away as far as possible. It's what they always do with the nut cases'

'Well,' concluded a much relieved Ginger, 'this is what happens when you're a stickler for detail. Isn't life a pisser?'

Sunday outing

In preparation for a 'flash' inspection by Wing Commander Barclay, an inspection everyone in the camp seemed to know about in advance, there was a flurry of activity taking place at the latrines servicing Huts 1-29. Urinals were sluiced, scrubbed and burnished, large quantities of Vim applied at random with total abandon, and the floors so vigorously polished they gleamed like the surface of the local ice rink.

'Nice one,' muttered Ginger as he recklessly threw a bucket of cold water over the top of a closed cubicle. There was a howl and the cubicle door opened to reveal a fellow orderly drenched from tip to toe.

'Have some frigging care, I'm working in here,' he protested loudly.

'Sorry mate'

'Look at me, look at the state I'm in,' complained the orderly with arms outstretched to indicate the damage. 'My uniform's soaked'

'You'll soon dry out,' replied Ginger unconcernedly as he withdrew a cigarette butt from behind an ear and lit up.

'Dry out? What do you mean, dry out? I've got a date in an hour with the girl who gives the bible readings in the NAFFI'

Ginger pondered this new information and suggested,

'Why don't you tell her you went up the padre's to get

baptised and fell in the font like?'

'Fuck off,' reprimanded the disconsolate airman as he squelched across the gleaming floor and exited stage right.

'You what Ginge?' enquired Sticky belatedly. He was atop a tall ladder cleaning the strobe lighting covers. 'You was saying'

'Only, nice one, I was saying. Stuck in here of a Sunday morning when we should be lying in us scratchers with the papers and a hot brew; shouldn't be allowed. We're not bleeding criminals, we've got rights'

'Aye, you're not wrong Ginge,' agreed Sticky.

As sometimes occurs in times of trial, serendipity stepped in to alter the complexion of the vexatious happenings that were so far blighting this particular day of rest; serendipity in the shape of two unexpected but nonetheless rewarding visitations.

The first of these came in the shape of Sergeants Hare and Withinshawe accompanied by a squat, fey looking gentleman wearing a pork pie hat and a floor length astrakhan overcoat.

'Ah, Widow Twankey, there you are', announced Bunny Hare. 'I've got some exciting news for you dearie'

'Oh aye, and what is that?' asked Ginger suspiciously.

'An offer to feed your dreams, trip the light fantastic, put on the greasepaint, tread the boards – '

'He means you get to dress up as a fat tart again,' summarised Stan Withinshawe.

'Not on your fucking Nellie, mate'

'You'll get paid this time,' said Bunny.

'Two hundred quid?' asked Ginger hopefully.

'Hardly, you're not in that league yet, ducky. However, I daresay the budget might stretch to twenty five pounds for seven nights, two matinees.' Bunny looked at the astrakhan coat for confirmation and got a nod of assent. 'Oh, and by the way, this is Mr Jerome Underwood. He has written a brand new forces revue which he's staging at the Warrington Repertory Theatre. Sergeant Withinshawe and I are directing and producing respectively'

'That's nice for you,' contributed Sticky.

'What'll I have to do asides from dressing up as a fat tart?' enquired Ginger.

Bunny placed his arms around the shoulders of Ginger and Sticky.

'I'll need the services of your oppo here as well. Now, why don't we all meet up to discuss matters at say, six o'clock tomorrow evening at the education section offices? I'll get a few bottles of something or other in. Hmm, what do you say?'

'Twenty five quid, right?'

'For you, yes. Five pounds for your friend'

'What's the show called then?'

'Shocks in Frocks'

'Come again'

'You heard me, Shocks in Frocks'

'Get stuffed'

'And this is the geyser what's wrote it up like?' asked Sticky, pointing to the astrakhan.

'Yes'

'Oh, I do envy anyone who can turn his hand to creative writing,' gushed Stan, and then to the astrakhan coat, he said rather earnestly, 'I suppose you have to spend a lot of time studying the works of famous playwrights to get your ideas?'

The astrakhan coat produced a huge cigar, clipped one end, lit up the other and replied, 'No. I never read anything I haven't written myself'

'Oh, fancy,' sniffed Stan.

Half an hour later came the second visitation. It was in the shape of LAC Barry Emerson, complete with a well-stacked golf bag that he placed against a cubicle door.

'All right for some,' greeted Ginger who was up beside Sticky on the tall ladder helping to replace the last of the strobe covers.

Barry folded his arms, leaned against a freshly scrubbed wash basin, looked up at them and grinned.

'How would you two like to come with me to Chester this afternoon?

'Chance'd be a fine thing,' replied Ginger. 'Sticky and me are skint. We haven't got tu'pence to rattle together for the bus fare'

'You won't need bus fare. Flying Officer Beamish has offered to take us in his car'

'Playing golf with him was you?' enquired Sticky

'Yes'

'What's t'do in Chester of a Sunday like?'

'Well, there's the cathedral – and the river'

'Good pubs?'

'I'd imagine so'

'Maybe Beamish'll stand us a few pints,' suggested Ginger eagerly.

'I wouldn't bank on it'

'What time?'

'Two o'clock. He'll call for us at the billet'

'Fine, we'll just clear up then and vamoose. That old git Barclay won't show up now. He'll be tucking into his meat and two veg by now'

Barry had heard footsteps approaching and was looking out of the window.

'Don't be too sure about that. Here he comes now with Flight Lieutenant Ashford and Pilot Officer Emery'

Barry picked up his golf bag while Ginger and Sticky raced down the ladder and carried it between them as all three departed hurriedly through the rear exit.

Right on two o'clock Flying Officer Beamish arrived at Hut 29 in his red open top, spoke-wheeled MG Midget sports car. Barry Emerson claimed the front passenger seat and his fellow passengers clambered into the back and onto the hard wooden rumble bench.

Flying Officer Beamish, who fancied himself as a racing circuit devotee, sped off with tyres screeching, and within minutes they were out of the camp and into the countryside. Between the roar of the engine and the whistling of the wind, sustained conversation was proving difficult.

'Look,' yelled Ginger to his backseat colleague. 'Them's cows in that field over there'

'Me bum's sore,' responded Sticky dolefully.

'You what?'

'Ah said, me bum's sore with this hard seat'

'Oh give over mithering,' yelled back Ginger. 'Them's sheep over there, them is'

Sticky was unimpressed and continued to complain. 'The seat keeps bumpin' up and down and me arse is red raw'

Being rather more substantially upholstered in the hindquarters, Ginger was short on sympathy.

'You're spoiling a good skive with your moaning. Give over and enjoy the scenery. Look, over there, them's goats, them is'

An hour or so later they approached the outskirts of Chester and Flying Officer Beamish took a detour to avoid the city centre. He pulled into a lay-by on the riverbank and stopped the engine. They sat in silence for a few minutes, absorbing the view and watching the local populace out for a Sunday afternoon stroll.

'Nice crumpet around here,' remarked Ginger.

'Harrump,' coughed Beamish.

'Look at them two. Skirts right up to their armpits. I wouldn't mind giving the one on the left a right good - '

'Ah, plan of action,' interrupted Beamish who was clearly uncomfortable with Ginger's predilections. 'Thought we might take in the cathedral first, then a punt on the river, finishing off with afternoon tea, what?'

'Oh aye,' enthused Sticky. 'Some tea and cakes would be champion'

'Barry?' Beamish ignored Ginger's look of disappointment and turned to Emerson for approval.

'Sounds good to me'

'Right then, let's walk. The cathedral is not far from here'

Beamish proved to be something of an expert on the history of the ancient house of worship and acted as tour guide for the group. Barry and Sticky feigned interest in his instructive commentary while Ginger remained in the background murmuring words of discontent.

'What a bleeding pisser,' he muttered to Barry. 'Hanging about this condemned property when we could still be down the riverside pulling some of the spare'

And so back it was to the riverside they trooped shortly afterwards but not to pull the spare; to select a punt for a leisurely cruise down the river.

'How do you steer it?' enquired Ginger.

'With this,' said Barry, indicating the punt pole.

'A chuffing pole?'

'Who'd like to be our navigator?' asked Beamish.

'Ah'll have a go,' volunteered Sticky.

'Good show'

The boat keeper pushed the punt out into the water and for a time Sticky did reasonably well at the helm while there were no other craft around. However, like all learner drivers, he began to panic when he hit the rush hour traffic further upstream.

'Have a care sir,' rebuked one irate lady whose dinghy he just shaved clear by a whisker.

Worse was to follow though when his pole stuck in the mud and Sticky released it almost gratefully. The free-wheeling punt drifted aimlessly to the right, heading for a stationary row boat whose crew consisted of a hefty naval rating and a slip of a girl locked in a passionate embrace.

'I say, ahoy there – 'hailed Flying Officer Beamish a smidgen too late.

The punt smashed into the side of the motionless vessel putting an abrupt end to the seafarer's lovemaking. He released his grip on the object of his affections, glared at Beamish with deep hostility and said,

'You wanker, I'll rip your fucking ears off, I'll – '

Ginger stood up and challenged, 'Oh aye, how would you like to make a start on me first?'

A voice cried out, 'Co-eee'

It came from a passing skiff that had Bunny and Stan applying themselves earnestly and energetically to the oars with the astrakhan coat sitting aft and aloof in the cox position.

'Spot of bother?' enquired Bunny pleasantly in the passing.

'No thanks,' replied Ginger. 'We got some already'

'Have fun,' called Stan, waving back at them.

On sizing up Ginger's girth for a second time, the matelot decided that desertion might be the better part of valour on this occasion, and so he picked up the oars and pushed off downstream leaving the punt stranded. They tried in vain for more than half an hour to interest the rapidly dwindling traffic in their plight and were eventually rescued by the river security launch, which towed the punt back to the landing area.

'Here,' said the boat keeper as he inspected the empty vessel 'Where's the pole?'

'Ah, stuck in the mud back there, I'm afraid,' replied Beamish.

'Stuck in the mud? That'll cost you three pounds ten shillings that will'

'Listen pal,' butted in Ginger, 'you can shove your three pounds ten shillings, you can shove your pole, and you can shove your rotten river'

They left the boat keeper to grieve over his lost punt pole and headed uptown in search of a late afternoon tea.

'Ah,' announced Beamish. 'Here's the spot. Anne's Pantry, she does a spiffing Devonshire tea, oodles of jam and cream'

'Great,' said Sticky.

'Smashing,' seconded Barry.

'Wonder if she's got draught bitter?' mused Ginger.

Anne's spiffing Devonshire tea consisted of six soft warm scones apiece, oodles of jam and cream as forecast by Beamish, and an enormous pot of hot steaming tea – all of which was scoffed down by the ravenous seafarers in jig time. So pleased was Anne at the reception to her cuisine, she supplied them with second helpings at no extra cost.

'Ah'll have to go to the bog,' said Sticky at end of the repast.

'Why can't you say crapper when you're in company,' rebuked Ginger.

As Sticky got up from table, Beamish also excused himself, saying, 'I think I'll also wash my hands, then I'll settle the account and we'll head back to camp'

'Queer bird that Beamish,' remarked Ginger when they'd gone.

'Queer is the word, as in bent,' replied Barry.

'You don't mean?'

'As a four-pound note'

'How do you know?'

'He sounded me out the first time we played golf, but he knows better now'

'Bloody hell'

'He fancies Sticky'

'What?'

'Saw him in the pantomime. Reckon that's why we're here this afternoon'

'Maybe I'd better check that Sticky's okay'

As he got up to go and investigate, the door to the men's loo opened and both Beamish and Sticky emerged. Beamish proceeded to the cash desk and Sticky came back to the table.

'Here, guess what? Flying Officer Beamish reckons he and I should go out on town some night. Do you think it'd be okay Ginge, what with him being an officer like?'

'Oh aye, as long as you don't let him shag you'

'What?'

'He's a whoofter'

'You're having me on, aren't you?'

'He fancies you'

'But blokes only fancy tarts don't they?'

'Not this one, he's different'

'Oh, fuck me'

'Don't say that to him' advised Barry.

The drive back to camp was accomplished in total

silence. Beamish dropped his passengers off at the approach to the billets. Barry walked one way to the NAFFI, Ginger and Sticky the other way to Hut 29.

They were alone and Sticky was full of misgivings about agreeing to an evening on the town with Flying Officer Beamish.

Ginger was at a window looking out.

'Bloody hell,' he said. 'Here he comes; he's heading for the billet'

'Beamish?'

'Aye'

'What'll ah do Ginge?'

'Get yourself into that empty locker and shut the door after you. I'll deal with the whoofter'

Seconds later Beamish entered.

'Ah, is AC2 Albright around?'

'Naw, he's out with his bird'

'He has a girlfriend?'

'Oh aye, been going steady for months, getting spliced next year'

'Ah, right. Would you give him this book from me? It's about ancient monuments. He expressed an interest this afternoon'

'Aye, I will'

'Thank you, carry on'

Ginger knocked on the locker door.

'You can come out now'

'Has he gone then?'

'Aye, your virginity is safe - for now'

Weekend in Wakefield

'That Flying Officer Beamish ain't such a bad bloke, Sticky' announced Ginger on his return from the village.

'I had a pint with him in the Farmers Arms'

'Oh aye'

'Lonely beggar, no family and never goes nowhere; seems marauding gunmen in India killed his folks when he were a kid at boarding school in Kent. He was only nine, poor sod'

'Oh aye'

'Is that all you can say? 'Oh aye'

'There's a letter for ye on the bed, I brought it back from the orderly room. They must have forgot to deliver it yesterday like'

'Dozy beggars,' said Ginger, picking up the envelope and ripping it open. 'Let's have a read of it then'

'From your mam is it?'

'No, it's a birthday card from me Auntie Maggie with a ten bob note inside'

'When's your birthday?'

'Yesterday'

'You should have said'

'Well, you don't, do you?'

Ginger continued to read the card then added,

'Here, she's invited me to stay over the weekend'

'Where does she live like?'

'Wakefield. Well, Boghouses, really. That's three miles from Wakefield. Do you fancy coming with me?'

'Oh aye'

'Right I'll nip up and see Simple Simon for us travel warrants'

He stopped on the way out, turned and said.

'How about I ask Beamish to come as well? Do him good to get away from camp for a few days. Auntie Maggie wouldn't mind, she's got loads of room since her lads moved out, and Uncle Herbert loves a bit of company'

'Well…'

'Don't worry. Beamish won't bother you. He's got the message now'

'Well…'

'I'll call in on Beamish at his quarters on the way back. He can get his own rail warrant if he's coming'

*

'That'll be thirty bob for the two warrants,' said LAC

Simpkins.

'No it fecking won't

'What?'

'Not if you still want me to collect your money next week'

Simpkins demurred without argument. He depended heavily on Ginger's expertise as a debt collector. Soon after taking over Smudger Jacobi's black market activities, he discovered that he had absolutely no talent for cash control.

*

A few minutes after three o'clock on Saturday afternoon, the steam train chugged and coughed its way along platform one of Wakefield Station. Messrs Harrison, Albright and Beamish were in mufti on the occasion of an away weekend. They removed their baggage from the rack, left the carriage, and headed down the platform towards the exit.

'I say,' said Beamish. 'Is it far? Should we hail a cab?'

'Naw, we'll get the bus,' replied Ginger.

The bus to Boghouses turned out to be a single-decker relic from the nineteen twenties with slatted wooden seating accommodation. It stuttered and spluttered along the main road, emitting a constant stream of black smoke from its rattling makeshift exhaust. Suddenly and without warning, it lurched left into a minor road sending Sticky flying along the passageway. He struggled to his feet, announcing,

'Me bum's sore'

'Now, don't start all that again,' reprimanded Ginger. 'Get yourself sat down'

Three miles on the bus ground to a thankful halt on the village square situated on top of a steep hill. The weekenders proceeded downwards, passing rows of tattered terraced houses on either side until they reached the foot of the hill where stood all on its own a large ramshackle detached villa with bits butted on haphazardly to the front and on both sides

Waiting to greet her visitors at the lopsided gate was Auntie Maggie.

'Oh Clarence love,' she called when they were a dozen or so yards away. 'Come 'ere and give yer auntie a hug'

'Clarence? Is that your real name Ginge?' asked Sticky unbelievingly.

'Shush,' replied Ginger sternly. 'Spread that around camp and I'll crack your head open.' He embraced his aunt and then introduced her to the guests.

'This here's Sticky and that's Flying Officer Beamish'

'Oh, an officer, well, I never.' She curtsied, adding, 'You're very welcome I'm sure'

'Peregrine, please'

'Peregrine, is that *your* bleeding name?' Ginger was relieved that someone else was similarly if not more severely appellation challenged.

'Come away in boys,' fussed Auntie Maggie. 'Uncle Herbert's watching racin' on t'telly.' She led the way through a dark cavernous hall into a murky sitting room where crammed into an armchair reposed the living image of Ginger. Older, fatter, bigger even, and with the same carrot red hair tinged with grey. He wore a collarless shirt with the sleeves rolled up, sported a four-inch broad leather belt around his ample belly, and had his feet encased in size fifteen pit boots.

'Sit ye down lads,' he growled. 'We'll have us tea and then I'll tak ye down t'legion'

'Legion?' enquired Beamish.

'British Legion, it's a club like, for ex-servicemen,' explained Ginger.

'Ah, yes, quite'

'Have they got snooker?' enquired Sticky.

'Snooker?' barked Uncle Herbert. 'Of course they got bloody snooker. Wha' d'ye think the legion is lad, bloody Sally Ann'?'

'Now dad, behave,' admonished Auntie Maggie softly.

'So, auntie,' said Ginger intervening brightly. 'What do you have for us teas?'

'Yer favourite Clarence, pig's trotters wi' mustard'

'Smashing'

She looked at the other two for a reaction to her proposed menu.

'Great, missus,' confirmed Sticky.

Flying Officer Beamish wasn't quite so enthralled at the prospect of pig's trotters for high tea. 'If it won't put you to an inconvenience, may I have a spot of bread and cheese instead please'

Auntie Maggie was horrified at the suggestion.

'Bread and cheese, that's for mice and such like. Nay, I'll do you up some steak and chips, if that's suitable'

'Admirably so, thank you'

'Could ah have steak an' chips as well missus?' pleaded Sticky.

'No, you chuffing well can't,' decreed Ginger. 'You'll have pig's trotters and like them. Auntie Maggie's made them special like'

'Look, if I'm being troublesome -' said Beamish.

'Nay lad, you shall 'ave steak and chips'

'Right then ma, now tha's settled, let's 'ave grub on t'table,' commanded Uncle Herbert.

'May I use your facilities before we dine?' asked Beamish.

'Facilities?' Auntie Maggie looked puzzled.

'Your bathroom'

'Bathroom?' Uncle Herbert was outraged. 'Ma, bring out tub and 'e can scrub down his arse while we 'ave us teas'

'D'ye mean the toilet, dear?' whispered Auntie Maggie.

'Yes'

'Shed at back o' t'garden. Key's on hook on t'back door'

As Beamish left the room Uncle Herbert commented, 'Bloody soft southerner'

'Now then, be reasonable.' Ginger came to the defence of his fellow guest. 'He's a toff, he don't know our ways'

Auntie Maggie repaired to the kitchen and Sticky called after her,

'Can ah give you a hand missus?'

'There's a good lad'

As Sticky departed Beamish re-entered the sitting room.

'All right then?' asked Ginger.

'Ah yes, slight problem though. No toilet paper'

'Toilet paper' Uncle Herbert was off again. 'No fucking toilet paper? Wakefield Gazette not good enough fer you? Let me tell you lad, there's backsides around

Boghouses that ha'n't seen toilet fucking paper since afore War o' t'bloody Roses – '

'Oh, give over dad,' called Auntie Maggie from the kitchen. 'Let's 'ave us teas in peace'

*

'By the left 'Erbert, yon lad's the spitting image of you.' The head barkeep of the British Legion was pulling pints for the new arrivals.

'Another ugly bugger then,' responded Uncle Herbert gruffly, as he proceeded to effect introductions.

'We've never had an officer in here afore to the best o' my recollection,' said the barkeep when he became aware of Beamish's status.

'Aye you have,' announced a member perched on a high stool at the other end of the bar.

'Who?' asked the barkeep.

'Me'

'Give over Harold; you were in the pioneer corps'

'I were and all but I were a second lieutenant in the pioneer corps'

'Did you graduate from Sandhurst?' asked Beamish innocently enough.

'No I feckin' well didn't lad. I graduated from a shit hole in the desert'

'Sorry, I don't quite follow,' replied the bemused flying officer.

'You would if you'd been in the North African Desert in 1942. None o' your lot, the toffs like, was keen on getting' their hands dirty building bogs in the sand alongside the men in their charge. Didn't bother me mind, so I volunteered and got promoted'

'Sounds like a tall tale t'me,' growled Uncle Herbert.

'Oh aye, you reckon?' Harold pulled out a wallet, thumbed through it, and produced a snapshot and a piece of paper. 'Have a look at these then'

Uncle H examined the exhibits, which consisted of a much handled, grainy black and white print of Harold in full dress uniform, and a copy of his discharge certificate. Without a word he handed them to the barkeep who said, 'Well, I'll go to the foot of our stairs'

'You're a dark horse,' complained Uncle Herbert. 'T'think we 'ave a bleeding officer as us shop steward'

'That were then,' replied Harold solemnly. 'This is now'

Uncle Herbert led the way to the snooker room where he proceeded to thrash each of his guests individually and then collectively in a foursome. As he was downing a celebratory pint of best bitter, Ginger whispered to the other two,

'We'd best leave now and have a night on the town'

They bade their farewells and set off for the square.

'What's the plan?' enquired Beamish.

'We'll have a few more ales in town and then it's Wakefield Palais'

'The dancing like?' enthused Sticky.

'Naw, embroidery class'

'Wish I'd driven us here. I must say I'm not looking forward to another journey in that dreadful omnibus'

'We'll get a taxi this time. Auntie Maggie slipped me a few quid'

Waiting on its own at the rank was a 1931 Humber open roadster.

'You a taxi then?' asked Ginger of the doleful driver.

'No, not personally, but ah'm sitting in one. Hop in'

'Wakefield centre'

'Cost you five bob'

'Give over,' protested Ginger. 'Half a dollar, take it or leave it'

'Ah'll leave it, you tak' the bus'

'Look here,' Beamish said to Ginger, 'Don't let's haggle. I'll throw in the extra few shillings'

*

Wakefield Palais de Danse was packed to the gunnels

and as they entered from the foyer into the hall, they were almost deafened by a recording of Al Martino blasting out his latest hit,

Here in my heart,
I'm alone and oh so lonely….
Here in my heart,
I just long for you only'

The threesome stood at the back absorbing the atmosphere and eyeing up the talent when Ginger was summoned from behind by a strident female voice. It was Mavis Ollershaw, an old flame from childhood days.

'You dancin' then or wha'?' she enquired.

'You asking'?'

'Ah'm askin' '

'Ah'm dancing'

Beamish had just spotted a likely looking filly and he too excused himself.

Sticky decided he'd best make a move. He looked around and opted for a tiny, plainly turned out young lady with a pronounced squint in one eye. She was standing alone against the back wall.

'You dancin' then or wha'?'

'Bugger off'

'Eh?'

'Ah said, bugger off. You're only after t'one thing'

After a few dances Ginger and Beamish returned to re-join a forlorn Sticky.

'Was your friend nice?' asked Sticky of Ginger.

'Oh aye, good solid lass that can hold a tackle. How did you get on then?'

'She told me to bugger off'

'Had she owt else to say?'

'What's the one thing Ginge?'

Ginger winked at Beamish and replied, 'We'll tell you later'

Sunday morning and afternoon were spent loafing around in the garden before and after Auntie Maggie's generous meals. In the evening they went back to the British Legion Club in the company of Uncle Herbert.

*

Five thirty am Monday morning found the weekenders back on the village square but this time waiting at the bus stop for the workers special. It eventually came into sight at the brow of the hill coughing, spluttering and fully forty-five minutes late, causing them to miss their train.

As they trooped though the camp gates, Beamish set off for his quarters while the other two were hailed by one of the guards.

'Sergeant Jordan wants you two pillocks to report to him immediately'

Jordan kept them waiting outside his door for half an hour before barking at them to come in.

'Right, you overgrown idle airman, and you, you great long streak of cat's piss, I'm putting both of you on a charge sheet for being absent without leave. How dare you appear before me in civilian dress; no alibis this time, no witnesses and no almanacs – '

His chastisement was interrupted by an urgent sounding knock on the door.

'Come in,' bellowed Jordan.

In walked Flying Officer Beamish in full dress uniform.

'I'd like a word with you sergeant. Alone'

Jordan dismissed the offenders, got to his feet and saluted.

'What can I do for you Flying Officer?'

'You can put away those charge sheets for a start'

'What?'

'I'm about to save you from making a fool of yourself. Those two men came to my rescue this morning and that is why they were late arriving back at camp from weekend leave. I too was away for the weekend and my car broke down outside Padgate station. They pushed the vehicle for fully two and a half miles to the nearest garage. Without their gratuitous assistance, it would still be lying where it conked out'

Sergeant Jordan wasn't about to have this poncified young titch snatch his prize away. He decided to tough it out.

'That's all very well, but I've only got your word for it, and the fact remains they was AWOL, and in my book – '

'Very well, then you leave me with no alternative other than to report to Squadron Leader Phartingail ffoulkes-Knight on an extremely serious incident I witnessed last Thursday evening, an incident involving you sergeant. I'd rather hoped I could overlook it'

'What fucking incident?' exploded Jordan, then quickly adding to save face, 'Begging your pardon Flying Officer Beamish, what incident?'

'The incident involving you in the uniform of His Majesty's Royal Air Force knocking seven bells out of a Royal Navy chief petty officer outside the Farmers Arms public house in Padgate. That incident, sergeant'

'You can't prove nuffinck'

'Oh, but yes I can. Pilot Officer Emery was with me. He saw it too and would be prepared to give witness to that effect'

*

'It must have been Flying Officer Beamish what got us off,' speculated Sticky as he threw a bucket of cold water into an unsuspecting cubicle.

'Told you he isn't such a bad bloke,' replied Ginger.

'Yeah, you said,' agreed Sticky as the cubicle door opened to reveal Sergeant Jordan drenched from tip to toe.

Shocks in frocks

'Let's have some order please,' announced Sergeant Bunny Hare to the packed audience of hopefuls gathered around the stage of the camp theatre. Sitting alongside him at table were Sergeant Stan Withinshawe and Mr Underwood, the tiny, fey looking gentleman dressed in his full-length astrakhan coat topped on this occasion by a natty straw hat.

'Featured artistes to the left – '

'Chorus and dancers to the right, and shit shovellers to the rear,' shouted the audience en masse.

'Cheeky devils,' rebuked Stan.

'Before I make a start on tonight's agenda,' continued Bunny, 'allow me to introduce our special guest, the well-known impresario Mr Jerome Underwood. Jerome is the author and executive producer of the revue we'll be staging at the Warrington Repertory Theatre'

'What's it called then?' someone yelled.

'Underneath The Arches,' yelled back someone else.

'Where's Chesney Allen then?' someone at the back cried out.

Bunny ignored the jibes and continued,

'As happened with the Christmas pantomime, some roles have already been cast but it won't take us long tonight to sort out the remainder because Sergeant Withinshawe and I now have a grasp on what you're all capable of contributing. Stan, will you give them the good news before we get down to brass tacks?'

'How many brasses are you looking for?'

'That'll be quite enough of that, thank you,' Stan reprimanded the wag. 'We've already identified our comedians for the revue. Right, the good news, you'll all get paid this time'

A roar of approval went up followed by questions about how much and when.

'All in good time,' shouted Stan, waving his hands about in an endeavour to quell the babble. 'You will be remunerated for your contribution to the production, which will run nightly over two weeks with matinees on both Saturdays. That's all you need to know presently'

'Right,' said Bunny. 'Our star on this occasion will be LAC Gropethorpe who will entertain audiences with his impersonations of famous film stars. Marlene Dietrich, Mae West, Carmen Miranda and Jean Harlow, to name but four'

'Does that mean he gets top billing over me?' called out Ginger Harrison in what seemed like a complaint.

'Do you have a problem with that?' sniffed Stan.

'No, I suppose not,' reflected Ginger. 'Just wanted to check like'

'Well now you know,' continued Bunny, 'and you also know that you'll be playing the part of Mrs McGillicuddy.

Bit of an Old Mother Riley act really,' he added by way of explanation, 'but with an idiot son as her sidekick instead of a beautiful daughter. AC2 Albright has been cast as the idiot son'

'Good casting that,' said Scrounger Harris.

'Supporting these star roles will be Betty Grable, Veronica Lake, Betty Hutton, Greta Garbo, Bette Davis, Joan Crawford, Dorothy Lamour, and we have our own thoughts on who we'll be casting for these parts'

An hour or so later the assembled airmen were doing justice to the customary hospitality provided by Bunny and Stan; pies, sausage rolls, sandwiches and cakes disappeared as if by magic; tea and coffee urns were drained dry.

Standing by the edge of the stage, Stan was holding court with Ginger and the astrakhan coat in attendance.

'You done a lot then in this theatre lark?' asked Ginger of the astrakhan.

'I'll say he has,' contributed Stan before the coat could answer. 'Musical comedies, summer shows, pantomime; Jerome's done the lot *and* he's worked in films. Written screenplays for Northern Productions, he has, *and* material for Sandy Powell, Frank Randle *and* George Formby'

'What's George Formby like then?' Ginger tried again to get the astrakhan coat to open up but Stan denied him the opportunity.

'Oh, he's all right but his wife Beryl is a right little needle in the derriere. Haughty madam, she is, tight as a ballerina's bum with George's money'

Ginger felt a tap on his shoulder and turned around. It was Bunny, who led him by the arm to a corner of the room.

'How would you like to earn some extra money, over and above what you'll be getting for appearing in the review?'

'Doing what?' asked Ginger.

'Assuming control of camp ticket sales; you seem to know everyone and everyone seems to know you. I'd give you a supply of posters to stick up in the NAFFI, the various messes, camp cinema, orderly room and wherever else you reckon would make good vantage points'

'What's in it for me like?'

'A shilling in the pound on sales'

'Get stuffed'

'Don't be too hasty. The theatre holds eleven hundred and there'll be fourteen shows in all over the two weeks. Do the sums. Admission prices will range from fifteen shillings for the front stalls right through to two and sixpence for the gods. As the official ticket seller, you'll get a shilling in the pound on all camp sales – and don't forget, we're not just talking forces personnel –there are a lot of civilians working here too'

'What about outside the camp? Like pubs and shops?'

'Fine, if you'd like to take that on too. We're looking for family audiences'

'And I'd give the cash to you, right?'

'No. As executive producer, Mr Underwood is in charge of banking for the revue. He'll be in my office every night at seven o'clock from now until we open. Just call in nightly and give the cash to him. He'll issue you with receipts so that you can keep check of your commission'

'Right, you're on'

A few days later Sticky was dispatched with an armful of posters and a can of paste to do some fly posting around the camp.

'What if Sergeant Jordan sees me?' Sticky had protested before setting out. 'He'll have me on another fizzer'

'No he won't,' replied Ginger confidently. 'Just tell him you was sent by Flying Officer Beamish. Jordan's shit scared of Beamish since he sorted him out the time we came back from me Auntie Maggie's'

When Sticky had completed his billposting assignment he was given another armful of posters and instructed to call on local pubs, garages and shops.

'Oh,' shouted Ginger after him, 'don't forget Mad Taffy down the village. He'll be good for a few ticket sales'

These front-of-the-house activities prospered in the weeks to follow and every night Ginger called in at the education offices and cashed up with the astrakhan.

*

'No, no, no,' screamed Bunny at the outset of the dress rehearsal. 'You are not a motionless tableaux in a cheap and nasty nude show. You are famous film stars. For heavens sake move around a bit, show a bit of leg'

'And some bum and tit,' contributed Stan.

'Betty Grable,' continued the exasperated producer. 'Who put you in a frock?'

The wardrobe master indicated that the decision was his.

'Well, get her out of it and into a skimpy sarong or tights. She's the million-dollar leg girl, not some frump from a Hopalong Cassidy oater'

'Bette Davis,' cried Stan, not to be left out. 'Make with the eyes, vamp, vamp, vamp; now wardrobe, what about costumes for the Andrews Sisters?'

'Andrews Twisters, dear,' whispered Bunny. 'They reckon it sounds sexier'

'Ooooh, cheeky devils'

After they'd put the dancers through their kicks, Stan called for Mrs McGillicuddy and her idiot son.

'Now Mrs McGillicuddy, open with line forty seven in your script'

'Oh, stop your mithering boy,' acted out Ginger forcefully. 'I'll find money for the rent somehow'

On this solitary line, the idiot son exited stage left.

'What about the stuff that went before?' enquired Ginger.

'We'll leave that for now,' replied Bunny. 'Now Mrs McGillicuddy, imagine this. Just as your idiot son exits, the stage suddenly darkens and stays that way for a few seconds until the floods and spots pop back on one by one. You are standing there alone. You are eating a fish supper out of a newspaper and your starched skirt is turned up at one corner, all the way up to your face, blocking your view to the fact that your polka dot bloomers are showing. Got that?'

'Aye'

'Cue comic policeman,' called Stan.

From stage right entered the comic policeman wearing an outsize helmet.

'Hullo, hullo, hullo. You can't do that there 'ere Mrs McGillicuddy'

'What?'

'Standing there with your skirts up, showing off your particulars for all to see'

Mrs McGillicuddy stopped eating, looked down, then resumed eating again before replying disinterestedly,

'Has that little sailor gone then?'

'Oh, bold, bold!' cried Stan.

'Not too bold though?' entreated Bunny.

'Much too bold,' wailed Stan. 'We've got family audiences to think about, we have. We don't want the kiddie winkies copping an earful of that adult pallare. We'd have the watch committee on stage before the final curtain'

'Perhaps you're right Stan,' considered Bunny and then, calling to the astrakhan coat who was seated in the very back row of the stalls, he added, 'that one's coming out Jerome. Too near the bone'

'That's it then, is it?' exploded Mrs McGillicuddy, clutching her handbag. 'Spent half the frigging night learning meself the routine, and now it's out. Is that it then?'

'Marlene Dietrich on stage,' called Stan, ignoring the outburst.

On walked Marlene Dietrich in her Blue Angel costume, complete with top hat, high heels and black fishnet tights. She ambled to the centre of the stage and sat astride the back of a hard chair.

'Hello boys,' she spoke in a husky whisper. 'You in the fwont rwow, miwitawy powiceman, is that a twuncheon in your twousews or are you chust pleased to see me?'

'She'll knock them dead Bunny, she's priceless, star of the show,' enthused Stan. 'I've said it before and I'll not apologise for saying it again; what a pair of lallies'

Marlene threw the chair aside and peeled off her jacket.

> *Fallinck in love again,*
> *Vot am I to do,*
> *Nevah vanted to,*
> *I can't help it.*

'Come and wisit me in the back woom at the end of the show, boys,' concluded Marlene as she swaggered off stage. 'Votevah you dwink, I dwink also'

*

The rehearsals progressed satisfactorily and ticket sales boomed. Ginger even had a special offer included in the orderly room black market menu. Free travel warrant with every two tickets purchased for cash. LAC Simpkins had objected when Ginger first mooted the idea.

'You've got it the wrong way round. It should be two free tickets with every travel warrant purchased'

'No it fecking shouldn't. Just do as I say if you still want your own cash collected – and don't hand out no tickets without cash in hand or I'll take it out of what I collect for you'

*

The opening night of *Shocks in Frocks* was a smash and audiences for the run were highly acceptable with full houses recorded for eight nights and half to three quarters for the remainder.

The only glitch occurred at the beginning of the second week when Bunny announced excitedly to Stan one afternoon,

'Guess what?'

'What?'

'I've only managed to persuade Anne Ziegler and Webster Booth to make a guest appearance tonight. I'm putting them on just before the interval; they've got to rush away immediately afterwards to catch a train back to London'

'What, your actual Anne Ziegler and Webster Booth? Singing stars of stage, screen and radio?'

'Not quite, look-a-likes. They take them off at soirees, tea dances and concerts - that sort of thing'

'Dirty devils'

'Don't be clever, you know what I mean'

'Is there a fee involved?'

'No. They said they'd do anything for the boys in blue'

'Hmm, did they now?' Stan pouted.

*

Just as the first half was drawing to a close, Barry Emerson resplendent in hired dinner jacket walked onstage to announce, 'It gives me great pleasure to introduce two surprise guests for this evening's performance. Ladies and gentlemen, Anne Ziegler and Webster Booth...'

'Thank you, thank you, thank you,' gushed Anne Ziegler breathlessly,' you are too, too kind. Webster and I have just this moment arrived hotfoot from the BBC studios in Manchester where we have been recording our weekly radio show. I do hope you boys all listen to it, tucked up as it were in your cosy little billets. Yes?'

Her enquiry was greeted with stunned silence, peppered only by a loud hacking cough from an elderly lady at the back of the stalls.

'Tonight,' broke in Webster Booth covering up the songsters' embarrassment, 'we bring you a melody of favourite love songs, starting with a snatch from our very own signature tune…'

In a shrill, trembling soprano, Anne Ziegler began

With a song in our hearts -

'Gerroff, you're nobbut impostors,' bellowed a fat bulbous-nosed man in the front row just as Webster was opening his mouth to grab the second line.

'Anne Ziegler and Webster bloody Booth my arse,' yelled someone else disgustedly. 'Laurel and Hardy more like'

The orchestra battled on manfully for a few more bars and then ground to a ragged halt as the guest songsters trooped sheepishly off stage on the prompt side

'Show us your knickers then Webster,' shouted a drunken voice.

'Surely he means *Anne*'s knickers,' remarked Bunny indifferently from the OP side.

'You leave Scrounger Harris alone,' rebuked Stan, sniffing.

'He knows whose nether garments he means'

*

And so by the final Saturday evening performance everyone connected with the revue was in high spirits with the exception of the astrakhan coat who was sitting in his customary seat in the last row of the back stalls seemingly impervious to the excitement surrounding him.

Following an enthusiastic rendering of frenzied Latin American dance music by the septuagenarian theatre orchestra, a drum roll heralded the last act in the evening's entertainment.

Bedecked in a fruit piled headpiece, Cuban high heels and slit skirt, magenta lipped Carmen Miranda congaed onto the stage to the delight of the full house.

> *Ay, ay, ay, ay, ay,*
> *I like you very much,*
> *Ay, ay, ay, ay, ay,*
> *I think you're grand,*
> *Si, si, si, si, si, si,*
> *Way up high above…*

Bunny and Stan were standing together in the wings with tears welling up in their eyes.

'She's worth more than the fifty quid we're paying her,' choked Bunny.

'I cannot but agree,' simpered Stan. 'She takes her part lovely. She's just wonderful, that LAC Gropethorpe is, just wonderful, and she's got gorgeous lallies as well'

'Maybe we could stretch to a hundred,' said Bunny in a

trembling voice which suddenly straightened itself out when he added, 'But only after we've had our fees'

'Ooooh ye-es,' squealed Stan, equally reinvigorated. 'We have to have our fees, we've earned them we have'

There was a discreet cough from behind and they both turned around to investigate the source. It was the general manager of the Warrington Repertory Theatre. He was short and stout, his sparse hair jutted forward in a slick, and he was wearing a black dinner jacket, fawn coloured slacks and light blue shoes.

'Sorry to intrude gents but I find myself in summat of what you might describe as an embarrassing situation'

'Oh dear,' commiserated Stan. 'What's that then? Can we help?'

'I do hope so gents. Y'see, your cheque for the hire of the theatre has not been honoured. It has been returned marked return to drawer, gone bad, bounced, as you might say. Difficult position it's put me in, theatre owner won't like it, local press'll catch on, writ'll be issued, I'll get sack'

'That can't be right,' protested Bunny with some indignation. 'I mean, have you spoken to Mr Underwood about this? He's in the back row. Have a word with him, he'll sort it out'

'I did, and he said he'd get back to me. Now he's not there, he's gone, scarpered, pissed off. I've called the police'

'Whatever for, what can they do?'

'They can apprehend the cheating bastard, that's what they can do, that's what they're paid to do, isn't it?'

So overcome were Bunny and Stan by the theatre manager's disturbing news, they hadn't even noticed the final curtain coming down.

Two embarrassed young police constables stood at the OP side observing the good-natured banter between the cast and crew. Bunny felt a pang of remorse at the thought of bursting their collective bubble but there was no alternative available to him.

'May I have your undivided attention,' he began. 'I'm very sorry to have to tell you this after such a successful run but – '

He proceeded no further because Ginger, still dressed as Mrs McGillicuddy, entered from the prompt side with a large black satchel in one hand and the astrakhan coat by the scruff of the neck in the other.

'Caught the little git at the railway station,' he announced to the astonished onlookers.

'But how, how did you know?' exclaimed Bunny.

'Because I never did take to him from the first time I clapped eyes on him and I became more and more suspicious every time I handed over the ticket cash to him of a night. He used to snatch it right out of me hands'

'Yes, but how did you know he was going to have it

away on his tippy toes with the cash tonight?' enquired Stan.

'Because I've been watching him in the back row of the stalls every night, looking as if butter wouldn't melt in his mouth. I've had plenty of time to do that because you cut down me part to next to bugger all. I noticed tonight that he had a black bag with him and it didn't take too much working out to guess what was in it. So, after me last spot I stood peeping out through the side curtain and then I saw him get up to leave. He hadn't been watching the acts during the run, he'd been timing them so's he could dodge off and catch an evening train before the final curtain'

'Bastard,' assessed the theatre manager.

'So you rushed out after him?' suggested Bunny.

'Yeah, I did, and I caught up with him at the station. You owe me five bob for taxi fares. Never mind,' Ginger added, 'all's well that ends well'

'D'ye know,' reflected Stan, hand on chin as he sized Ginger up and down. 'You'd make a great Falstaff'

'Piss off'

Summer love

Barry Emerson, Scrounger Harris, Ginger and Sticky were sitting at a table in Betty's Café on a warm Sunday evening in early summer.

'Look at them GIs from Burtonwood pulling the spare,' complained Scrounger bitterly. 'It's like shooting fish in a bloody barrel'

It was to Betty's famous little Nissen hut snack bar that the local talent gathered most evenings; some out of curiosity, others with a view to fixing up an assignation.

'Small wonder,' replied Ginger resignedly. 'What with their gabardine clobber and wads of notes that would choke a donkey, we've got no chance'

'Hold up,' announced Barry. 'Look over there. The fancy uniforms and the money didn't work for those PFCs; they've just been given the elbow'

Ginger sneaked a glance and observed two GIs departing from a table where a couple of well-turned out young ladies were sitting.

'How about moving in on them?' suggested Scrounger.

'There's four of us,' countered Ginger

'Count me out,' said Barry. 'I'm off now, got to be up early in the morning. First intake of new recruits arrives at half past eight and I'm down for attestation duty'

'I fancy the little brunette,' continued Scrounger, staking an early claim. 'She's called Barbara. I heard one of the Yanks call her that. The other one's Dorothy'

'Well, I wouldn't be in a hurry to crawl over Dorothy to get to Barbara,' vouchsafed Barry as he made to leave the group.

Ginger and Scrounger got up from the table but Sticky remained seated.

'Come on,' instructed Ginger.

'Ah wouldn't know what to say like'

'Best leave him be,' advised Scrounger. 'He wouldn't be able to pull'

'What makes you think you will?' rebuked Ginger. 'Come on Sticky, we'll all three of us go over. Leave me to break the ice'

Barry made his way out and Ginger, followed by the other two, headed towards the prey.

'Them chairs free?' asked Ginger.

'I wouldn't know,' replied the brunette snootily. 'You'd best ask the proprietor if you're thinking of taking them away'

'No one's using them,' said Dorothy, smiling.

'Mind if we join you then?'

'Three's only two seats and anyway, three's a crowd,'

said the brunette.

'Shove off Scrounger,' said Ginger.

'But – '

'Shall ah go instead?' offered Sticky.

'No,' and turning to Scrounger, Ginger whispered in his ear, 'Shove off short arse, you're queering my pitch'

Scrounger grumbled on his way out of the café while Ginger sat down beside Dorothy and motioned Sticky to do likewise beside Barbara.

'What happened to the Yanks then?' enquired Ginger as an opener.

'We told them to push off,' volunteered Dorothy.

'Bullshitters,' added Barbara.

'So, Barbara, Dorothy - we heard your names mentioned earlier - what do you work at?' pursued Ginger.

'We don't,' replied Barbara. 'We're students at Padgate Teachers Training College'

'Get away'

'Seriously'

'Hear that Sticky – '

'Sticky?' repeated Dorothy incredulously.

'Oh aye, sorry, introductions; I'm Ginger on account of me hair, he's Sticky – on account of you don't ask why'

'Right little chatterbox, isn't he?' said Barbara.

'He can be once he gets fired up'

'What does it take to light his fuse?'

And so the banter continued for half an hour or so until the girls made noises about getting back to their living quarters. Ginger suggested that he and Sticky escort them back to the college gates.

*

'So, what are you waiting for?' asked Barbara, rubbing her leg against Sticky's genitalia, 'Inspiration?'

'Ah've never been with a girl afore,' mumbled Sticky in his embarrassment

'Not ever?'

'No'

'Jolly hockey sticks, I've plucked me a virgin'

'What?'

'Well then, best make a start then, hadn't we?'

*

It was well past lights out when Sticky made it back to Hut 29. Ginger was the only one still up and he lay stretched out on his bed in his underpants reading the comic cuts with the aid of a flashlight.

'How did you get on then?' he asked.

'How d'ye mean?'

'Did you get your leg over?'

'What?'

'Did you get your rocks off?' clarified Ginger.

'Ah don't know'

'You don't know?'

'He don't know?' smirked Scrounger who was eavesdropping on the conversation from under the covers.

'What d'you mean you don't know?' flared Ginger. 'You either know or you don't'

'Ah don't know because ah've never done shagging afore'

*

Ginger completed the cheerless chore of polishing the chrome fittings on a row of wash basins and began to fill his bucket with cold water from a wall tap. As he was doing so, he glanced at Sticky hunched in a corner, staring into space and sighing intermittently.

'You've been sat there since we got here, squawking like a lovesick parrot'

Ginger picked up the bucket and walked towards the

regimented row of toilet cubicles, the first of which appeared to be occupied. He rattled on the door and called, 'Anyone in there?' There was no response. Rattling the door once more, he repeated, 'Anyone in there?' Still no reply was coming forth. He knocked loudly for a third time and cautioned, 'this is positively your last chance to reply'

The silence persisted so he tipped the contents over the top in the time-honoured manner of the seasoned bog orderly.

Screaming erupted from inside, the door opened and Scrounger emerged, dripping from head to toe.

'Look at me,' he yelled. 'Look at what you've done'

'I did ask three times if there was anyone at home,' replied Ginger politely. 'I've had complaints in the past about not enquiring before sploshing'

'I was having a kip,' protested Scrounger.

'Well, you shouldn't have been. No kipping allowed in the crappers. Anyway, you should be up the hospital by now tending to the skiving sick and wounded'

'Bastard,' shouted the victim as he peg-legged it out of the latrine.

Ginger turned his bucket on its end and sat down beside the distressed Sticky.

'What's wrong with you mate?'

'Ah in love or summat; ah'll have to get married'

'No you won't,' snorted Ginger. 'You're not in love, you're just in lust'

'What if ah've put her up the duff?'

'You haven't'

'Ah might have, Scrounger said'

'He knows nowt. Listen, that lass is too smart to get caught out. She'd have taken precautions. She knew what she were about last night'

'Ah've got a date with her tonight. Do ah have to go Ginge?'

'Of course you have to go'

'Will ah have to shag her again?'

'No, you great wassock, where are you taking her?'

'Pictures, in Warrington'

'Then meet up with her, enjoy the film, take her back to the college gates, bow politely, say thank you, goodnight, kiss her on the cheek – and that's it. You're off the hook. Can you remember all that?'

'Oh aye'

'Right then, pull yourself together before the match this afternoon'

'Ah don't want to play; ah'm no good at football'

'Tough chuck, we're a man down for the game and you're taking his place'

*

Fifteen minutes into the second half RAF Padgate were down three-nil in their home fixture against Kirby AFC. Worse was to follow though because ten minutes later Barry Emerson twisted his ankle and was forced to retire. Sticky took his place in the middle of defence but proved hopelessly inadequate at marking the opposition target man who was having a field day.

As Ginger picked the ball out of the net for the fifteenth time, he said to the referee,

'Blow your whistle mate. Put us out of our misery'

Drastic reorganisation was called for and Sticky was drafted to centre forward, not in an endeavour to put some respectability on the scoreline, but to get him out of harm's way.

In the dying seconds and to the astonishment of his team mates, he rose to a cross from Scrounger, soared above the Kirby centre back and headed the ball cleanly into the net.

As he luxuriated in the suds of his post-match bath, Sticky eavesdropped on a conversation between Scrounger and Tiny in adjoining cubicles.

'What a pisser,' said Scrounger. 'If Barry hadn't got crocked we'd have murdered them in the second half'

'Pity the ref didn't abandon the game at half-time,'

reckoned Tiny.

'Never mind, Sticky got more fame out of that last minute strike than their centre with his twelve goals'

The unlikely icon lay back and luxuriated once again in this news of an unexpected mention in the roll of honour.

*

As he hung around the entrance to the Regal cinema, Sticky had a premonition that Barbara wasn't going to show. He was right. Dorothy turned up instead.

'Barbara couldn't make it tonight,' she reported by way of explanation.

'That's all right, ah didn't really fancy her anyway. It were only lust'

'Oh yes,' replied Dorothy, eyeing him curiously. 'Let's go in, you can tell me more later on'

*

'Well, that's it. I give up on women,' said Ginger on learning of Sticky's new romance. 'He tubs the two of them and I end up wi' nowt as usual, maybe I should change me tactics and start playing the daft lad'

Sent to Coventry

'By the left, it's pelting down stair rods out there'

Ginger had just entered the billet. He removed his groundsheet, shook it vigorously over Scrounger's newly made bed and then stopped to look at the assorted bundles of kit dumped on the empty bed adjoining.

'Whose gear is that?'

'New bloke, just arrived, gone up the NAFFI,' replied Sticky hurriedly. He was in the process of donning his own groundsheet and forage cap.

'You going out?'

'Aye, camp cinema'

'Must be a chuffing good film to venture out in this weather'

'Dunno, it's the Flash Gordon serial ah'm goin' to see. Chapter 13 an' Emperor Ming has just chucked Dale Arden into a pit of molten metal'

'Nice for her'

'No Ginge, it's not, she'll get all hot and gooey like. Ah want to see if she gets out okay'

'I wouldn't worry. Flash will break off from whatever he's doing, nip down and sort it'

'You reckon?'

'Oh aye, forced to'

*

Half an hour later another sodden groundsheet appeared, dripping rainwater on the floor where it stood. Its occupant had a bale of polythene covered bedding on its shoulders.

'You'll be the new bloke then,' called Ginger from midway up the passage where he lay flat out on his bunk reading the comic cuts. He was the only other one in the billet.

'Yes, Len Armitage, just arrived. Well, best get started on unpacking my kit I suppose'

Ginger got up and walked down towards the newcomer.

'Here, I'll give you a hand, but you don't want to be sleeping there next to Scrounger. He'll only try tapping you before you get your jammies on.' Ginger picked up the bedding bale and continued, 'Bring your kit bags and follow me. We'll fix up you with a bunk next to the stove, beside my mate Sticky and me. I'm Ginger, Ginger Harrison'

'Thanks, I could use a good warm'

Ginger unwrapped the polythene and began to make up a bed. 'Just been posted, have you?'

'Yeah, from RAF Credenhill'

'You'll have just finished your clerk's course then'

'That's it, and now I'm to be working in the attestation section'

'You'll be all right there, that's where Barry works. Nice feller, you'll meet him on Monday. He's away for the weekend. Only me, Scrounger and Sticky here to keep you company'

They sat chatting by the stove and sharing Ginger's last cigarette. Ginger listened with interest as AC1 Armitage related how just before his call up he had been spotted by a scout when playing for his local amateur football team. The scout's interest had resulted in a series of trials with Exeter City FC after which the manager had signed him up on a professional form.

'What position do you play?' asked Ginger eagerly.

'I've got a good left foot so they signed me as a left winger, but I can play centre-forward or outside right just as well. In fact, the week before I left for basic training the manager called me in and told me I'd be playing in the first team the following Saturday because the regular centre was injured. I scored a hat trick'

Ginger eyed him curiously before saying,

'I'll tell Barry. He's captain of RAF Padgate and he's been looking for a goal-scorer for ages. You could play for us next Saturday'

'I can't do that right now'

'Why not?'

'Two reasons. I pulled a hamstring in my debut and the physio has forbidden me to train, never mind play, until it clears up completely. On top of that, even if I was fit, I'd have to get club permission because I'm a professional with first team experience'

'Never mind lad,' said Ginger quietly, 'you'll most probably be fit and cleared to play for us when the inter-services cup games start next month'

'Oh yes, It'll be okay by then, I'm sure'

*

During the course of the following week there were rumblings among the residents of Hut 29 about the newcomer's apparent propensity to spin long tales.

'Armitage even told me he was a champion ballroom dancer,' revealed Barry. 'I'd like to see all those cups he's supposed to have won'

'And maybe he could show them to you,' replied Ginger.

'How do you make that out?'

'I took him to the Carlton Club last Sunday evening and he had the birds queuing up to dance with him. He's a fantastic ballroom dancer. Take my word for it'

'Well...'

'Ah don't believe a' that crap aboot him bein' a professional fitba' player,' growled Jock Burns. 'Signed for Exeter, my arse; ah could jist as easy say ah play fur Glasgow Celtic'

'Ah yes, but then we all know you don't play for Celtic,' Ginger pointed out, 'because you couldn't kick your own arse even with someone giving you a leg up'

'Watch it pal'

*

The unrest reached boiling point several weeks later when AC1 Armitage was accused of stirring it up with his fellow boarders. Levelled against him was the charge that he had maliciously misled Tiny Loftus regarding a crude remark purportedly made by Scrounger when Tiny had proudly shown around the billet a snapshot of his new girlfriend.

'I had to separate them,' said Barry. 'I thought Tiny was going to murder Scrounger'

'Serve him right if he did,' countered Ginger. 'He deserves murdering, the lying little scroat'

'I never lied,' croaked Scrounger.

'No? Well it wouldn't be the first time you spread bollocky rumours around about your mates'

'Look, this is getting us nowhere,' interrupted Barry in an effort to cool the situation. 'The fact is Ginger, we had a meeting and we've decided unanimously to send Armitage to Coventry until he gets the message and stops shooting the shit'

'You what?'

'It means naebody talks tae him,' volunteered Jock. 'An' if you keep talkin' tae the waster, you'll get sent tae

Coventry as weel'

'I know what it means you Scotch prick,' snapped Ginger. 'What I want to know is why I wasn't invited to the meeting'

There was no reply forthcoming, so he continued, 'Oh, I get it, leave big fat Ginger out so he won't cause a rumpus. How about you Sticky, were you at the meeting?'

'Aye'

'How did you vote?'

'Ah voted with the lads because ah don't want them not speaking to me'

'Did you now, well, I'm not talking to any of you. I'm sending myself to Coventry'

*

Len Armitage was taking it badly and the stress of being shunned by everyone except Ginger began to tell on him. He decided to confide in his only source of conversation and asked Ginger out for a drink. They sat in silence in the snug bar of the Farmers Arms until Ginger broached the subject of Len's distress.

'You know why they're doing this to you, don't you?'

'I don't,' he protested. 'I only told Tiny what Scrounger had said, I didn't make it up, honest I didn't'

'I know lad, but you should have said nowt'

'What else then? What have I done?'

'You've been telling a lot of porkies, you're a bullshiter. I'm sorry, but I have to be cruel to be kind'

Len was crestfallen and the tears began to well up in his eyes. 'I'm not a bullshiter Ginger, I'm not.' he said mournfully.

'Len, you've got a problem separating fact from fiction. You talk about being good at things you know fuck all about. Why aren't you proud of being a champion ballroom dancer? You never talk about that, and you should. It's what you're good at'

'They'd only think I was bragging,' replied Len.

Ginger sighed and let matters rest.

*

Some days later Len was admitted to the camp hospital where he was diagnosed as suffering from depression. Ginger went up to visit him only to be told that he was no longer there.

'He's been sent to the psychiatric unit of a clinic that specialises in mental disorders,' advised a helpful medical orderly. 'They'll keep him in for a few months and then he'll be discharged from the RAF on the grounds of emotional instability'

*

'Well, I hope you lot are satisfied now,' announced Ginger on his return to Hut 29. 'They've only bunged the poor bugger into a loony bin'

There was a hush of misgiving as Ginger repeated what the orderly had told him.

'He's better off there,' advocated Scrounger sheepishly. 'Pathological liar, that's what he is'

'You reckon, do you?' accused Ginger harshly. 'Become a brain specialist in between sloshing out bedpans up the hospital, have you? Do any of you have any idea what Len Armitage is facing now? Can you imagine what will happen when he goes looking for a job in Civvy Street with 'nervous breakdown' written on his discharge papers?'

'Maybe he were a professional footballer after all,' speculated Tiny.

'No, he weren't,' answered Ginger abruptly.

'How do you know?'

'Because the Monday after he arrived here I contacted the Exeter Evening News and asked them to send me a copy of the Saturday sports edition when he was supposed to have been playing in the first team. He wasn't on the team sheet and there was no hat trick'

'Why did you do that?'

'Because I suspected as much. I've got a brother back home just like Len Armitage. He can't say owt either to impress unless it's made up. Poor buggers'

Inter-round summaries by Barrington Dalby

RAF Padgate had been chosen to host the Inter-Services Boxing Finals and No 1 Hangar was earmarked as the venue.

Local interest in the tournament was heightened by the fact that one of their own, AC2 'Spiffy' Spiffington, had successfully negotiated the preliminary rounds and was boxing for the flyweight crown. Hopes were high among the enlisted personnel that Spiffy would bring glory to the base by winning its first ever sports title.

'Everyone is bucking for our scrawny little airman to knock the socks off that naval type,' Squadron Leader Phartingail ffoulkes-Knight had confidently informed the commanding officer. 'Load of old bollocks,' was the sentiment expressed by Sergeant Jordan to his fellow NCOs in the mess. For Ginger Harrison though, this was a temptation he could not resist. He decided to open book on the outcome, which according to him was a foregone conclusion.

*

Several days before the scheduled event excitement reached fever pitch when it was announced that the BBC was to broadcast the entire proceedings on both the Light and Overseas programmes.

'I can't wait for the announcement on the radio,' enthused Scrounger Harris, affecting his best endeavours at BBC enunciation as he swabbed the latrine floor, 'Your commentator tonight is Raymond Glendenning with inter-round summaries by Barrington Dalby'. It's what they always say, you know'

'Well, while you're waiting, you can get some brass on Spiffy,' countered Ginger.

'What odds are you offering?'

'Fifteen to two on'

'Hardly worth placing a bet,' reckoned Scrounger.

'And the other bloke?' asked another airman.

'Three to one against'

'Bit on the generous side, I'd have thought,' opined Tiny Loftus. 'Spiffy's opponent might turn out to be pretty handy with his fists'

'No chance,' contradicted Ginger. 'Spiffy will murder the poncy matelot; he's taken more dives than Esther Williams; any roads, only the tars will want to lay money with me on that bugger. None of our mob will'

'I wouldn't bet on that,' forecast Tiny with equal conviction.

*

The OB unit was set up outside the appointed hangar and the BBC engineers spent the afternoon laying out cables, positioning the microphones, and conducting extensive sound tests. Elsewhere inside the hangar RAF personnel were attending to other essential matters: erecting the ring for the pugilists, setting out seating accommodation from mounds of stacking chairs, and restructuring the strobe lighting to meet the requirements of the occasion.

'That's him over there, talking to Farty Night,' observed Scrounger, pointing to a distinguished looking bespectacled gentleman sporting an outsize handlebar moustache.

'So that's Raymond Glendenning,' replied Ginger. 'Bit on the short side. I thought he'd be much taller'

Their conversation was interrupted by Sticky who arrived breathless at their side.

'Ginge, some sailors called in at t'bogs looking for you'

'What do they want me for?'

'To place some bets'

'Are they still there?'

'Aye, ah told them ah'd go fetch you'

'Good man. Let's get back and rake in their dosh'

*

'Three to one against, our man, those are the odds, right?'

Confirmation was being requested by the burliest of the three able seamen lounging against the latrine door to the right of which another thirty or so other sailors had lined up.

'Three to one if he comes out on top over the distance,'

replied Ginger.

'We'll have some of that'

As he collected the money and issued betting slips the queue started to dwindle but Ginger noticed that several airmen had tagged onto the end.

'Right lads,' he addressed the group brightly. 'Come to bet on Spiffy?'

'No, the other bloke'

'Traitors,' accused Sticky.

'Nay lad, if they want to toss away their brass, who am I to argue?'

Sticky resumed lavatorial duties as with a wire brush he attempted to restore the surface of a grime-encrusted worktop while Ginger retired to a cubicle where he sat on the toilet seat to tally up his takings.

*

'Co-eee, is Ginger about?' The request emanated from Sergeants Hare and Withinshawe.

'By the left, it's all go in here today,' called Ginger.

'Where are you?'

'I'm in me office. I'll be with you in a tick'

He emerged, beamed at the visitors and enquired, 'What's it to be, Spiffy or the other bloke?'

'Eh?'

'The match tonight, Spiffy's boxing in the flyweight final. You'll be wanting to place a bet'

'No, we sodding well won't,' replied Bunny firmly.

'We never engage in games of chance,' added Stan.

'If it's not the boxing match what then?'

'Funnily enough, it has to do with match, indirectly'

Ginger looked from one to the other and as no further intelligence appeared to be forthcoming, he pursued the matter. 'Am I suppose to guess then?'

'Well, it's this way,' volunteered Stan. 'Bunny's written up some radio scripts, which he's desperately keen to show to someone in authority at the BBC but he can never seem to reach the right people. The scripts always come back with a rejection slip attached'

'So?'

'So, we'd like to approach Raymond Glendenning ourselves while he's in camp and we wondered whether you could suggest some way we could gatecrash the cocktail party they're laying on for him and Barrington Dalby after the show'

'Show, what bloody show?'

'You know what we mean. Is there? Could you?'

'No chance,' said Ginger. 'As usual, it's for officers, wives and tarts only. However, I'll talk to him directly myself if you want'

'You know Raymond Glendenning?'

'Yeah, well, you know how it is; brothers in the sporting fraternity always have time for each other'

'But Ginge -'

Sticky's protestation was quelled by Ginger's admonition, 'You get back to that worktop with your brush. It's still as manky as a badger's backside'

'Your sporting fraternity sounds a bit like the Water Rats and their sunshine coaches, don't you think?' suggested Stan.

'Similar, very similar,' replied Ginger sagely. 'I do Raymond a turn here; he does me a favour there'

'So it's all for charity then?'

'In a manner of speaking, yes'

'You'll approach him then?' asked Bunny eagerly.

'Of course I will, but there'll be a price to pay'

'You just said it's all for charity and now you've got the cheek to ask Bunny for money after all we've done for you,' snapped Stan. 'Is that the way of it?'

'Not as such, no, just a small wager on Spiffy to keep the flag flying; Raymond would appreciate that'

'Oh, go on then, how much?'

'Five pounds apiece'

They handed over the cash together with copies of the radio scripts.

'Mind you don't lose those,' instructed Bunny.

*

With the microphone pressed up close to his handlebar moustache, Raymond Glendenning opened the broadcast with an enthusiastic flourish, 'Boxing tonight comes to you from RAF Padgate, host to the inter-services finals, where the first bout is for the flyweight championship. The contenders are local hero Aircraftsman Spiffy Spiffington based at this very camp and Able Seaman Bigsworthy from HMS Bulwark. By all accounts we're in for a great contest which might well go the full distance over seven rounds...'

Alas though, the local hero's shot at glory lasted all of ten seconds, including the count. He was knocked out cold by the very first blow of the contest.

*

'So, how did it go with Raymond? Is he prepared to show my scripts around to the right people at the BBC?'

'Ah, well now, there's a bit of a problem there I'm afraid'

'Why, didn't he like the material?'

'No, no, it's not that'

'What then?'

'He had to miss the party and dash back to London before I'd a chance to give them over to him'

'You rotten liar'

'We'll have our cash back then'

'Ah, sorry squires, can't do that, it's against Marquess of Queensberry rules'

'What?'

'Spiffy lost, so you forfeit the cash'

Sergeants Hare and Withinshawe glowered venomously at Ginger, turned on their heels and minced off in the huff.

*

'Bloody hell,' squealed Scrounger as he peered through a chink in the drawn curtains of the billet window. 'There's about fifty of the buggers heading this way and they don't half look hacked off'

'How would they know where I live?' asked Ginger plaintively.

Barry Emerson advanced a possibility, 'I saw Bunny and Stan talking to some of them earlier. I reckon our thespian friends have taken their spite out on you and given those tars the billet number'

'Dear, dear, I am surprised,' replied Ginger nonchalantly. 'Now why would they want to do a thing like that?'

'What are we gonna do Ginge?' wailed Sticky. 'Them sailors won't be best pleased when you tell them you can't pay out'

'Tiny here will act as my handler. He's about seven- foot tall. That should scare the shit out of them'

'Leave me out of it,' contradicted Tiny. 'I'm not about to be beaten to a pulp because of your shenanigans'

'Best handle it myself then'

Ginger opened the door to face his debtors who were now just a few yards away.

'How can I help you jolly matelots?'

'You can pay us out, you Brylcreem ponce'

'There's nowt to pay out lad'

'You bloody welsher'

'Watch it sailor. I mean there's nothing to pay out because your man failed to come out on top over the distance. That was the bet, you all heard me say that when you put down your money'

'But Bigsworthy knocked out your man in ten seconds'

'Ah, but he didn't go the full distance'

'Ten seconds was all the fucking distance there was'

Just as matters were about to get out hand leaving Ginger to the tender mercies of an enraged lynch mob, a service lorry drew up alongside the billet. Out stepped Sergeant Jordan followed in tow by a burly, bull-necked Chief Petty Officer.

'What's all this then?' barked Jordan. 'What are you doing with them sailors?'

Picking up the thread on cue, the CPO bawled at his charges, 'We've been searching the camp for you idle jack tars. Get your arses aboard the truck at the double'

'But Chief, we -'

'No buts, seaman. I don't care if you was invited by the King to have tea and muffins with this shower of airy fairy poufters, move it!'

'I never thought the day would come when I'd be glad to see old Bandy Jordan arrive at the billet,' announced Ginger.

'Jammy beggar,' scorned Scrounger. 'You didn't have to pay out a penny to anyone'

'What about them sprogs who backed the other bloke?' posed Sticky.

'What about them?'

'You'll have to pay them out'

'No I won't. Traitors, all of them, you said so yourself'

'Personally speakin' fur masel' like,' snarled Jock Burns who had just clumped into the billet having concluded a particularly tedious back shift at the cookhouse, 'ah think you're a thievin' fuckin' bastird'

'I ask you; is that nice?' replied Ginger feigning hurt.
'Now, to more serious matters, who's for a snifter up the
Farmers Arms? I'm paying'

'Mine's a gless o' whusky an' a pint,' said Jock.

Can I do you now sir?

It was *National Help The Aged Week* and in his capacity as shepherd to the disparate flock at RAF Padgate, newly promoted Flight Lieutenant The Reverend Willoughly-Goddard had with the blessing of his superiors launched an initiative of his own conception.

'You have to hand it to him,' observed Ginger as he scanned the notice. 'He comes up with some right fair skives'

'What's this one,' asked Sticky.

'Befriending the aged'

'Be what'?'

'Calling in on old folks down the village'

*

The padre leaned back in his chair as he addressed the volunteers. 'I am indebted to you chaps'

'How's that sir?'

'Sadly, you are the only ones to respond to my appeal'

'Well padre, 'said Ginger expansively, 'the way I see it is, you only pass this way but once, so you ought to do your bit to help others'

'Goodness, I wish there were a few more upright fellows like you two around the camp. Now to business, are you familiar with the requirements of the task at hand?'

Sticky could answer this one and he did.

'Oh aye, visiting old folks down the village like'

'Exactly so, precisely, you will of course receive liberal release from your latrine duties and reimbursement of out-of-pocket expenses'

'You what, padre?' enquired Ginger interestedly.

'Bus fares to and from the village together with any other minor emoluments you may see fit to dispense in the fulfilment your undertaking; flowers for an elderly lady on her own, pipe tobacco for a gentleman. That sort of thing'

There was a gleam in Ginger's eyes as he enquired.

'How long would you want us for?'

'Well, if you could give me a whole day, I would be most obliged'

'We'll give you the whole week sir'

'Oh I say, how splendid, most generous. Here is list of addresses I obtained from the local vicar. It should keep you occupied in your good works for most of the week'

*

'Be-fucking-friending the elderly?' screamed Sergeant Jordan, kicking over a bucket of dirty water onto the newly swabbed latrine floor. 'All fucking week, not fucking likely'

Ginger and Sticky were crestfallen at Jordan's thunderous reaction to the news when an unlikely ally came to their rescue.

'Not only likely, but most definitely,' contradicted Squadron Leader Phartingail ffoulkes-Knight who had crept up on Jordan from behind, sending a shudder of terror down the spine of the latter.

'But -'

'But me no buts, sergeant, I have wholeheartedly endorsed the padre's scheme and I commend these two chaps for their willingness to participate. Pity no one else in your squad proved to be so public spirited'

'But sir -'

'Jordan, be quiet man! Speak to me only when you have something constructive to say. Has it not occurred to you that the padre's initiative is an opportunity? A heaven-sent opportunity to repair the damage inflicted on our image by the constant, unacceptable stream of drunken off-duty escapades perpetrated on the village, including those of a certain senior NCO who ought instead to be showing an example to the men under his command'

Jordan sprang to attention in a clumsy endeavour to regain his composure, but he was clearly perturbed by the allegation.

'I have one more thing to add,' concluded the officer. 'We pass this way but once. Think on sergeant'
*
On the very first port of call in their mission of mercy, the

volunteers were greeted by a hastily hand written note pinned to the door of Flat 2, South View Terrace. It read, 'Gone up the bingo. Back Friday'

'Chuffing hell, it's only Wednesday morning,' protested Ginger, not unreasonably.

Two doors down proved marginally more fruitful. A patriarchal lady sporting a beehive of shocking pink hair encased in plastic curlers answered the knock.

'What d'yer want?'

'Blessings on you missus,' began Ginger fervently. 'My mate and me have come to befriend you'

'Piss off, replied the householder, slamming in door in his face.

As they were departing a male voice bawled from inside, 'Who was it?'

'Bloody do-gooders'

'Silly cow, you should have asked then in. We could have tapped them for a right few bob'

On the third call they struck oil.

'You'd best come in,' responded the octogenarian. 'I'm Obediah Outhwaite'

'What are you doing sitting in the dark grandad?' asked Ginger as he stumbled through the tiny hallway.

'Ha'n't got a bob for the meter'

'It's perishing in here Ginge,' observed Sticky.

'By the left, you're right mate. Freeze the nuts off a hazelnut bar it would. Haven't you any family or a neighbour who'd lend you a bob?'

'No, I'm on me own'

'Well, if I had one going spare, I'd give it you. Sticky, how are you fixed for brass?'

'I've got nowt. I borrowed you me last two bob yesterday'

'Not to worry grandad. I'll soon get you some light and heat. Have you a screwdriver I could borrow?'

The elderly gentleman rummaged through the contents of a drawer in his rickety kitchen table and produced the required object.

We'll be back in a couple of ticks,' said Ginger.

*

As Ginger swiftly and expertly dismantled the coin depository in a nearby call box, Sticky enquired anxiously, 'What are you doing Ginge?'

'Getting some brass in for old Obediah'

'And we'll get six months' wailed Sticky.

'Stop mithering and hold your cap out so I can fill it up. There's bound to be a few shilling coins in here - and the rest of it we'll keep for us expenses.' He added magnanimously, 'It'll save the padre paying us out of his collection box'

'Where did you learn how to do that Ginge?'

'Just a trick Old Jez taught me'

'Who's old Jez?'

'I met him in Borstal'

'But Borstal's only for kids isn't it?'

'He weren't an inmate, he were a warder'

*

'I have to say, I'm very disappointed in you chaps,' Phartingail ffoulkes-Knight admonished the volunteers. 'I had anticipated a more favourable outcome to the padre's initiative. Now clear off.' As Ginger and Sticky trooped out in disgrace, he called after them. 'Not only will you be up before me on a serious charge, you also face court action from the civil authorities'

He turned his attention to Sergeant Jordan who was standing beside the desk. 'Wheel in this union chappie; what's his name?'

'Clapstick, sir, Cyril Clapstick, general secretary of NUTS'

'Nuts?'

'National Union of Telephonic Staff, sir'

The officer groaned. He glanced at the angry bruise on Jordan's face and enquired, 'What happened to your right eye? And don't even think about advancing the theory that you walked into a door'

'Got set upon by some thug in the village, sir'

Phartingail ffoulkes-Knight groaned once more in his despair.

*

The general secretary of NUTS proved to be a bulky thickset individual sporting a pork pie hat and a disreputable Macintosh raincoat that wafted off a nauseous fusion of stale beer, tobacco and chips.

'Now Mr, er -'

'Clapstick,' volunteered Jordan.

'What, ah,' continued Phartingail ffoulkes-Knight uneasily, 'what precisely is your interest in this case, Mr Chopstick, ah, Clapstick?'

'Case, what case?'

'Well, I mean to say, the GPO will almost certainly instigate legal proceedings against the two airmen'

'No they won't,' the union leader answered briskly. 'I've already made arrangements to pull the plug on them'

'Pull the plug?'

'That's what I said'

'Right, well, we'll leave that for now. Just exactly what is your interest in this, ah, incident?'

'Victimisation of one of my members'

'Eh?'

'Clarence Harrison'

'We appear to be at cross purposes here,' flustered the officer. 'Harrison is an enlisted man undergoing national service. He couldn't possibly be a member of your union'

'He bloody is an' all.' Clapstick was gathering up a healthy head of steam. 'Fully affiliated member of NUTS who is being victimised by the GPO and his current employers, the Royal bloody Air Force'

'I say, steady on'

Sergeant Jordan decided to intervene with what he reckoned to be a cunning ploy to thwart the general secretary in his negotiations.

'You've got no right to be representing Harrison because he ain't paid no dues since he was called up'

'Members doing military service don't pay no dues,' growled Clapstick. 'Any roads, the lad made his first payment three weeks before he were enlisted an' in my book that makes him a bona fides affiliate of NUTS'

'Touching on the matter of 'pulling the plug -'

Phartingail ffoulkes-Knight's tentative endeavour to cool the temperature of the discussion was seized upon by the general secretary.

'You want to know what it means, well, I'll tell you, like I told the GPO. If they refuse to recant on legal action by midnight tonight, there won't be no GPO because I'll call all my members out on a national strike. Any roads, they haven't got a leg to stand on. Their only witness is some doddery old fart with dodgy eyesight an' a pair of wonky binoculars who alleges he saw my member dismantling their poncy coin box from a distance of five hundred yards and three flights up'

'Be that as it may,' Phartingail ffoulkes-Knight came back strongly, 'I shall nevertheless have no hesitation in pursuing charges against your member under RAF jurisdiction'

'Then you won't have any bleeding internal 'phones working either, mate'

As he got up to leave, Clapstick turned to address Jordan. 'How's your eye then?'

'Healing up'

'I must be getting old. It was the other eye I was aiming for when I clobbered you in the pub last night'

Phartingail ffoulkes-Knight buried his head in his hands in abject despair.

*

The door was ajar and Ginger rattled noisily on the panelling as he entered and called out, 'Can I do you now sir?'

'You'd best come in'

'Why are you sitting in the dark again?'

'Ha'n't got a bob for the meter'

'What about all them bobs I gave you the other day?'

'Lost them down the bookies'

Ginger sighed and replied in mock indignation,

'I have to say, I'm very disappointed in you Obediah Outhwaite. You're making a mockery of this befriending lark'

Smog sale

There was a new boarder in Hut 29, one Harry 'Snaffles' Tipping, who when asked on arrival how he had come by his nickname, cheerfully announced, 'I nick fings. Know what I mean?'

His candour had resulted in the odd arched eyebrow and an unspoken bond among the inmates to keep a close watch on the sprightly Cockney newcomer.

'Looks as if we've been lumbered with another tealeaf like that thieving sod of a corporal we had here a few months back,' speculated Scrounger Harris.

'And look who's talking,' said Barry Emerson.

'I never stole nothin' from none of you,' Scrounger reacted angrily.

'No, you just borrow from everyone and conveniently forget to pay back *anyone*'

*

'How's business Taff?' enquired Ginger who had called in at Mad Taffy's emporium with a view to browsing through his collection of second hand records.

'Terrible boyo, terrible bad, yours is the first clean face I've seen in here all day. If things don't pick up soon I'll be forced to shut up shop'

'Well, look on the bright side. You could have a closing down sale like my Uncle Harry. His ran for nigh on five months'

'Out of business now, is he?'

'Not likely. On the sixth month he switched to a Grand Re-Opening Sale and that's still going great guns, nine months on. Strategic marketing, he reckons it's called.

Taffy looked doubtful.

'No, we never went in for such like in the valleys. Anyway, I've got those overalls on the line out there to see to. All soiled they are with that smog we had last week'

A light switched on in Ginger's brain. 'That's it, the answer to a trader's prayer'

'What are you on about boyo?'

'You can have a smog sale'

'Smog sale?'

'I can see it now, big bill in the window saying, 'SMOG SALE - everything slightly soiled, everything greatly reduced'. They'll break down your door to get inside'

'But I've only got but six pairs of working men's overalls that's smog soiled and they're outside. All the stuff in here is perfect'

'Ah, but the punters won't know that'

'So?'

'So, I'll nip back to camp and nobble that big tin of stage dirt left over from the panto'

'Stage dirt?'

'Aye, it looks like the real McCoy but it brushes off easy. All you have to do is sprinkle it over your stock and tell the punters you've knocked down every price to rock bottom because the stuff is smog soiled. Then Taffy, you demonstrate how simple it is to brush away the smog'

'You mean I've got to reduce all my prices?' Taffy sounded almost apoplectic

'My uncle Harry didn't. He hiked all his up by thirty per cent and still they flocked in for five months.

'You know boyo, for someone without a drop of Celtic blood in your veins you're as nimble as a mountain goat. You could be as smart as a native born Welshman if you put your mind to it. Are you sure your granny didn't come from Llandudno?'

During the following ten days Mad Taffy's little emporium rocked to the sound of jingling cash registers. Customers poured in from all over the district as a direct result of Ginger's promotional aplomb. Persuading Taffy to part with a few pounds to have a six-line classified ad run daily in the Warrington Guardian Series was proving inspirational. It had resulted in attracting several coach parties to visit the premises.

So busy was he, Taffy was obliged to engage the services of Ginger and several other inmates of Hut 29 as temporary sales assistants over Saturday and Sunday. Included in their number was Snaffles who observed the proceedings with mounting enthusiasm.

'Go on, missus, get your purse out,' encouraged Ginger as he sensed his prey was having second thoughts about her proposed purchase. 'You know you want them outsize long johns for your old man'

'But they's all smudged. He won't like that, y'know. He puts a right face on when owt don't suit'

'Watch this missus'

Ginger proceeded to blow away the stage dirt effortlessly and then for good measure gently stroked the fabric with a pastry brush.

'See, good as new they are now'

'Well, I never, I'd best have six pairs then. He's right hard on long johns, he is'

'Wise decision missus. You'll not get these for four times the price come next winter'

*

'Taffy doesn't know whether to laugh or cry now'

Ginger was holding court in the Farmers Arms and buying drinks all around courtesy of the considerable wad of notes Taffy had given him for services rendered.

'He's completely sold out but doesn't want to continue the smog sale with new stock in case the punters catch on'

Snaffles moved in for the kill.

'I could fix him up with some new lines and a new idea

for a sale,' he announced.

'Dodgy gear is it?'

'No mate, it's kosher, straight up. I've got a mate down the smoke who specialises in salvage stocks. You know, fire and flood damaged goods, liquidations, receivership offloads, that kind of thing'

'Is he reliable?' asked Ginger suspiciously.

'Totally legit, he's even got his own wholesale business; 'Salvage Stores', with six outlets around London. Look, here's his business card'

Ginger examined the card, which on the face of it seemed genuine enough.

'What's in it for me?'

'I'll split my commission with you, fifty-fifty'

'Okay, let's go talk to Taffy - but this had better be on the level mate or I'll split you right down the middle'

*

Taffy listened intently to Snaffles' sales pitch and then turned to Ginger for a considered view on the proposed venture.

'What do you think to it then, boyo?'

'Well, the way I see it, you can't run another smog sale this side of the year any roads, and if you want to keep the punters pouring in, you'll not do better than order this gear in bulk

'But is it knocked off? That's what I'm asking myself'

'Snaffles reckons it kosher'

'Okay lad, let's have a look at your lines and the price list.' Snaffles spread out several sheets of paper on the counter. Taffy studied them carefully and after a few minutes came to a decision. 'The prices seem fair and there's some stuff here I know I can shift. Okay boyos, I'll give you an order - but cash on delivery, mind. I'm not parting with as much as a Welsh farthing until I inspect the merchandise'

'No bovver, guv. COD is how we do business. I'll nip down the smoke Friday night and come back with a truckload Saturday afternoon'

That's settled then,' said Taffy cheerfully. 'I'll stock up the shop over the weekend and start trading on Monday'

'Just one more thing squire, I've got some posters and handbills to help you shunt the gear.' Snaffles unfurled a window poster and held it up for inspection. It read,'SALVAGE STOCKS - you profit from other people's misfortune'

Taffy was horrified.

'I can put that up in my window'

'Why not?' asked Ginger.

'What would they say in chapel of a Sunday morning?'

'But you don't go to chapel'

'That's true. I'll have a think on it'

*

Come Monday evening after work, Ginger strolled down to the village to see how matters were progressing on Taffy's new promotional drive. As he approached the emporium, a huge Day-Glo poster all but covering the entire window dazzled him. The message screamed out, TAFFY'S SALVAGE STOCKS WAREHOUSE - Trade Only.

Inside there was no evidence of the newly delivered merchandise. Instead, it appeared that Taffy had stocked up on fresh quantities of his usual second hand ranges.

'What gives Taffy,' enquired a bewildered Ginger.

'I'm going in for a change of direction as we call it down the valleys'

'Have you gone barmy?'

'No boyo. Let me explain. I never did take to that fellow you brought down here. He's got crook stamped across his forehead. So, I had a think and decided to go in for wholesaling as well as retailing'

'But Taffy,' pointed out Ginger, 'your regular punters won't come in no more with that great sign in the window saying 'trade only' '

'Oh yes they will, boyo. They'll come in out of curiosity because they know Mad Taffy's always good for a bargain'

'How does the wholesale side work then?'

'I flogged off his gear to a market trader for four times what I paid for it. He told his mates and now I've got orders for six more truckloads of salvage stocks'

'Right,' said Ginger, warming to this unforeseen opportunity. 'I'll get Snaffles down with his order book'

'No, you bloody won't boyo'

'But -'

'I'm not in business to make you and that cockney devil rich. I'm going direct, see'

'Now Taffy mate,' concluded Ginger with genuine admiration, 'that's what I call strategic marketing. You could teach my Uncle Harry a thing or two'

The choristers

'Hello, what have we here?'

'What's that then?' enquired Sticky.

Ginger studied the contents of the announcement on the Naffi notice board before replying, 'It says here, "Volunteers required for camp church choir" '

'Never volunteer for nothing, no time, never,' advised Tiny Loftus. 'My dad told me that before I got conscripted'

'How come then you volunteered to hump all them instruments for the bandmaster?' countered Scrounger.

'Well, he asked if any of us was musical and I put me hand up'

'It also says,' continued Ginger undeterred, "Liberal release from duties to participate in a series of external community choral activities" '

'What's all that mean then?'

'It means pal,' clarified Jock Burns, 'it's a fucking good skive'

'I'm up for that,' said Snaffles.

'You, what makes you think they'd take you?' asked Ginger with an edge of sarcasm.

'I was in the choir at borstal, mate. Got a certificate of

commendation, I did, straight up'

'Soprano or baritone?' asked Barry.

'Baritone, I suppose'

'Sound in the canticles, were you?' persisted Barry in a quest for further and better particulars.

'Well, if I wasn't, I'd have been a sodding soprano, wouldn't I?'

'Here, that gives me an idea'

'What's that Ginge?'

'We could all say that, like Snaffles, we've been in a choir before. Let me check that bill again'

He repaired to the notice board, running his finger along the lines as he read.

'What time is it?' he snapped.

'Going on half past six,' answered Tiny.

'Right, let's get us up to the camp prayer hut and nobble old Holy Willy-Goddy before seven o'clock. That's when the doors open for volunteers'

'Count me out,' said Barry. 'I'm an agnostic'

'Aye, me an' all'

'You, you don't even know what that means, Sticky'

'Well, ah'm not fussed any roads'

'Get on with you,' ordered Ginger. 'I'll not let you miss out on a chance to get away from them evil smelling bogs now and again on a right fair skive

*

On arrival at the 'prayer hut' a hand-written notice directed them to the games room where Ginger and Sticky had whiled away many pleasant hours as temporary church orderlies. To the dismay of the group though, a host of other hopeful choristers were already occupying three-quarters of the space on the benches surrounding the four walls.

'We'll join the head of the queue,' announced Ginger.

'How do you know which end is the head?' enquired Snaffles, not unreasonably.

'That one,' replied Ginger, pointing to a door on the extreme right. 'It's where the padre enters the hall from his vestry'

They strode noisily as a unit across the linoleum covered floor to a barrage of protest from the other occupants.

'We was here first,' complained a burly LAC seated next to the door.

'That's your hard bun mate,' Ginger replied unsympathetically.

'Well I'm not shifting,' said the LAC, folding his arms in an act of defiance.

Ginger eyeballed him and whispered menacingly,

'Move your fat arse or I'll set your trousers on fire'

His protagonist reflected on the situation for a moment, murmured some words of discontent, and then shoved his companions along the bench to make room for the intruders.

Moments later the door opened to admit not Flight Lieutenant The Reverend Willoughby-Goddard but Sergeants Hare and Withinshawe.

'Bloody hell,' exclaimed Ginger. 'Is this a ruse to get us lined up for another show?'

'Language, AC2 Harrison, language,' chided Stan. 'Remember where you are and have some regard for the sanctity of the holy precincts into which you've wandered - for whatever reason - because Gawd help us, you are no singer'

'Who says? I sang regular in the church choir back home'

'But you're a Rosicrucian, aren't you?'

'So what, we sing the same hymns as the other chapels'

'Right, settle down,' interrupted Bunny. 'Sergeant Withinshawe and I are handling the auditions tonight because of the padre's unavailability. Now, while it's heartening to see such a wealth of volunteers, the sad news is that we have vacancies for only twelve choristers. So, let's press on'

Ginger and his entourage managed to convince the

management of their collective bona fides and together with a handful of other hopefuls, were invited to attend an initial rehearsal the following evening.

'We'll soon get you whipped into shape,' concluded Bunny with a degree of confidence.

'Well, I never, 'remarked Stan, winking licentiously at the dancing queen LAC Gropethrope who was one of the chosen few.

On the walk back to Hut 29 Snaffles sidled up to Ginger and engaged him in conversation.

'You're a dedicated driver for Sergeant Jordan's new jeep now, aren't you?'

'Yeah, Corporal Blackstock and me because we're the only ones in the squad that can drive apart from you; old Bandy lost his licence when he got pissed down the Farmers Arms the first night he took the bugger out of camp'

'Lucky for some,' assessed Snaffles. 'Look Ginge, how would you like to earn some easy readies?'

'Doing what?' asked Ginger suspiciously.

'Driving me down to the vicarage tomorrow lunchtime'

'You what?'

'I've done a deal with Mrs Vicar on some bits and pieces she don't need no more. You drive me there, help me load the stuff onto the back of the jeep and then it's back to camp. There's more than a drink in for you -

there's twenty oncers'

'Have you been nicking again?'

'No mate, straight up. I got wind she was having a house clearance and I got in smartish ahead of Mad Taffy'

'Well...'

'Listen,' Snaffles continued conspiratorially, 'didn't I see Bunny Hare give you the vestry key?'

'He did and all. The vestry is where we get togged up in surplices for the rehearsal. Why'd you ask?'

'Because if you let me leave Mrs Vicar's gear in there for handing over to my contact tomorrow night, I'll double up the wedge to forty quid'

'You're on'

*

'What's in the big black box then?'

'None of your business Sticky,' said Ginger. 'Just get yourself kitted out with a surplice'

'Here Snaffles, you shouldn'y be eatin' they hosts an' drinkin' the altar wine,' reprimanded Jock Burns. 'That's sacrilege, that is, you'll go to hell you will'

'No bovver mate. They don't become holy until the padre says his words over them. Anyway, I'm fair starved - I ain't had no tea'

*

It transpired, much to the delight of Messrs Hare and Withinshawe, that Snaffles was the possessor of a quite extraordinary singing voice that blended the notes in almost perfect pitch. His solo rendering of 'Amazing Grace' brought tears to their eyes and an enthusiastic commendation from Wing Commander Peregrine de Vere Chalfont, an honoured guest at the rehearsal and acknowledged aficionado on all matters choral.

'I say, that was most awfully good. Ra-ther'

'Yes, well, I have to agree sir,' preened Bunny, 'and a very pleasant surprise in the circumstances'

'Now, turn to number 127 in your Westminster Hymnal,' announced Stan, seizing the moment. 'Let's try this together as a group. Sergeant Hare, will you start them off with the first line?'

'Praise him for his grace and favour,' sang Bunny in a pleasing baritone.
'Have you got the vestry key?' followed Snaffles, sotto voce.
'Yes I have, it's in my pocket,' sang Ginger.
'Good, then pass it on to me,'
'Leg it, leg it, leg it, leg it, advised Tiny
'Here comes sergeant you know who'

As Snaffles disappeared behind the makeshift curtain to the rear of the choristers, Sergeant Jordan made his entrance.

'Saw a light on in the games room, thought I'd investigate,' announced Jordan by way of explanation. 'What's all this then? And what are my men doing here? They should up the billet preparing for tomorrow's kit inspection'

'They are assembled here in their official capacity as members of the camp church choral society,' replied Bunny with some authority.

'Oh yes? More likely a poncified rehearsal for another of your fucking fairy shows'

'There's a senior officer present, Sergeant Jordan,' revealed Stan gleefully as he pointed out the Wing Commander.

'Begging your pardon sir, I didn't know you was in the room'

'Clearly not,' said the WC briskly. 'That sort of language is best reserved for the barrack square, sergeant. Hardly acceptable in a house of reverence'

'Sir'

*

Snaffles regarded the large wooden box in the vestry with some concern and wondered how he was going to shift it without assistance or transport when he heard a vehicle pull up outside. He pulled back the curtain, opened the window and looked out.

'Now there's a bit of luck,' he reflected.

The driver got out of the cab and seemed to be heading for the games room when Snaffles hailed him.

'Here, Corporal Blackstock, come inside'

'What for?'

'It's important. Come on in and I'll tell you'

'Have you seen Sergeant Jordan around? He told me to pick him up at the mess but he's not there'

'That's all right, he's here; I've just been talking to him'

'*You've* been talking to him?'

'Yeah, he'll be along in a minute. Come in, I'll explain'

Blackstock lumbered into the vestry.

'Why are you dressed in a surplice?'

'I'm to be an altar boy'

'What's it all about then?'

'There's a flap on. The padre and the local vicar are holding a special service up the CO's house on account of the old man's silver wedding anniversary. I've got to get this box up there pronto. Give us a hand mate to lug it into the jeep'

'Not on your nelly, the sarge'd have a fit'

'No, it's okay; he gave me a set of keys'

'I don't believe you'

'Straight up' vouched Snaffles, dangling the keys.

'We'll wait for Sergeant Jordan'

'Suit yourself corp, but it'll be too late if we do. They're screaming for the box right now and I wouldn't want to be in your shoes when the padre and the vicar tell the CO he can't have his service because you wouldn't help the altar boy load up their gubbins'

'Well...'

'Go on mate, lift your end. We'll have this lot shunted in a jiffy'

Corporal Blackstock complied reluctantly, and then gasped as he struggled to maintain control. 'Blimey, what have they got in here; the lead off the vicarage roof?'

'It's their holy chalices and fings. They're gold and they weigh a bit. Know what I mean?'

Between them and with extreme effort, they managed to haul the box outside and onto the jeep.

'Here squire,' said Snaffles, 'just sign on the dotted line. No need to read it; it's just a load of old bollocks Sergeant Hare made up to get me out the main gate'

'Why didn't he sign it then?'

'Cos he's not my immediate superior, is he?'

Corporal Blackstock obliged by scrawling illegibly on the document without attempting to verify the content.

'Are you sure this is okay?'

'Ask Jordan yourself. Here he comes now'

Sergeant Jordan appeared on the scene just as Snaffles drove off with the rear wheels burning up the tarmac.

'Who's making off with my jeep then?' snarled Jordan.

'AC2 Tipping, sarge'

'What?'

'He's had a message to get the holy things up to the CO's house for the special service like'

'What are you gibbering about man?'

'The special service the padre and the vicar are holding for the CO and his missus being married for twenty-five years. Silver wedding, like'

'And he used my frigging jeep?'

'Says you gave him a set of keys'

'I did what?'

'Showed them to me, sarge'

Jordan bit his lip, thought for a moment and said, 'He won't get past the guardhouse'

'He has a pass'

'Who gave him it?'

'Sergeant Hare'

'Did he now? Well we'll see what that poncified whoofter has to say for himself'

*

Sergeant Jordan burst in upon the fledgling choristers followed by a worried looking Corporal Blackstock.

'Really, Jordan,' protested Bunny brusquely. 'This is intolerable. It's the second time you've disturbed us tonight and this time you've caught us in the middle of our apercu'

'What you and this bunch of queers get up to is of no concern to me. What I want to know is why you gave that layabout Tipping permission to leave the camp in my jeep without arsking me first'

'I haven't the vaguest idea what you're talking about'

'Did you or did you not tell him he could use my fucking transport to shift the padre's gear?'

'No, I did not'

'What gear?' enquired Stan eagerly, 'Is it kinky, whips, manacles, masks, that sort of thing?'

'The holy gear,' screamed Jordan, 'for the padre and the vicar to hold their special service up the CO's house'

'Are you quite mad?'

'I think he must be,' contributed Stan, 'The padre and the vicar are off together on a cycling holiday in France, and the CO is at a conference in Gloucester'

'And what's more,' added Bunny for good measure, 'the aforesaid CO turns a peculiar shade of puce at the very mention of the name Willoughby-Goddard'

The sergeant glared fiercely at his corporal and then turned his attention to the row of choristers.

'You, Harrison, what do you know about this?'

'Nothing sarge'

'And the rest of you?'

'Nothing sarge,' they chorused innocently.

'Nothing eh, you lying shower of barstards'

'That remark is quite out of court,' rebuked Bunny. 'While these men are in my charge, I will not have them addressed in such a crude and vulgar fashion'

'Piss off Vera Lynn,' replied Jordan as he strode from the hall.

'Where to now sarge?'

'I'm taking you up the sergeants mess for a piss up'

'Cheers sarge,' said Blackstock brightly.

'We're going up the guardhouse, you pillock' shouted Jordan, 'to see if they apprehended the thieving sprog'

*

Jordan regarded with bewilderment the document he'd

just been handed by the guard commander.

'He must have forged the signature'

'Reckoned your corporal here signed it,' volunteered the commander cheerfully.

'Didn't you think it a bit odd like,' asked Blackstock, 'him being dressed as an altar boy?'

'Not really, we get all sorts coming in and out'

'Tell me this isn't your scrawl,' pleaded Jordan in desperation as he thrust the paper in front of the corporal who looked it over and replied,

'Yes, sarge, it's my signature right enough'

'What? You signed this knowing what was written down?'

'I don't know what's writ down sarge'

'Are you taking the piss?'

'No, sarge, I can't read'

'Here Jordan,' broke in the guard commander, 'have you heard? The vicarage has had all its lead stripped from the roof. The local plods suspect one of your mob; they always do - and they're usually right'

*

After the rehearsal the choristers repaired to the Farmers Arms at Ginger's invitation.

'What I don't understand,' posed Scrounger, 'is how Snaffles got his hands on the keys for the jeep'

'Nicked them out of my battledress top I reckon,' volunteered Ginger.

'Crafty sod'

'Any roads, at least we can have a drink on the sticky-fingered scroat,' continued Ginger, holding court at the bar and fanning himself with a spray of ten-pound notes. 'Get them in squire'

The landlord held one of the notes up to light and requested,

'Let's have a look at the other three'

'What's up?' said Ginger anxiously.

'They're duds'

'No watermark?' enquired Tiny.

'No, and take a look at the face on the notes'

'Whose face is it Ginge?

'Snaffles'

As his lordship pleases

It was four-thirty in the afternoon and the three remaining latrine orderlies were packing away their mops, buckets, squeegees, soap powder inter alia, and wondering what was for tea when the door opened to admit Corporal Blackstock accompanied by a bull-necked warrant officer clutching a well-worn swagger stick.

'This here is WO Blood. He's got a lorry outside to take you lot up before the unit cleansing commander,' announced the corporal in stentorian tones.

'Why?' protested 'Spiffy' Spiffington. 'We ain't done nuffinck'

'Shut your row and follow me,' bawled the warrant officer.

The conversation in the back of the rumbling lorry was muted although Sticky ventured to suggest that they might be in trouble because someone had reported Ginger for selling off substantial quantities of regulation Vim to Mad Taffy down Padgate village.

'Bollox,' reckoned Ginger loudly but not convincingly.

*

'As you were, chaps,' began Squadron Leader Bexley-Boddingham as he reviewed the trio of orderlies lined up before him. 'I have a very important mission for you three airmen, a mission I wish to have accomplished with the utmost dedication and dexterity; hush-hush and confidential, official secrets and all that. Do I make myself clear?'

'Sir', they responded in perplexed unison.

'As to the background: last night I dined with Lord Silkworthy at the Towers.' He stopped, looked them over, and then enquired, as though it were common practice for the rank and file to call in at Silkworthy Towers for a glass of bubbly and a game of croquet, 'Are you acquainted with his lordship?'

'No sir,' they replied as one.

'First class type, frightfully good egg'

'Sir'

'Anyway, I digress. The fact of the matter is; his lordship confided in me that the Towers had been broken into the previous evening. Some local louts apparently made off with the silver and that sort of thing. However - and this will distress you - before departing they desecrated the urinals in the servants ablutions'

'Sadists!' exclaimed Ginger in mock indignation, instantly sensing the opportunity of an up-market skive.

'Knew that would throw you, being in the trade as it were,' mused the Bexley Boddingham.

'Indeed sir, right off that is'

'It's a damn poor show all round and calls for a cleansing blitzkrieg. I promised Lord Silkworthy that we'd step into the breach, so to speak, and I am seconding you chaps to the Towers where I require the ablutions attached to the servants quarters to be thoroughly sanitized throughout'

'Eh?' said Sticky blankly.

'Look to your front airman!' bawled Warrant Officer
Blood, 'and don't speak until you're spoke to. What the
hofficer means is he wants the place spruced up good
and proper'

'Exactly so - and what is particularly distressing,' he
continued gravely, 'there would appear to be evidence
of excrement in the general vicinity of the porcelain
basins'

'Eh?'

Blood lent forward and whispered hoarsely in Sticky's ear,
'He means the dirty sods crapped in the jaw boxes'

As they clambered aboard the lorry again the warrant
officer addressed them, 'The driver will drop you off at
your hut to pick up some kit and then it's off to the
Towers. You'll stay overnight and spend tomorrow bulling
up the aristocratic bogs. Make sure you're all through by
1600 hours when the lorry comes back to collect you -
and no skiving - or I'll have you'

One hour later they passed through an impressive set of
ornamental gates and all the way up a winding
driveway to where the lorry came to a juddering halt
outside the ornate Gothic double-door entrance.

As the blitzkrieg crew looked up admiringly at the
balustrade and turrets on the rooftop, the doors opened
and out strode a tall dome-headed, sepulchral man in
butler attire.

'You'll be the shite house wallahs'

'Cleansing operatives to you cock,' corrected Spiffy.

'Whatever, but you'd best behave yourselves while you're here. Sergeant Jordan is a member of my lodge and he's told me all about you lot. Don't even think about nicking anything because I'll be watching you, night and day'

'Well, it wouldn't the silver, would it mate' countered Spiffy. 'You've had that half-inched already we heard tell'

The butler looked Ginger up and down.

'You're the troublemaker'

'Listen baldy,' reacted Ginger angrily, 'let's get one thing straight right now. You're not wearing stripes so I don't take any snash from you. Call me that again and I'll split you, stately home or not, makes no difference to me'

The butler glowered at him but made no reply and motioned to the party to follow him through the double doors into the great hall and along a wide passageway at the end of which stood a tall distinguished looking gentleman with closely cropped silver hair. He was wearing a monocle and leaning on a pogo stick.

'Ah, the shite house wallahs,' he announced cheerfully.

'Yes sir,' replied Ginger without a trace of rancour.

'You address his lordship as 'your grace',' rebuked the butler.

'Nonsense, stuff and nonsense, no need for the high hat, these chaps are here on a mission of mercy. Now, Graves, take our guests downstairs where Mrs Grimes is laying on some tiffin. Then be off with you and set up a bedroom for them. Look to it man, look to it'

'As his lordship pleases' said Graves, bowing slightly.

*

'They've gone where?'

Back at RAF Padgate, Corporal Blackstock was briefing Sergeant Jordan on the developments of the day.

'Silkworthy Towers, sarge, on the direct orders of the unit commander'

'Well, my mate Bill Graves had best lock up the silver'

'Too late, someone's already had it away on his toes with the silver'

*

Doris Grimes had welcomed the guests into her kitchen with open arms and within minutes was giving Ginger the glad eye. 'Tiffin' transpired to several racks of lamb, a mountain of roast potatoes, a tureen of freshly gathered garden peas, and several large jars of assorted ice-cold mineral waters. To follow, she had prepared an enormous sherry laden cream trifle. Her only other diner that evening was Walter, the gardener. 'This'll keep you going for a while lads,' she advised, 'and for supper I'll give you double egg, sausage, bacon, tomato, mushrooms and chips. Will that be enough or would you like me to lay on a few steaks as well?'

'Oh aye,' said Sticky, 'some steaks on top for us teas would be right champion' She looked him over. 'I don't know where you put it and that's a fact. You're nobbut skin and bone. Still, you're a growing lad and you need a bit of filling up'

'Oh aye missus'

'Ginger love,' Doris Grimes was now sounding vaguely amorous. 'Shall I fetch you another rack of lamb, pet?'

'Aye Doris, thanks. Just the one mind'

'Ah'll have one too missus,' requested Sticky.

'How about you Spiffy?' she fussed.

'No ma'am, I couldn't eat another morsel of lamb'

'You've got trifle to get through yet, remember,' she cautioned.

'Oh, I'll manage that okay'

Graves the butler descended the stairs, opened the kitchen door and entered the room. He observed the largesse on the table and rather recklessly began to harangue the cook.

'Mrs Grimes, have you lost your senses? These people are here to work as labourers. You shouldn't be feeding them as if they were proper guests. They should be having scrag end'

'Scrag end?' She looked appalled. 'Scrag end, you say,

Mr Graves? I'll have you know, no one's never had no scrag end in any of my kitchens.' She turned to the gardener. 'Have I ever served you scrag end, Walter?'

'No missus, I baint never had thaat'

'And you never will. Scrag end, huh, I ask you'

Graves retreated back upstairs silently and morosely

'Scrag end, I'll give him scrag end all right,' she continued indignantly. 'He can have some for his supper'

'That's telling him Doris,' complimented Ginger.

'Now love,' invited Doris, pinching his ample right buttock, 'how about a drop of port or a brandy?'

As she went off to fetch the spirits, Spiffy nudged Ginger. 'You've pulled there, I reckon'

'She's fifty or maybe more'

'So what, many a good tune played on an old fiddle'

'How about an old bow fiddle though?'

*

Going on ten-thirty, the blitzkrieg crew was tucked under the covers of the king-size bed in the Mace Room, reserved for lower-echelon guests. Ginger was in the middle with Sticky and Spiffy on either side.

'This is the life lads,' Ginger remarked. 'Beats the buttons off Hut 29'

'Doesn't it just,' agreed Spiffy.

Ginger drew his vast bulk upright on an elbow and addressed Sticky.

'You don't take after your brothers, do you?'

'How do you mean like?'

'You don't make rude noises in bed do you?'

'Only when ah've had baked beans for tea'

'That's all right then,' said Ginger, reposing his bulk in grateful relief.

'Spiffy'

'Yeah'

'Have we finished the flask of tea and the bacon butties Doris gave us?'

'Yes'

'Good, weren't they?'

'They were that'

'And we heard Victor Silvester on the radiogram,' contributed Sticky appreciatively.

'Did we have to have that row?' asked Spiffy.

'Leave him be,' said Ginger magnanimously, 'It's just his way. Here, Spiffy, put the light out'

'Right mate, night all'

'Goodnight'

'Aye, it were an' all,' concluded Sticky.

*

Early next morning Sticky was the first to arise, wash, dress and have breakfast. He decided to indulge in an exploratory stroll around the gardens before the cleansing activities commenced - and while his mates were still pulling themselves together.

Doris Grimes and the parlour maid had departed on sundry housekeeping assignments and the only ones left in the kitchen now were Ginger, Walter the gardener, and Spiffy who was still at table scoffing a second helping of breakfast.

'You're not from around here, are you Walter?' speculated Ginger.

'I be's from Dorset, I be'

'Who's that geyser and the scrawny bird talking to Sticky - over there by the trees?' asked Ginger with elbows on the sill and looking out of the window.

Walter got up to observe and replied,

'That be Master Plank and his fi-awncee, Lady Cynthia Winterbottom-Smythe'

'Master Plank?'

'Waal, thass what we calls him'

'Why?'

'He be as thick as one'

'Who is he anyway?'

'He be the lordship's son and his real name be - oh, it's a big bugger - The Honourable Plan-taaginet Fortesque-Beauville Chateaux dee France Silkworthy. Thass it'

'Blimey.' Spiffy all but choked on a piece of bacon. 'If he took that to a chemist, they'd make it up for him'

'Here, Lady Cynthia is dragging Sticky into the woods and Master Plank is heading back to the house'

'Waal, thass nobility for thee, likes a bit of rough now and then, they does. Never know who they's going to pick on next. But she's fussy thaat Lady Cynthia, she likes her rough big and strong in the taad-ger way'

'What?'

'Just saying, best if the lad be waal taad-gered, that's aal. She'll be vexed if he baint be waal taad-gered, I'll be bound'

Ginger and Spiffy exchanged puzzled glances.

'She be taking him to greenhouse,' continued Walter.

'Where's that?'

Walter pointed to the pathway leading into the woods

and directed, 'You furck off to left, furck off to the right and furck off the left again'

Spiffy looked at Ginger and tentatively suggested, 'Maybe he means 'fork off' '

Walter pulled in a notch on the buckle of the four-inch deep belt strapped around his slim waist, tightened his braces, adjusted his gaiters, and wandered off splayfooted. Ginger turned to Spiffy in search of a translation.

'What was all that about Spiffy?'

'Buggered if I know mate, never could understand the bumpkin lingo'

*

Ginger and Spiffy reviewed the damage to the servants' ablutions and in particular the despoiled wash basins. They arrived at a rapid and unanimous assessment.

'That's not too bad,' said Ginger. 'I've seen much worse in the jaw boxes back at the camp bogs the morning after the lads have had hot curried eel for supper'

'Easy, wiv a bit of Vim and vigour, we'll be through in jig time'

*

Graves was taking a telephone call in the great hall.

'How much did you get? Good. Bring my share to the back door of the Towers at two o'clock this afternoon'

*

The depleted cleansing crew had all but completed their chores in the ablutions when they had a visitor in the shape of Master Plank.

'I say you chaps; awfully decent of you popping round like this to sluice out the servants' biffy. Pater will be pleased'

'No bovver, guv,' said Spiffy.

'I say, has either of you spoken to the Lady Cynthia this morning?

'Can't rightly say as we have, squire,' replied Ginger.

'Odd, haven't seen hide or hair of her since she took some lanky type into the woods to watch the crocuses coming out. Rum, wouldn't you say?'

'Maybe they went for a stroll,' suggested Ginger.

'That's it, of course, should have thought of it myself. The Lady Cynthia loves to show guests around the grounds. Well, best be off now. Spot of croquet on the lawn before lunch, what?'

'That'll be nice for you'

Minutes later Sticky rolled in, looked around, and remarked, 'You've finished then'

'No thanks to you, you skiving sod,' rebuked Spiffy. 'Where have you been? As if we didn't know'

'Lady Cynthia an' me walked in the woods an' has us tea in the glasshouse'

'You mean the greenhouse,' corrected Ginger, 'but you'll be heading for the glasshouse next if Master Plank finds out what you and his bird have been up to'

'Who's Master Plank?'

'Lady Cynthia's boyfriend'

'She reckons he's a plonker'

'Does she now? So, did you?'

'Yeah, twice afore the picnic, once when we was having the picnic, and twice after'

'Bloody fair; he knocks up the aristocracy at will and all I can manage to pull is a bow-legged old biddy from downstairs with bits hanging off her'

'I tried it on wiv the parlour maid,' admitted Spiffy.

'How did you get on?'

'I didn't. She told me to piss off'

'Shows sound judgement that girl,' reckoned Ginger.

'You're back early, love,' observed Doris Grimes with a glint in her eye.

'Yeah, well, it wasn't too bad,' responded Ginger, sensing impending danger. 'We got stuck in so we'd be ready for the lorry coming to take us back to camp'

'But that's not for hours yet. I'll make you something nice

for lunch and then we can go up to my room for a bit while your transport arrives. It's my afternoon off and I've got a bottle of gin I've been saving for a special occasion. You know what I mean love, don't you?'

'Well, it's like this Doris,' Ginger blustered, 'I never sup during the day. It gives me tummy gyp. Any roads, me mates and me are planning to, ah...' He looked at the wall for inspiration and his eyes fell upon a drawing of a flight of Ospreys. 'We're planning to go bird watching'

'Oh yes,' sniffed Doris. 'Well, you'd best have these then.' She walked across to a wall cabinet where she picked up a pair of binoculars, handed them to him and said, 'They belong to Walter. You'll need them for bird watching'

She made to leave the kitchen but stopped, looked back, and announced caustically 'It's scrag end for lunch today'

*

Suffering from hunger pains, the blitzkrieg crew trawled disconsolately across a hillock overlooking the Towers.

'Bird-bleeding-watching,' grumbled Spiffy. 'You're a wally. What made you say that?'

'Well, she'd got me on the hook,' pleaded Ginger. 'It was the only thing I could think of'

'You could have said we was going to the pictures,' advocated Sticky.

'What, and have her come with us, feeling my balls in the back row?'

'Those scraps she served for lunch tasted as if her cat peed in them first,' complained Spiffy bitterly. 'Here, give me them binoculars'

'Why?'

'I'm going to have a look in the greenhouse to see if Lady Cynthia has pulled again. It might take my mind off the taste of moggy piss in my mouth'

'You what?' protested Sticky.

'Gordon bloody Bennett, Graves is at the back door talking to a couple of yokels wearing caps and knotted white silk mufflers. They're flashing readies at him'

'Give us them back,' snapped Ginger, snatching the binoculars. He was just in time to witness the hand-over. Zooming in on the focus he saw a wad of notes being passed over to Graves.

'Right, let's get downhill and grab the villains'

Puffing, panting and wheezing, they scrambled down the slope and managed to secret themselves behind a bush before their prey reached the end of the pathway.

The trio jumped out to accost the villains.

'Gotcha!' gasped Ginger, winded and aching.

'Gerroff, you're nowt but squaddies'

Recovering his composure, Ginger grabbed one of them by the throat as the other scurried off into the woods, hotly pursued by Spiffy.

'You and your mate broke in last night and nicked the silver'

'Naff off, ouch, you're hurting me'

'I'll hurt you some more if you don't come clean'

'Okay, okay. Just let me breathe'

Ginger released his grip and continued,

'Graves was your accomplice, right?'

'He left a window open for us'

'How much did you get for the silver?'

'A fence gave us two hundred and fifty oncers'

'How much did you give Graves?'

'Two hundred'

'Daylight robbery, that is,' said Spiffy who had arrived back, clutching the other villain by an arm. 'You was done mate'

*

Lord Silkworthy sat behind the desk in his study glowering at Graves who was wedged between two police officers; to the left of his lordship stood Ginger, Sticky and Spiffy.

'You are a bounder sir, an unspeakable bounder, and

you are dismissed from my service. I never want to set eyes on you ever again'

'As his lordship pleases' spoke Graves, bowing his head the merest fraction.

'Constables, do your duty'

*

'Look at the lovely wedge his lordship give us,' said Ginger, swaying about in the back of the lorry as he counted out fifteen crisp new one pound notes

'Here Sticky, where did you get the medallion?' asked Spiffy.

'Lady Cynthia give it me'

'She must hand them out as trophies'

'It's gold, she reckons'

'Blimey, looks as if it's worth a right few bob'

'She says ah've to wear it next to me heart'

'Like hell you will,' contradicted Ginger, snatching the jewellery out of Sticky's hands. 'We'll take it down to Mad Taffy tonight. He'll give us thirty bob for that'

'As his lordship pleases,' concluded Spiffy, bowing extravagantly.

Blackpool ballroom blitz

'Right lads, it's pay-up time for the Blackpool weekend and I need three quid from each of you. Strictly cash, no IOUs'

Chalky White, in his capacity as organiser and treasurer for the billet outing, had entered Hut 29 carrying a clipboard and fingering the pencil lodged behind his right ear.

'How do you make that out then?' enquired Ginger, 'how come three quid?'

'There's the train fares and an overnight stay at the digs to be accounted for,' explained Chalky exercising due diligence. 'That comes to the best part of three notes each - with a little left over for emergencies'

'What emergencies?' asked Sticky innocently enough.

'Shut up, you big girl's blouse,' reprimanded Ginger. 'How many rooms are you allowing for Chalky?'

'Three. With six of us travelling, that'll be two people per room'

'We don't need three rooms,' Ginger disagreed vehemently. 'You're throwing away good ale money. We can all bunk up together in the same room like we do here'

'What, six in a bed?'

'You can get four in a double,' asserted Ginger.

'Four?'

'Yeah, two at the top, two at the bottom'

'Jist like back hame,' protested Jock Burns. 'Stuff me'

'Only as a last resort,' qualified Scrounger.

'Count me out of that deal mate.' Spiffy shook his head. 'I ain't having no geyser's smelly feet stuck up my hooter'

'Then you and Chalky can bring your sleeping bags and kip on the floor,' reasoned Ginger.

Sticky, who was meanwhile counting on his fingers, observed, 'That leaves some bugger with nowhere to sleep'

'No it doesn't. We'll fix you up in the bath up with some cushions and a rug'

'Eh?'

'Well,' reflected Chalky cautiously. 'There's some merit in what you say Ginger. Doing it your way will certainly hike up the ale kitty'

'I'll go along with that,' seconded Spiffy.

After some persuasion, Jock Burns, Scrounger Harris and Barry Emerson also agreed to the revised accommodation arrangements.

'That's that then,' said Ginger grinning broadly. 'You'll thank me when there's still money left for a few jars on the way back'

On Saturday morning the party assembled at Padgate station to board the train for Warrington, then on to Preston where they would change to an excursion special bound for Blackpool Central. They carried haversacks, wore casual civvies and had their spear-point collar shirts open at the neck. All except Sticky who was wearing a luminous mustard poplin suit with matching shirt and tie. He was carrying a battered old suitcase.

'That's a wide-awake piece of schmutter, mate,' observed Spiffy.

'Me Uncle Harry give it me. He got it from a Yank when he got torpedoed in the North Sea during the war'

'Your Uncle Harry?'

'No, the Yank'

'You're having a laugh, aren't you?'

'Never mind all that bollox,' broke in Ginger. 'Here comes our train'

Once aboard, Chalky immediately set about his duties as the official outing organiser. He opened up his haversack and withdrew a handful of brochures and leaflets, which he passed around the party. 'These will give you an idea of the amenities and places of interest in the Blackpool area. I thought we'd start with a visit to Stanley Park where we could take a boat out on the pond'

'Pond, whit dae we want a pond fur when we've got the sea?' complained Jock. 'Ah don't see the sense o' that. Anyway, we'd huv tae tak a bus an' that's mair expense'

'Ah, but you see,' countered Chalky enthusiastically, 'After Stanley Park I thought we'd visit the maritime museum nearby-'

'Bloody Nora, Chalky,' interrupted Ginger. 'What do you think you're organising, a girl guides outing?'

'Oh well,' Chalky replied huffily, folding his arms and scowling, 'if that's the way of it, you'd best take over'

'Aye, I will. We'll check in at the digs first, take a stroll down the front, have a dip in the sea, go back and have us teas, get freshened up, call in at Yates' Wine Lodge for a few ales - and then on to the dancing'

'Winter Gardens or Tower Ballroom?' enquired Barry.

'Tower, forced to be'

'Hold up,' interjected Scrounger, 'we don't have no cossies for a dip in the sea'

'Didn't you pack your drill shorts then?' asked Ginger.

'You can't wear drill shorts to bathe in the sea'

'I chuffing can'

'I reckon we should go t'Pleasure Beach,' proposed Sticky.

'The Pleasure Beach, in that suit, they'll stick you in a

sideshow, mate'

'Mair likely use him fur target practice at the rifle range,' opined Jock.

'What's the talent like at the Tower?'

'No' bad, but no' as good as the Albert'

'The Albert Hall?'

'Naw, ya mug, the Albert Ballroom in Bath Street'

'What's he on about?'

'Brawest lassies in Glesca go there on Seterday nights,' Jock reminisced fondly.

'Fancy that'

*

Gladys Moakler, landlady of number ten Balmoral Gardens on the South Shore reviewed the new arrivals with unconcealed distaste.

'No alcohol in the room, no smoking, no gambling, no bringing in your own food, no cooking, no shenanigans, no sneaking in members of the opposite sex; is that understood'

'Aye, missus, you're all right there,' confirmed Ginger. 'Would it be okay though if we had us a prayer meeting tonight? We usually do of a Saturday evening'

'As long as you're not Baptists; I'll not have no Baptists in this house'

'How about Rosicrucians?'

'Aye, well, happen.' She eyed Ginger curiously. 'But no Baptists; they give me the hump they do'

'Why is that missus?' asked Scrounger.

'One o't them, big red hair hussy she was, made off with my husband a few months back and turned him into a bible thumping street preacher'

'Leave you a bit short-handed, did it?' suggested Ginger.

'I'll say. He did the shopping, cooking, serving, washing, ironing and bed making'

Spiffy whispered in Barry's ear, 'Bet the old duffer was glad of the conversion. Talk about the Road to Damascus...'

'Front door closes ten o'clock sharp every night- including weekends,' concluded Gladys fiercely.

*

Five open-necked spear-points and one highly luminous poplin suit promenaded along the front debating where to go first.

'I vote the quick flicks,' advanced Scrounger.

'You dirty bugger'

'We could have us photos took,' suggested Sticky, espying some yards ahead a busy street photographer who had a queue of punters forming up

'Good idea. How much are you charging, squire?' shouted Ginger.

'Four bob a go'

'You're opening you're mouth a bit wide,' remonstrated Scrounger.

'How about a discount for national servicemen?' proposed Chalky.

The photographer pulled away from his current assignment, looked them over, relented, and replied as he was resuming his duties, 'Well, two bob apiece for you lads, seeing as how you're doing your bit - but you'll have to wait until I'm through with this lot'

'Sounds reasonable'

'Are we 'having our photos took then?'

'You'll be the ones who gets took if you give him two bob each,' warned Spiffy.

'How d'you mean?' asked Ginger.

'He's a con artist, ain't got no film in his camera'

'How do you know that?'

'I've seen him on the prom at Margate. He and his mates dodge from resort to resort down the south coast. Makes it difficult for the rozzers to catch up with them'

'What's he doing in Blackpool then?' said Barry.

'He gets on an early morning train in the smoke, travels up here, rooks the day trippers Saturday and Sunday, then vamooses back down south wiv a stash of cash'

'You still haven't explained how you know his camera's empty,' persisted Barry

'Look, it works like this. He clicks away like a good 'un, takes the money, gives the marks a dodgy address to pick up their snaps on Monday - but there ain't no snaps, no film, no address - and he's back down the smoke when they go looking for their prints'

'I just gave him eight bob to have me grandchildren's pictures taken,' contributed an elderly lady who had been eavesdropping on the conversation.

'Did you now mother?' replied Ginger. 'Well, let's have a gander inside his camera. Here mush, give me your magic lantern'

'You what?' exclaimed the photographer, taken aback.

'You heard'

'Piss off. I'll have the law on you'

'No you won't.' Spiffy moved in, eyeballing the happy snapper. 'You've been working the front up and down all day to avoid them'

'Hand the box ower,' growled Jock, 'or ah'll throw you and it in the sea'

'Gerroff'

Ginger snatched the apparatus and opened it. 'You're right Spiffy, no film, as empty as the vicar's collection box. Right, give the lady her money back - plus another two bob so her nippers can have some candy rock as they got no photos'

'Here comes a copper,' observed Spiffy.

'All right, all right, here's ten bob for the old dear. Fine thing when a honest man can't make a living,' complained the photographer, scampering off up a side street.

*

'Hello, come for a sitting, have you?'

It was Stan Withinshawe accompanied by Bunny Hare. They had just spotted the party entering Tussauds wax museum.

'Yeah,' riposted Ginger, 'Scrounger's up for melting down next week. Thought we'd have a look around first'

'Here, we're going clubbing tonight,' said Bunny enthusiastically. 'Would you like to come with us?'

'You'd be perfectly welcome, I'm sure,' added Stan.

'No thanks, we're off up the Tower'

'Ah well, you'll get great views tonight, what with the illuminations'

'They don't need the illuminations,' Stan disagreed. 'That mustard suit will shine like a beacon for miles around'

'Not that tower, the Tower ballroom,' advised Ginger.

'Oh'

'I'll come clubbing with you,' volunteered Chalky.

*

Yates' Wine Lodge had the usual Saturday night crowd in comprising hawkers, dockers, rockers, navvies, comic singers and dancers. The party found it difficult to make themselves heard above the din and when Ginger was almost through his fourteenth pint, he announced loudly,

'Time gentlemen please,' and swallowing the remains in a single slurp, he thumped the tankard down hard on the counter. 'It's off to the Tower and on with the crumpet'

'Why are we having crumpet now,' enquired a mystified Sticky. 'We've just had us teas'

'No, you dozy beggar,' explained Scrounger, 'he means the talent up the dancing'

*

Three hours had passed without incident at the Tower Ballroom when Ginger turned to speak to Barry in the upstairs spectators' gallery. He had to shout to be heard above the Joe Loss Orchestra as they belted out their version of 'Bewitched, Bothered and Bewildered'.

'Grand night, grand night, good ale, good dancing, good lasses, what more could we ask for?'

'Certainly not what I'm witnessing downstairs,' replied

Barry, pointing to a disturbance on the floor.

Ginger looked down. 'Trust some idle josser to ruin everything. Best go sort it out'

Jock Burns had also witnessed the fracas. He'd been standing quietly one his own at the edge of the dance area watching Scrounger displaying his expertise at the slow foxtrot and engaging in animated conversation with a young lady when they were rudely interrupted.

A mountainous GI in dress uniform had pushed Scrounger aside roughly and whisked off his partner in a bear hug. She was pummelling him with her fists in protest at his unwanted advances.

Jock shoved his way through the mass of dancers to the middle of the floor and addressed the Yank.

'Get yir jukes up. It's a squerr go'

'Go take a walk, buster'

'Ah've hud a walk'

Three other American soldiers made to rush to the assistance of their comrade when Ginger appeared on the scene and with outstretched arms halted their progress.

'You heard the man. It's a square go. No butting in - Marquess of Queensberry rules'

However, as a precaution and to ensure that they fully understood the terms of his dictate, he head butted each of them in turn.

'Hadn't we better give Jock a hand?' said Barry.

'Naw, he'll be okay. He's sturdier than a red brick wall'

Back in the centre of the floor, the Yank released his grip on the distressed young lady and moved in on Jock. He towered over his adversary, advising, 'You don't know what you're taking on here buddy. I'm the va-va-va-va-vroom-boy'

'Oh aye, is'at right Jimmy? Well, here's a Maryhill kiss tae stick on the end o' it,' at which Jock too executed a perfect head butt, knocking the gargantuan Yank in a heap to the floor.

Several burly bouncers arrived belatedly to escort the combatants forcefully from the ballroom.

'Are you okay mate?'

Ginger was endeavouring to help the Yank to his feet where he lay crumpled on the pavement.

'Ouch, no, leave me. I've hurt my foot.' As an afterthought he added, 'And I've missed the last bus back to Burtonwood'

'He can come back wi' us tae the digs,' growled Jock.

'He'll have nowhere to sleep,' argued Sticky.

'Aye, he will. He can have the bath; you can kip in the corridor outside'

'Eh?'

The revellers staggered all the way from the Tower down the Golden Mile to the South Shore, Balmoral Gardens and a locked front door. Supporting the lame Yank between them were a bedraggled Ginger and Jock.

'The old scroat has shut us out,' said Spiffy, hammering on the door.

Immediately above them a light was switched on, a window opened, and a head full of curlers emerged. 'I told you ten o'clock. You'll not get in here tonight' yelled Gladys Moakler.

'But we've brought back a wounded American soldier from the front,' protested Ginger equally loudly.

'It's okay but, missus,' added Sticky, ''he's not a member of the opposite sex'

'You what?'

'Wounded American soldier from the front'

'What front?'

'Blackpool front'

'Right, I'm throwing down a key. Catch'

Jock had gone out early to accompany the Yank to the nearest bus stop; the others were at table when Sticky strolled into the breakfast room wearing a stylishly cut navy blue serge suit.

'Now that's what I call a tin flute,' remarked Spiffy admiringly. 'How did you come by it?'

'Mrs Moakler give me it, belonged to her old man'

'Where's the monstrosity you was wearing yesterday?' asked Ginger.

'She wrapped it up with brown paper an' string and sent it to Mr Moakler wi' a note inside telling him to wear it when 'he goes out preaching in street'

'Was it cold outside in the corridor last night?' enquired Scrounger.

'Dunno'

'How d'you mean you don't know?'

'Ah weren't in corridor. Ah slept in the missus' bed'

'Where did she sleep then?'

'With me'

*

Jock arrived back with some disturbing news.

'Chalky's up fur sentencin' at the Sunday Court they huv fur weekend trippers that ur out of order'

'What's he done?'

'Got himself arrested at a club Bunny and Stan took him tae'

'Did they get nobbled too?'

'Naw, some pal let them oot a side door'

'Oh, one of them funny clubs'

'Best get down to the court then,' said Ginger.

They arrived at the court towards the end of the proceedings to witness Chalky standing dejectedly in the dock, the object of concerted stern glares from the magistrates on the bench.

The chairman was a short, round little man with flowing locks of stringy white hair. He spoke in a rasping voice.

'We don't hold wi' lewd, late-night drinkin' clubs in Blac'pool where men dress up as women and vice versa, gives the town a bad name. An' we don't hold wi' day trippers what frequents them neither. But seein' as how you're a first offender, I'll go lenient on you like. Fifteen shillin's fine an' bound over for twelve months'

*

'Well, that's it lads, no ale on the way back,' groaned Ginger. 'We'll have to pay his fine'

Why?'

'He's got no brass. I know that for a fact'

'How come?'

'Because there's only fifteen bob left in us kitty I tapped him for yesterday morning'

'You mean you used our cash to fund your weekend?'

'That's why he had us sleeping three in a bed'

'And Chalky and me in sleeping bags'

'Aye, an' me out in the corridor'

'Shut up, you got a new suit out of it'

'And his wicked way with the landlady'

'You're a thievin' bastird,' growled Jock.

'Steady on now lads. It's only money,' soothed Ginger, 'how about a whip round?'

Poison chalice

The last thing on their minds was a visit to the rifle range but that was the fate in store for the latrine orderlies on a wet and windy day in late March. Pilot Officer Dawkins called in unexpectedly on Ginger and Sticky to relay the news.

'When was the last time either of you did any shooting?' he enquired.

'Eh?' mumbled Sticky.

Ginger put down his mop and bucket, and leaned against a cubicle door as he pondered the question.

'Do you mean like on a rabbit shoot?'

'No, I do not. I mean like at the rifle range'

'Square bashing, that was the last time,' retorted Ginger brusquely. 'There's been no call for it since'

'Well there is now. I want you and your oppo to report to the corporal instructor at the range. Two o'clock sharp. What with the turmoil in Korea and general unrest elsewhere in the world, we've had a directive from Area Command to have you chaps licked into shape on rifle proficiency. I'm charging you AC2 Harrison with the responsibility of advising everyone in your section accordingly.' He looked around the latrine, sniffed, and added. 'It will save me the trouble of traipsing around any more of these foul smelling, germ infested establishments'

As he departed, Ginger withdrew a half spent Woodbine from behind an ear, lit up, coughed, and remarked to Sticky,

'Nice one, nice little skive'

'No, Ginge, they'll maybe send us off to war next'

'No chance, never, we're too important. Cleaning out bogs is a reserved occupation'

*

They stood in line, the massed ranks of latrine orderlies, cold and shivering in the face of a hostile gale. Those who had exercised the foresight to don greatcoats fared best but for the remainder, an icy wind billowed mercilessly up the legs of their flimsy denim trousers. 'Bloody Nora,' observed one of the unfortunates. 'What are they preparing us for - the Russian front?

'Right then,' announced the instructor. 'Have you all been issued with a rifle and live ammunition?'

'Yes corporal,' sang out the freezing brigade.

'First six in line, move out and take up your positions'

Ginger and Sticky who had been at the head of the queue lay down flat on their fronts beside one another at the firing line.

'What do we have to do?' asked Sticky nervously.

'Just do as I do. See them targets?'

'Aye'

'Look through the sight finder and focus on the target facing you. When the corporal tells you, fire at the fucker and keep firing at it until he tells you to stop. Got that?'

'Ah think so'

'Get ready,' called out the instructor. 'Take aim, fire!'

The crackle of rapid rifle fire filled the air for several minutes and then ceased as abruptly as it had begun.

'Where did you learn to shoot like that lad?'

Ginger looked up to find looming over him a giant of a man, the sergeant instructor who was examining the targets through field glasses.

'At the shows sergeant'

'Fairgrounds, you mean?'

'Yes sarge. The target finders on their guns are always crooked. If you can shoot accurately with them, you can hit the target with any rifle'

'Didn't you get a marksman's badge at basic training?'

'Yes sarge'

'Why aren't you wearing it?'

'I lost it somewhere'

'Right, I'll give you a chit before you leave the range. Take it to the stores and they'll give you a replacement.'

As he departed to the other end of the line, the sergeant boomed out, 'Wear it with pride lad. Six shots, six bulls, best of the bunch, I'll be bound'

'How many bulls did ah get then?' enquired Sticky

'Just the two,' replied Ginger. 'They're lying dead in that field over yonder'

'He couldn't hit a cow's arse with a banjo,' added the corporal instructor snidely.

As they were preparing to leave the range, the sergeant reappeared with the requisition order for Ginger's marksman's badge. 'Take more care of your insignia in future,' he cautioned.

'Yes sarge, I will'

'Now then, before you leave,' said the corporal, 'check out your rifles to make sure you haven't left one up the spout'

'What do ah do now Ginge?'

'Do as the man says,' replied Ginger testily. 'Open the bolt, hold your rifle up in air and check that the chamber is clear'

Sticky fumbled with the bolt for a few seconds and then yelled out in pain, 'Ah've caught me thumb in the hole'

'Fucking hell'

'Let's have a look,' said the corporal, easing Sticky's injured thumb free from the bolt hole. 'No bleeding but badly bruised. Better get yourself up the MO.' Turning to Ginger, he added, 'You go with him. I'll get word back to Sergeant Jordan'

*

As they sat huddled together in the cheerless medical reception area awaiting attention, Ginger asked,

'How's your thumb feeling now?'

'Sore. It hurts like 'ell'

'Well, it would do,' replied Ginger unsympathetically. 'Getting it caught in the chuffing hole. Fat lot o' good you'd be in a Korean punch-up'

'Ginger'

'What?'

'You told the sarge you lost your badge, but you didn't Ginger, you flogged it'

'Aye and I'll be flogging the new bugger too. Mad Taffy'll give me ten bob for it'

Sticky's injured thumb was given the customary five second examination by a patently disinterested medical orderly who briskly dabbed the affected flesh with a damp sponge before handing the out-patient a bottle of tablets.

'Take one of these three times daily before meals'

'What are they?' asked Ginger.

'Aspirin'

'Aspirin for a bruised thumb?'

'It's what we always prescribe for minor ailments,' replied the orderly with some authority.

'Shouldn't he be examined by a doctor?' persisted Ginger.

'We can't be wasting doctor's time on service personnel who are too thick to look after themselves'

'Watch it, shirt lifter,' threatened Ginger.

*

Work over for the day, the residents of Hut 29 trooped in one after the other to collect irons and mugs prior to departing again for their evening meal at the canteen.

'What's up with you then?' asked Barry Emerson on observing Sticky's glum face.

'Caught his thumb in a bolt hole up the rifle range,' volunteered Ginger.

'Sure he wasn't groping Big Trixie up the NAFFI?' suggested Scrounger Harris. 'He'll get a dose of the pox if he was. Best get some tadger cream on it straightaway'

'Piss off'

*

As the mess mates tucked into a salad tea consisting in the main of rabbit droppings, crisp brown paper and sheets of soggy cardboard, Sergeant Jordan approached the table.

'I hear you got yourself on the roll of honour at the rifle range today Harrison'

'Yes sarge, six bulls,' replied Ginger proudly.

'Well, no surprises there. You're always full of bullshit, you are. Let's see what you can do with a brush'

'What?'

'When you've finished your meal you can make up for the time you lost skiving off to the MO by cleaning out my quarters'

'But sarge – '

'No buts. Here's the key.' He looked around the assembled diners and added, 'You, Harris'

'Sarge'

'Go with him'

Jordan marched off but stopped again midway up the dining hall and called back, 'Just to make sure the fat barstard don't nick nothing'

'Sarky sod,' muttered Ginger.

*

Jordan's quarters had been completely redecorated and refurbished following the trashing effected by the now departed Corporal Butterfly. As Scrounger energetically brushed the highly polished linoleum floor,

Ginger busied himself opening and closing the drawers of a dressing table.

'What are you doing Ginger?'

'Seeing if he's got owt worth nicking'

'Pack it in mate'

'Hello, hello, hello'

'What?'

'The dirty old man, this drawer's full of porn magazines'

'Leave them be'

'Gordon bloody Bennett, there must be at least fifty or maybe sixty. Now we know why he spends so much time in the crapper'

'Like I said Ginger, leave them be'

'Piss off. I'll have half a dozen. He'll never miss them and Mad Taffy'll take them off me at two bob a piece.

As they entered the billet some fifteen minutes later, there was a groan coming from the direction of Sticky's bedplace.

'What's afoot?' asked Ginger.

'He's none too good,' replied Barry Emerson. 'Got a high temperature and he's shivering badly. Oh, and I had a look at his thumb. There's a red line moving up his forearm'

'Let's have a butcher's,' said Scrounger who worked as an assistant to the orderlies at the medical unit.

He rolled back Sticky's shirt for a closer inspection and exclaimed, 'Forearm be fucked, the line is only a few inches away from his armpit'

'Is that bad?' asked Ginger anxiously.

'Bad? It'll be fatal if it's not attended to immediately. The bruised blood is septic now and it's heading straight for his heart'

They tried lifting Sticky to his feet but his knees wobbled and he fell back onto the bed again.

'Leave him to me,' said Ginger who lifted up his sick mate in his arms. 'Shove a blanket around him Scrounger and come with me. You can explain it better'

With Scrounger scurrying after him, Ginger walked the half mile to the camp hospital at a brisk pace, stopping not once for a breather.

'When we get there Scrounger, you'd best get a doctor to look at him right away – or I'll punch some bugger – I mean it'

'Don't worry Ginger; Doc Hollis is on duty tonight. He's a surgeon; he'll know what to do'

*

'At what time did the injury occur?'

'Half past two sir, at the rifle range' replied Ginger.

'Has he had any attention at all?'

'Medical orderly gave him some aspirin'

'Did he now?' said Squadron Leader Hollis without elaborating further on the prescription. 'Right then, young man, it's gone too far for simple lancing. I'm going to give you a sedative which will relieve the pain and ensure you a sound night's sleep'

'Thank you sir,' replied Sticky dolefully.

'I'll operate first thing in the morning and cut out the puce'

At which Sticky fainted.

*

The following evening Ginger visited the patient who was propped up against several pillows in his hospital bed. He was also in the act of composing a letter to his mother with the writing implement poised awkwardly between his forefingers.

'How do you spell sufficient, Ginge?'

'Same as a drill sergeant's blessing; two 'ff's' and one 'c''

*

Several days passed and Sticky was released from hospital to convalesce in the care of Flight Lieutenant Willoughby-Goddard.

'Light duties in the recreation room, what? Would that be convenient for you?' asked the toothy padre.

'Oh aye, vicar, right champion,' said the new arrival whose heavily bandaged right thumb was sticking bolt upright.

'Good, excellent, first class'

Sticky settled down comfortably in his new quarters and spent the next few hours trying out the newly installed pool table. To his delight he discovered that he could follow the game plan much more easily than snooker; the balls were all numbered and the colours were less confusing. He was also an avid fan of the 'Behind the 8 Ball' comedy shorts which seemed to be a regular fixture at the camp cinema and even with his injured thumb he was soon potting the balls accurately and in sequence in every game.

Ginger walked in on one of these games just as Sticky was slotting away the final six balls in rapid-fire order.

'By the left, you might not be able to hit a cow's arse with a banjo but you sure can clear a table. Where did you learn to shoot pool like that?'

'Don't know. Just seems easier like, now that me thumb's stuck up in the air'

'Right, let's make the most of it'

'How do you mean?'

'We'll go down the NAFFI and clean up with the sprogs. They've also got a new pool table and there's a fresh intake just arrived this morning with pockets stuffed full of oncers their aunties gave them'

'Ah don't right follow you Ginge'

'Look, this'll be like money from home. We go down the NAFFI, get ourselves a table, and make out we're a couple of lummoxes. You just hang around looking like a spare prick at a wedding and I'll make a right arse of meself on the table. This is the first night in camp for the new intake; they've all got brass and they'll all be showing off. If a couple of them don't come up within ten minutes and ask us to play for money, I'll wear me Auntie Maggie's knickers on parade tomorrow morning'

*

'Fancy a game? Bet on the side?'

Ginger looked up from the pool table at the Brylcreem slicked youths in civvies.

'You mean for money like?'

'Makes it more interesting'

'Go on then'

'Say five bob a game?'

'Well – I'm not much cop and me mate here is crocked'

'Okay, half a dollar'

'Over ten games?'

'If you like'

Ginger fluffed his first shot and then Sticky took over,

clearing ball after ball, game after game.

'You're a couple of con artists,' said one of the youths as he handed over thirty shillings at the end of the session.

'What us? We're rubbish. Lucky you wasn't playing our mate Scrounger Harris tonight. He's hot stuff, rattling away them funny little balls'

As they walked back to Hut 29 Sticky announced, 'Think ah'll take off me bandage. Me finger feels better now'

'You chuffing won't. There's another intake of rookies due in tomorrow morning. That's our beer money for the rest of the week you've got sticking up in the air'

Extravaganza!

'Have I got news for you or what?' announced Ginger on entering the billet.

'Well, shut the bleeding door before you let us in on it,' rebuked a recumbent airman. 'It's cold enough in here as it is - and all because your dopey mate forgot to stoke up - as usual'

Ginger's entrance had blown in a howling gale together with Sticky Albright who removed his rain sodden groundsheet and shook it vigorously in the direction of the complainant.

'What's your news then Ginge?' enquired Barry Emerson.

'Bunny Rabbit and Stan the Flan are up for posting'

'Bloody hell,' said the victim of Sticky's indiscriminate spraying. 'Those two arrived here when Pontius Pilate was still in basic training'

'Even before that,' contributed another airman from the back of the billet. 'Bunny and Stan came here with the ark. In fact, some people reckon -'

'How do you know, Ginge,' interrupted Barry. 'How do you know about them being posted?'

'Read it on the bulletin board up the Sergeants Mess. Sticky and me was there all day cleaning out their bogs'

'Dirty buggers, them sergeants,' added Sticky.

'Bunny's drawn Hamburg and Stan, poor bugger, is heading for Cardington'

'When?' asked Barry

'End of next month'

'Wonder if they'll stage another show before they leave?'

'Shouldn't think so,' surmised Ginger. 'They'll have too much on their minds to be bothered with shows. Anyway, there's not enough time'

*

'I feel the vibes Stan, I feel the vibes. It's coming through I tell you, it's coming through'

Bunny Hare closed his eyes in silent meditation for a moment or two, opened them, and sighed, 'It's no use, it's ebbing away, it's gone'

'How about...extravaganza?' suggested Stan who was consulting a large dusty volume of Chambers Dictionary. 'Extravaganza, noun, it says here, "an extravagant or eccentric musical, dramatic or literary production. Extravagant conduct or speech..." Well, I'm not so sure now, sounds a teeny weeny bit on the melodramatic'

'Stan, you're a genius, 'enthused Bunny. 'It's the perfect title! I can see it now writ large on the marquee. Extravaganza - complete with screamer - perfect'

'Marquee?' enquired Stan incredulously.

'Well, perhaps marquee is stretching it a bit - but we could use that disused hanger at the back entrance to the camp'

'That draughty old place, nowadays that's only used by the ORs and WAFFs as an after-hours knocking shop'

'We'll have it converted'

'We'll what?'

'I'll have words with Phartingail ffoulkes-Knight and my first two words will be Madame Golightly'

'Frankly Bunny, I don't see the point of putting ourselves to all that trouble. Why don't we just use the camp theatre? It worked well for the panto; we had no complaints'

'Too small, too restrictive, no ambience,' Bunny was adamant. 'Extravaganza will be a big show, a master production. We'll need all the space we can harness'

'Oh fancy,' exclaimed Stan who was still consulting Chambers Dictionary. 'Ecstasy, Noun: "state of exalted pleasure, happiness or rapture". All right for some I suppose'

'Right Stan, let's draft a notice and post it on the bulletin board straightaway'

Ginger was on one of his numerous skives around the camp when he was seized by a sudden notion to call in on Barry Emerson at the Attestation Section where new recruits underwent initial assessment.

The telephone trilled stridently as he entered Barry's office. 'Homicide, Lootenant Emerhiem,' announced

Barry by way of a deep drawl into the mouthpiece.

There was evidence of an angry response in the crackle emanating from the other end of the line

'Sorry Flight Sergeant,' said Barry meekly.

'Who was that?' asked Ginger.

'Old Chiefy Bulstrode'

'Bullet balls, some call him'

'I thought it was one of the lads'

'So, what's been happening around here?'

'Guess who I attested this morning?'

'Surprise me'

'Anthony Newley'

'Who's he then?'

'The film actor, you must have heard of him'

'Naw, can't say as I have. Never bother with the flicks meself'. Ginger paused for a moment. 'You should tell Bunny though. He might want to use this geyser in the show'

'Good thinking Ginger. I'll phone Bunny later'

*

'What do you want a hangar for?

Squadron Leader Phartingail ffoulkes-Knight was seated at his desk facing an unwelcome deputation in the shape of Sergeants Hare and Withinshawe who proceeded to elaborate on the purpose of their requirement.

'Out of the question,' said the squadron leader when they had concluded their presentation. 'The Commanding Officer would never sanction indiscriminate expenditure on such a piece of tomfoolery, frippery and fandangle'

'But it wouldn't cost much,' countered Bunny. 'I'll have my crew do all the graft - and the props and scenery I can get for free from Warrington Rep'

'Crew, what crew?'

'The cast and the production team'

'Sergeant Hare,' snapped Phartingail ffoulkes-Knight. 'Your crew, as you call them, are enlisted men undergoing national service, not a bunch of prancing fairies in a school entertainment'

'Really, how crude' protested Stan.

'Will you at least submit our request to Wing Commander Barclay?' reasoned Bunny.

'No, I will not, and that's my final word on the matter'

'Well, suit yourself squadron-leader,' said Bunny, standing up to leave.' If you don't mind having your sordid goings-on at Mrs Golightly's splattered all over the *News of The*

World, that's your business'

'Are you threatening me?'

'Heaven forbid. No, I was just saying, that's all'

When they had departed, Phartingail ffoulkes-Knight braced himself, picked up the telephone and requested the orderly corporal to connect him with the CO's office.

*

It was six o'clock in the evening and despite the foul weather, the auditorium was filled to near capacity in expectation of news of the format of Bunny's final production.

'Wonder what the theme will be this time?' mused an airman.

'Tarts and farts as usual,' replied another.

As raindrops peppered the roof in a constant downpour, the producers took up their positions onstage, accompanied by a stoutly proportioned little man with a red face and a loud check suit. Bunny kicked off the proceedings.

'Thank you, thank you one and all for coming out on such a dreadful night, and I promise not to detain you for long. There's not really much to tell right now except to say that our final production will be the biggest, the best, and the most ambitious of all; an extravaganza, an irresistible piece of theatre. Watch out for details on the bulletin board because we aim to knock your socks off with this show'

'Not giving much away is he, the crafty sod,' remarked Ginger to Barry Emerson.

'First though, introductions,' continued Bunny as he called out, 'Would AC2 Newley kindly identify himself?'

A tentative hand was raised to a ripple of mild applause.

'AC2 Newley, better known to you as film actor Anthony Newley, will be featuring in the show and I'm sure you will all want to give him a warm welcome'

An even milder ripple of applause greeted this announcement.

'Now gather around everyone, gather around the stage please,' announced Stan with some authority. 'I want you all to pay particular attention to what our second guest Happy Harry Hopwood has to tell us tonight. Mr Hopwood, as I'm sure you know, was for many years before his retirement, one of the most revered top of the bill comedians in the variety circuit. Harry has kindly consented to coach us on the essential tenets of high comedy – and high comedy is to be the essence of Extravaganza'

'You'll throw in some tips on satire, won't you Harry?' whispered Bunny urgently to his honoured guest.

'Satire, as you wish squire. Let's kick off with satire then'

'This should be fun' gushed Stan.

'May I use your blackboard?' requested Happy Harry.

'Of course, feel free'

'Chalk'

'On the ledge'

Harry picked up three stalks of chalk and the blackboard duster, which mundane objects he proceeded to juggle with some expertise as he strutted back and forth across the stage. His impromptu little act drew an enthusiastic round of applause. Harry took a bow, beamed at his captive audience, and began his dissertation.

'I've always found that getting laughs from satire is all to do with how you use words, and not the actual words themselves. For instance, I'll give odds of one hundred to one that this word gets a belly laugh.' Harry chalked up the word 'knickers' on the board and won his bet before he had reached the final literal.

'Well, really,' objected Bunny quietly.

Harry then added the word 'bum' to louder ribaldry

'Are you sure he was a pro?' enquired Stan of his producer.

Then Harry chalked up 'tits' followed by 'cock' and bedlam broke out.

'I'll not work with that man, I will not work with him,' complained Stan bitterly. 'He's rude, he is, very rude'

'Now a few words on milking your audience at camp shows.' His warm up act over, Harry was going for the kill. 'During the war I worked with ENSA – '

'Ah, thank you, but no thanks' called out Bunny. 'You can leave camp comedy to the management. We've got oodles more experience'

Stan put an end to Harry's shenanigans by abruptly closing the meeting – but not before requesting AC2 Newley's presence onstage.

What's your speciality?' asked Bunny when order had been restored, the others had gone, and the three of them were seated around the table.

'I'm an actor,' replied AC2 Newley succinctly

'Yes, but what do you do besides? Do you sing, dance, tell jokes, or what?'

'I've never done stand-up and my singing and dancing isn't up to snuff yet for a live performance'

'Not over-stretched in the repertoire division, are we ducky?' assessed Stan indifferently.

'I've got it,' said Bunny. 'We'll re-enact a scene from one of your films. How about, say *Vice Versa*? A piece of business between you and that girl thingy perhaps?'

'Petula Clark,' advised AC2 Newley.

'Whatever'

'What about a script? I certainly don't remember the lines'

'Oh, we have access to film scripts – as far back as *Little Nell*'

'Who'd play Petula's part?' asked Stan.

'Let me see now...' Bunny rustled through several pages of his draft script. 'I know, we'll create a slot after scene 15, Greta Garbo. We'll shove in Albright as thingy; he's free then. Stick on a wig and some make-up; that should do it'

'We are taking into account, are we not,' pursued Stan with pronounced sarcasm, 'that Petula Clark is four foot eleven, petite and pretty. Albright, on the other hand, is six foot two, rangy, clueless, inarticulate, thick as a brick, and ugly as sin'

'Mmm, yes, well... point taken, we'll sort something else out'

*

The first rehearsal call was brief on two counts; the management had already chosen their cast, but more essentially, they were still frantically working on a final script.

'Next,' called Stan.

Out strutted LAC Gropethorpe who gave a lack lustre three-minute impersonation of Mae West, ending with the legendary and boring, 'Come up and see me sometime'

'Bit shallow, that was.' complained Stan. 'What about your Greta Garbo?'

Greta Garbo turned her head to glare at Stan as she pouted her lips to elicit,

'I vant to be alone'

Dressed in his Mrs McGillicuddy attire, Ginger remarked to Bunny, 'If Gropey performs like that on the night he'll most likely get his wish'

*

'What's all this then?' protested Leading Aircraftsman Gropethorpe as he unfurled a theatre bill on top of Bunny Hare's desk.

'What's all what?'

'You know very well what I'm talking about, Sergeant Hare. That sprog, over me, in the billing'

'Sprog he may be,' retorted Stan, 'but AC2 Newley also happens to be a famous film star'

'Unknown bit player more like. I've never heard of him,' countered Gropthorpe huffily.

'What's this really all about sweetie?' soothed Bunny.

'I'll tell you what it's all really about.' LAC Gropethorpe was gathering up steam. 'My Agent reckons I shouldn't do the show'

'Agent, hark at the mouth on her,' said Stan. 'She'll be telling us next she's joining Sadler's Wells'

'No, but what I will tell you is this, I've got a summer season and a panto lined up after I'm demobbed and my agent reckons I have to be careful about my image meantime'

'Image, image?' spluttered Stan. 'The only image you've got bitch is the one we gave you when we dragged you out of the chorus line and made something of you, you ingrate–'

'Now then Stan,' appeased Bunny. 'Let's keep this in perspective.' He looked LAC Gropethorpe straight in the eye and calmly asked, 'is that your final word on the matter, you won't be appearing in the show unless you get top billing?'

'Yes, my agent says – '

'Never mind what your agent says. He's not producing Extravaganza. We'll make alternative arrangements'

'Yes, but, I mean…' LAC Gropethorpe wasn't so sure of himself now. 'It's *only* a question of the billing. It's not as if – '

'Goodbye Gropethorpe. Sergeant Withinshawe and I have a great deal to get through this afternoon'

The Fairy Queen, also known as Marlene Dietrich and Carmen Miranda, departed in some distress.

'Well, I never,' commented Stan.

'Did you vada her eek when I told her what she could do with her act?' asked Bunny mischievously.

'She goes too far. She's getting my wild up, she is'

'Greta Garbo will return. She doesn't *really* want to be alone'

'Have you heard the news?'

Barry Emerson entered the latrines as Ginger was in the act of pitching a bucket of ice cold water over the closed door of a toilet cubicle.

'Arghhh!' screamed the startled airman inside.

'Sorry mate,' apologised Ginger. 'Didn't know you was in there. You should have said.' Ignoring the distressed airman's protestations, he put down the bucket and addressed Barry.

'What news?'

'It's all off'

'What all off?'

'Extravaganza, the postings for Bunny and Stan came through earlier then they expected. They left in a hurry last night to catch a flight to the Outer Hebrides'

'The sods'

'Bunny and Stan?'

'No, the CO and Farty Night, I reckon Bunny had something on those two old perverts'
'Well, you know what they say'

'What?' enquired Sticky.

'Never mind'

'Right, you idle layabouts. Let's be having you,' stormed Sergeant Jordan, emerging from another cubicle.' He glared sternly at each of them in turn and said forcefully, 'You're all on a charge'

'Back to reality,' muttered Ginger.

Hangman's noose

'Does this mean we're like NCOs now Ginger?'

Sticky was examining his newly affixed armband that bore the legend 'Security Patrol'. He had a large torch in one hand while in the other there was clasped a single typewritten sheet of instructions to which he now turned his attention.

'Oh aye,' replied Ginger, winking to Barry Emerson. 'Right up there alongside old Bandy Jordan'

'It says, app-, apper- "

'Give us it here,' said Ginger, snatching the instruction sheet.

'Apprehend wrongdoers,' he read out.

'Like SPs then?' asked Sticky eagerly.

'Aye, more like SPs. Let's be having you then. We'll look for wrongdoers an' have some fun'

'Watch out for the bogey man,' called Scrounger Harris.

'Naff off'

*

It was ten o'clock on a bitterly cold foggy winter's night and already tiny particles of white frost were appearing on the ground as they set out on their first two-hour stint of camp patrol duty. Wearing balaclavas and mittens, they had the collars of their greatcoats turned up and

Sticky wore a doubled-up scarf around his face for added protection.

'You'll get a bollocking if we run into the real SPs. They'll say you're improperly dressed,' cautioned Ginger.

'But it's freezing cold Ginge,' mumbled Sticky from behind his muffler.

'Never mind, we'll do a quick tour of the offices and stores on your sheet and then we'll call in at the back door of the canteen. Slimy Jake will do us a brew an' some bacon butties'

'Someone's coming towards us Ginge,' announced Sticky anxiously as he pulled down the lip of his scarf.

Out of the mist emerged two shapes.

'Halt, who goes there' bellowed Ginger.

The shapes froze on the spot and stood rigidly to attention.

'What have we got here?'

'New recruits sir,' answered one of the shapes. 'D Wing sir'

Ginger shone his torch in their faces and said, 'Just been issued with your kit then?'

'Yes sir'

'You,' continued Ginger, focusing on the shortest of the pair. 'You look like George Formby, get your forage cap adjusted properly'

'Sir'

'And you,' turning to the other shape, 'you look like a pregnant duck. Now get on with you, back to your billet at the double'

As the recruits disappeared rapidly into the mist, Ginger said, 'Told you we'd have some fun. Now for a brew'

'But Ginge we haven't checked out stores an' offices yet'

'We'll do that on the four o'clock shift'

*

'Where's the country bumpkin then?' asked the senior man of the D wing intake.

'Dunno,' answered a recruit lying atop his bed reading a magazine. 'Haven't seen him around all night'

'Done nothing but blub since we got 'ere, the soft bugger,' added another recruit who was energetically applying spit and polish to his newly acquired drill boots.

'He'd better be back before lights out else the corp'll have his guts for garters,' asserted the senior man with some conviction.

*

'Ginge, wake up,' whispered Sticky.

Ginger stirred, turned around in his bed and looked up at the balaclava helmet looming over him. 'It's never four o'clock, is it?'

'Yeah, time to get up and go'

Ginger heaved himself out of bed, ruffled his unruly mop, and began to pull on his trousers.

'Will ah bring the sandwiches Jake give us?'

'Aye, go on'

As they were leaving the billet Ginger stopped at Scrounger's bed space and pulled the covers away roughly.

'What? What did you do that for?' asked the startled occupant. 'I were chatting up Betty Grable just then'

'Well you shouldn't have been,' reprimanded Ginger. 'She's a happily married woman. What would Harry James say?'

'Who?'

'Her Husband'

Scrounger pulled the covers back over his head and snarled, 'Bog off'

'I shouldn't be at all surprised'

*

Although the fog had lifted it was even colder outside now and there was a pronounced wind rising.

'Bloody fair, isn't it,' complained Ginger.

'Never mind,' comforted Sticky. 'We get to lie in late in the morning'

'Late, late you call it? Half past eight an' we don't get to bed while six o' chuffing clock'

'Where'll we check first?'

'We'll do the stores'

They walked past several rows of dark silent billets and turned right at the end up a narrow passageway to where the stores section was situated.

'What's that banging noise?' asked Sticky.

Ginger shone his torch. 'Look, over there, some twat's left a bog wide door open. It's banging against the wall.' Although he didn't have a key to lock the door, Ginger decided to investigate before proceeding with the patrol duties. He entered the latrine cautiously, followed in close attendance by Sticky who whispered,

'What's that creaking noise?'

'You and your bloody noises, where?'

'At the far end'

Ginger could hear the creaking plainly now as he approached the last cubicle. Very gently, he opened the door.

'Fucking hell' he gasped, as Sticky yelped and turned aside to throw up.

Focused in the beam of his torch was a naked body rocking slowly and steadily from side to side. The head jutted forward grotesquely from a hangman's noose constructed of thick heavy duty rope, the other end of which was affixed to a large hook screwed into the wooden beam above.

'Have you got a knife?' Ginger called out.

'No –no-' squeaked Sticky.

Ginger edged his vast bulk past one side of the swaying weight and clambered onto the lavatory basin. He placed his right arm around the lifeless buttocks and eased the body over a shoulder while with his left hand he started to unscrew the stubborn hook from the beam. It took all of his considerable strength but with supreme effort, he managed to pull the hook free.

'Give us a hand here,' he instructed Sticky. 'Take the legs. No, not that way, you pillock, don't push them, pull them towards you'

Ginger stepped down from the basin and between them they carried the body out of the cubicle and laid it carefully on the passageway floor. Sticky shone his torch on the outstretched shape. It was that of a young male. It was cold and it was dead.

'Your fingers has blood on them Ginge,' said Sticky.

His observation was a gross understatement. The flesh on the fingers of Ginger's left hand was badly lacerated and the bleeding was profuse. Taking a murky handkerchief from a trouser pocket and wrapping it around his painful hand, he spoke quietly but urgently, 'Go up the guardhouse as fast as you can and get the SPs down here. I'll hang around with this poor bugger.' He double-checked for the remotest sign of life: heart, pulse, and breathing. There was none.

*

The main office of the guardroom was rapidly converted into an emergency control centre and one of the cells allocated as a temporary mortuary for the remains. Roused from his bed at four-thirty five am, the Commanding Officer had telephoned Squadron Leader Phartingail ffoulkes-Knight and charged him with the responsibility of conducting a preliminary investigation into all events likely to bear relevance on the tragedy. They were now in conference.

'Damn bad show,' announced the agitated Wing Commander Barclay. 'Damn bad timing too. We've got the finals of the RAF recruitment base of the year coming up next month. No chance of a first this time, I fear'

'Indeed not sir,' replied the next in command, eyeing his superior curiously.

'Area Command will have to be informed, then the Home Office'

'Not to mention the next of kin'

The Commanding Officer appeared oblivious to the acidity of the tone in which this observation was delivered. He continued, 'There will be a public enquiry of course and, God help us, a ministerial visit. Well, best crack on. Let me have your report as quickly as possible'

'Sir' The squadron leader stood up, saluted the departing CO, and called for the guard commander to enter the control centre.

'Right Flight Sergeant, wheel in the airman who discovered the body'

'Sir,' replied the guard commander, bawling out an appropriate instruction.

Into the room walked a crumpled looking Ginger with his left arm in a makeshift, bloodstained sling.

'Ah, we meet again AC2 Harrison, and yet again under distressing circumstances'

'Sir'

'I've just been reading the notes. First class effort, you displayed great presence of mind and initiative in what must have been a very tricky situation.' He stopped to examine the bloodstained sling. 'What happened to your arm?'

'It's me hand sir, me fingers'

'Have you received medical attention?'

'No sir, it's nowt but scratches'

'Nonsense, we can't have you contracting blood poisoning or worse in the course of duty. I'll converse with you later. Meanwhile, have this man escorted for treatment immediately, Flight Sergeant'

'Sir, you 'eard what the hofficer said, Corporal 'Oskins'

'But sarge,' protested the misguided acolyte. 'The medical block'll be closed'

'Then have the fucking thing opened up man,' screamed the guard commander who turned then to apologise to the presiding officer. 'Beg pardon sir'

'Not at all flight sergeant, I could not have phrased the instruction more appositely myself. Now, let's press on with our enquiries'

*

Dawn was breaking when Wing Commander Barclay arrived back at his home in Padgate village. He removed his shoes and tiptoed through the hallway so as not to disturb his sleeping wife. Entering the living room, he poured himself a large whisky and sat down in his favourite armchair to reflect on the tragedy.

*

'I understand it was you who attested the deceased on the day of his arrival'

'Yes sir'

Phartingail ffoulkes-Knight was now interviewing Barry Emerson, turning over the pages in a slim document folder on the desk as he spoke. 'Pearce, Leonard; domiciled at Home Farm, Padgate. Good God, that's only around the corner from here. He could hardly have been suffering from homesickness'

'I think he might have been sir'

'What makes you say that?'

'He seemed very remote and withdrawn when I attested him, disoriented almost'

'Did you make a note of that?'

'Yes sir, in the remarks box on the final page'

The enquiry officer referred to the back page, read the annotation and asked,

'Did you relay your suspicions to a superior?'

'Yes sir, I informed Flying Officer Beamish'

'What did he say?

'He said he'd look into the matter'

'Why has this recruit got 'knowe' written down against questions asking for a yes/no answer?'

'Because that's how he spells 'no' sir'

'But why does he spell 'no' as 'knowe'?'

'Because I reckon he's dyslexic sir'

'Hmm...I see you also recorded that in your assessment'

'Yes sir – but no one ever reads the reports'

'Shut your row,' shouted the Flight Sergeant. 'I'll put you on report for insolence'

'No you won't,' said the squadron leader. 'I do believe

LAC Emerson makes a valid point. I doubt anyone ever does bother to read them. By the way, what happens to these reports when you chaps are finished with them?'

'They're passed through to the Flight Lieutenant Rawlings for review'

'And then?'

'They come back to us at the end of the week for copying, data collation and dispatch to central records at RAF Unsworth'

'And hence entombed unread in perpetuity presumably,' added Phartingail ffoulkes-Knight.

*

'Ouch, that hurt,' squealed Ginger.

'Well, it would do,' replied the disgruntled, sleep-deprived medical orderly. 'I've just poured half a bottle of disinfectant over your grubby fingers'

*

'What do you know of the deceased, Flying Officer Beamish?'

'Absolutely nothing sir'

'Allow me to refresh your memory,' said the enquiry officer, handing Beamish a document.

'What's this?'

'Read the attestation clerk's comments on the back page'

Beamish duly obliged and replied, 'I've never seen this particular report before. It may of course have been reviewed by either Flight Lieutenant Rawlings or Pilot Officer Emery - but most certainly not by me'

'You were not aware of LAC Emerson's observations?'

'Categorically no'

'You do not recall him relaying to you verbally exactly what he's written down there?'

'He may have done, I suppose.' Beamish had been caught offguard and rambled on nervously, 'It's difficult to remember. We have chaps popping in on us every five minutes with some observation or another. It's impossible to keep track of them all'

'Need I remind you that the subject of this particular observation has just topped himself?'

Flying Officer Beamish was beginning to feel hot under the collar and blustered, 'Look here sir that remark is out of court. We work damn hard in the attestation section. There are substantial daily intakes to contend with, week in, week out. We can't be expected to double up as behavioural psychologists into the bargain. Besides, recruits are subjected to rigorous intelligence testing at the medical prior to enlistment'

'Shoving square pegs into round holes,' snapped his interrogator. 'Hardly the ideal benchmark for assessing mental stability, a little more attention to detail at this end wouldn't hurt'

'Sir,' responded the suitably chastened Flying Officer.

'I understand Rawlings is unavailable for interview. Is that correct?'

'Yes sir. He's in sick bay suffering from a minor ailment'

'You are misinformed. He is drying out - yet again – and my source of intelligence is beyond dispute; the chief medical officer'

*

Wing Commander Barclay was dozing when the light snapped on and his wife entered the room in her dressing gown.

'Why don't you go back to bed Humphrey, you look all in'

'Too much to do, too much to think about; dreadful business; must press on.' He dragged himself to his feet, poured out his fifth large whisky of the morning and added, 'No first for the base this year old girl, and no invitation to the Royal Garden Party I fear'

'Oh dear, how upsetting,' replied his wife. 'I was so looking forward to meeting the King and Queen again.

A strident ring from the telephone interrupted their conversation.

'Commanding Officer,' barked the CO into the mouthpiece.

'Sorry to disturb you sir, I have just completed my preliminary investigations. Shall I bring the report over to your house now? I see...'

Squadron Leader Phartingail ffoulkes-Knight replaced the telephone receiver, wondering to himself whether the old soak might have preferred a quick whip-round and a secret burial rather than the bothersome task of going through official channels.

*

'What kind of breakfast is this to be serving a man just off security patrol?'

Ginger was at the canteen counter examining the contents of the plate he'd just be handed by a surly looking duty cook.

'It's the same as what everyone has this time of a morning' replied the cook, dropping ash on the hotplate from a cigarette wedged in a corner of his mouth.

'Burnt toast and two slices of cold greasy bacon?'

'Breakfast don't start while seven o'clock'

'Oh yeah, I'll bet you don't eat this crap'

'What happened to your hand then?'

'Caught it in a revolving door'

'What revolving door?'

Ginger leaned across the hotplate, grabbed the cook's collar with his one good hand, and replied, 'The one that's going straight up your jacksy if you don't serve me up a decent breakfast'

Now that he was in possession of the interim report, Wing Commander Barclay convened an urgent meeting of his senior officers. It was going on nine-thirty when they trooped in, one by one.

'I want a damn good show here, the best ever, better even than when Air Marshall Lord Tedder visited the base. On the day the Minister and his entourage descend upon us, I want to see the place sparkling like a new penny. Complete bulling sessions everywhere and re-decoration inside and out, not a nook or cranny overlooked. Do I make myself clear?'

'Sir,' chorused the senior officers.

'New bedding for all officers, NCOs and enlisted men; new crockery and cutlery in the canteen and the messes; new carpeting and linoleum as required in all administrative offices – and on the day of the visitation, all ranks will be served turkey and all the trimmings for lunch'

'Turkey sir?' enquired the catering supremo. 'We only ever have turkey at Christmas time – '

'Turkey!' shouted the commanding officer. 'Turkey, dammit, you'll serve turkey for lunch or I'll have you scrubbing out the kitchens for a month'

'Sir'

'Now, Flight Lieutenant Willoughby-Goddard'

'Sir'

'I want all of your padre bods sobered up on the day. Last church parade I inspected, I detected something stronger than altar wine'

'Oh, I say...' protested the senior padre rather meekly.

*

Work over for the day, Ginger and Barry were standing at one end of the drill square, watching a myriad of men and machines carrying out the commanding officer's instructions.

'Look at them,' observed Ginger bitterly. 'Painting the grass green and sloshing white on owt else that don't move. Not one of the bastards gives a toss for the poor bugger whose remains were shipped back to his folks in the back of a service lorry'

'Strikes me Ginger,' replied Barry reflectively, 'that it could just as easily have been Sticky hanging from that noose – if he didn't have you looking out for him'

'Yeah, well...'

'Let's go up the NAFFI and get pissed'

'I'm skint

'I'm not'

'You're on'

*

On the morning that the findings of the public enquiry were made known to the nation, the eminent novelist RK

Tattersall all but choked on his boiled egg.

-What's the matter dad?

-Look-there-front page –Daily Express

-Oh that, the body found hanged at an airforce base. I read it earlier. Death by misadventure, they say'

-What they don't say though is that the bloody thing is stolen from one of my books

-Don't be silly dad. This is reality - your book is fiction

-I'll sue

-Who will you sue?

-The scruffy looking airman, the one who found the body, the one in the picture, showing off his medal'

Idle on parade

Sticky Albright and Scrounger Harris were walking towards the main gates on their way out of camp and into town on a night out when Scrounger espied the guard commander Flight Sergeant Hallsworth scrutinising them from the guardhouse bulwark.

'What's he looking at?' said Scrounger.

'Dunno,' replied Sticky nervously.

The guard commander casually descended the steps to face them. 'I'm putting both of you airmen on a charge sheet' he announced.

'But we haven't done anything,' protested Scrounger.

'Haven't done anything, what?'

'Haven't done anything, flight sergeant'

'You are in breach of station orders'

'How do you mean flight sergeant?'

'You're walking on the wrong side of the road'

Scrounger and Sticky looked at each other blankly.

'Ignorant as well as guilty,' asserted Hallsworth. 'Clearly unaware of the regulation stipulating that within the confines of the camp you must always walk on the side of the road facing but opposite to oncoming traffic'

'But sir, we was facing the traffic,' Sticky pointed out meekly.

'Yes, you dullard, but you weren't on the side opposite the traffic. You were on the right, which is wrong. You should have been on the left, which is right'

None the wiser, Sticky and Scrounger were duly cautioned and informed that they would be appearing before their flight commander the following morning.

*

'Well, can't help you Sticky mate,' said Ginger on hearing the news back at Hut 29 later in the evening, 'Can't be your witness this time.' Ginger thought for a moment and then called to Barry Emerson who was talking to someone at the other end of the billet. 'Is that right? About always walking on the left in camp?'

Barry walked back to join them.

'Yeah, it's in station orders okay, but no one else pays any attention to the regulation. Bandy Jordan marches up and down any side of the road that takes his fancy and Farty Night strolls down the middle most times'

'How come then Hallsworth's put them on a charge?' asked Ginger.

'I know why,' announced AC2 'Del' Delano, the billet's only serving regular who had been busted to the ranks on several occasions on sundry misdemeanours. He carried on blacking his boots with gusto but was pressed by Ginger for an explanation.

'Go on then, tell us why'

'Because,' said Delano, laying aside his boot brushes, 'the crafty sod wants summat done and puttin' them on a charge is his way of gettin' volunteers wi'out askin' by your leave'

'How would you know?'

'Because I run foul of him last time he were stationed here. He said I were idle on parade an' pulled the same stunt on me. You could ask Corporal Jacobi if he were still around. Smudge would never do business wi' him. Reckoned he were a bad lot. Smudge always did a check on officers and NCOs before he'd do them a turn on the black market and what he found out about Hallsworth put him right off. Smudge told me the old buzzard had been a bootlegger an' a gunrunner in America during the nineteen twenties. He also reckoned he's a sadist'

'That's handy,' replied Ginger.

*

There were three cavernous disused hangars in the grounds of RAF Padgate and at night they were dark and uninviting places; uninviting that is for all but amorous couples en route from the NAFFI, the camp cinema, or the local boozer.

Flight Sergeant Hallsworth stood alone at the far end of the drill square observing the stark outline of the buildings against a starlit backdrop. He decided to make for the middle hangar. It was proving to be the most fruitful of the three as a hunting ground.

*

'Bob Crapper fancies his chances with Jenny Murray,' remarked Barry to Ginger. 'He's been chatting her up all evening'

They were in the NAFFI and it was getting close to last orders as they watched LAC Crapper romancing ACW2 Jenny Murray, a substantially upholstered young lady from Glasgow.

'She'll eat him if he tries owt,' replied Ginger.

'We're off now,' called Bob Crapper. 'I'm walking Jenny back to her quarters'

'Watch he don't try to put his hand up your kilt Jenny,' advised Ginger good humouredly.

'Ah'm no' werrin' ma kilt, ah'm werrin' troosers,' retorted Jenny unabashed.

'You know what I mean'

'If he tries onything, ah'll brek his neck'

*

Squadron Leader Phartingail ffoulkes-Knight examined the particulars on the charge sheet, glanced first at the accused and then turned his attention to Flight Sergeant Hallsworth to whom he addressed his remarks.

'Look here was it really necessary to bring this matter before me?' The presiding officer was clearly irritated. 'Piddling little misdeed you could have dealt with yourself out of court. I meant to say, I've got a damn busy schedule ahead of me today without this ridiculous piece of nonsense cluttering up my morning'

The guard commander was unmoved by the officer's protestation.

'Flagrant disregard of station orders is a serious matter, sir.' Then he added with undisguised emphasis, 'Irrespective of rank, status or seniority'

There was a flash of anger in Phartingail ffoulkes-Knight's eyes but he decided to ignore the impertinent inference he had drawn from the remark.

'Very well, let's press on.' He looked at Sticky and Scrounger and proceeded. 'To save precious court time, I am taking the unusual step of having you both appear before me at the same time, on the same charge. Airman Harris, how do you plead?'

'Guilty as charged, sir'

'Airman Albright, how do you plead?'

'Not guilty, sir'

'What?'

'Not guilty, sir, ah were facing the traffic, sir'

'Yes indeed you were, but not on the side opposite oncoming traffic, contrary to station orders,' countered the presiding officer patiently.

'He's not very bright, sir,' contributed the flight sergeant.

'That remark is quite uncalled for,' replied the presiding officer. 'Airman Albright has made previous appearances before me and I am perfectly aware of his behavioural shortcomings without having them pointed out to me in such a callous manner. Do I make myself clear?'

'Sir'

'Airman Albright, unless you are anxious for me to increase my award in your particular case, I recommend that you change your plea to guilty'

'Yes sir, ah mean no sir. Guilty sir'

'Accused, I find you both guilty of the alleged offence. You are confined to barracks for three days.' He turned again to Hallsworth and added, 'I daresay you'll find something or other to keep them occupied'

'Indeed, sir'

*

Jenny Murray sobbed as she unburdened herself to Ginger in the NAFFI during the lunch break.

'The dirty old man, Del was right, he's a bloody sadist,' said Ginger.

Jenny had just related how on the previous evening she and Bob Crapper had been snogging in one of the hangars when they were disturbed by Flight Sergeant Hallsworth who had sent Crapper packing and then suggested to Jenny that they have sex on the spot. If she refused, he would report Jenny to the WAAF commanding officer, have her charged with licenscious behaviour, and personally write to her parents exposing the offence. She had spurned his advances, walked away, and the following morning confided in her flight commander

'What did Waggy say?' asked Ginger, referring to Jenny's superior, Squadron Leader Maggie Wagstaff.

'She was great Ginger, she really calmed me doon. She said she suspected he wis at it for a while but she could never pin anythin' on him. But she can noo. She got a' the girls in an' pit it tae them straight. Eight o' them admitted they'd drapped their drawers for him an' noo Miss Wagstaff's tryin' tae a build a case against him'

'Great'

'Aye, but it'll no' be easy. She says it's all 'male domination' in the RAF. She says they're no' very good at believin' wummen in a court case. She could dae wi' a male witness tae his shenanigans'

'Tell her she's got one. I'll be your decoy. Wait though, how will we know when he's on the prowl again?'

'Nae problem, he's at it every bliddy night'

'Right, here's what we do and we'll do it tonight...'

*

Ginger burst into Hut 29 with a thunderous look on his face and headed straight for Bob Crapper's bed place. He picked up the astonished airman, threw him against the wall and smacked Crapper's jaw with the back of his right hand.

'Ginger, what's got into you?' said Barry Emerson as he pulled his friend away from the beleaguered Crapper.

'This spineless piece of shit pissed off last night and left Jenny Murray to fend for herself against that sadist bastard Hallsworth'

When they'd heard the full story, the inmates of Hut 29 set about Crapper en masse.

*

'Gotcha!' said Flight Sergeant Hallsworth gleefully as he interrupted the courting couple. At his command the airman departed hurriedly into the darkness and Hallsworth honed in on the girl.

'Well, well, well. You must be desperate for it. Now come across this time or – '

'Or what, you pathetic old pervert'

Hallsworth turned around sharply to observe the airman he had just sent away.

'This will do you no good lad. You need another witness'

'I've got two'

At that, Sticky and Scrounger joined Ginger in the beam of the flight sergeant's torch.

*

The following morning in their paint splattered denims they watched, as two of his own military policemen led Hallsworth away from the guardhouse.

'Some say bollocks to Ginger, some say good old Ginger,' remarked Scrounger to Sticky, his partner on jankers. 'I'm with them, the good old Ginger mob'

*

'You're in the *News of The Screws* Ginger,' announced Barry on a Sunday morning several weeks later.

'What?'

'Yeah, you and Jenny, bloody hell-'

'What is it?'

'It says here,' continued Barry. "He's my hero, a braw lad. Ginger and I are to be married in the spring," announced kittenish WAC2 Jenny Murray'

'Give us it here,' replied Ginger, snatching the paper.

'Kittenish?' shrieked Scrounger. 'She's got an backside on her the size of a bullock's'

'Aye, an' Ginger's got its balls,' added Del.

'Stuff me,' groaned Ginger as he read the front page story.

'Just what the kitten intends if she has her way,' predicted Barry.

'Here Sticky. Fancy hitching with me to Wakefield for the weekend? We could go to me Auntie Maggie's'...

Final curtain

'They're back'

'Who?'

'Bunny and Stan'

The news was spreading fast and everyone wanted to know why Education Sergeants Hare and Withinshawe had suddenly arrived back at RAF Padgate from their mysterious posting to the Outer Hebrides. Barry Emerson had the answer.

'When the new CO discovered what that old pervert Barclay had done to Bunny and Stan,' Barry informed his fellow boarders at Hut 29, 'he issued instructions to have them transferred back here and reinstated to their posts. He's also shopped Barclay to Area Command on accusations of negligence and gross misconduct'

'Where does that leave Farty Night?' posed Scrounger Harris. 'He'll be due for the high jump as well because he was in on it'

'Farty'll be okay,' said Ginger knowingly. 'He's too smart to get caught out. I'll lay odds he covered his tracks well in advance'

'And,' continued Barry, 'they're resurrecting Extravaganza, Stan's issued a casting call for tomorrow night'

'Well, he can count me out,' replied Ginger. 'Sticky and me are up for demob in a couple of months, so it'll be a no-show from us for this show'

*

'The show must go on, the show *will* go on,' decreed Bunny.

'You're a trooper, you are. When I think of what they did, sending us all that way up there with only bracken and seagulls for company, I could spit. Spit I could'

'That bitch Barclay should be put down. Ostracising me was bad enough but to send you away as well. That was an outrage Stan'

'No, I'll not have that Bunny, I will not have it. We're soul mates us and after what he called you, I wouldn't have stayed a second longer under his rotten command'

Bunny looked in the mirror on his dressing table and sighed. 'It's put years on me this has. I've got crow's feet'

'Never,' countered Stan comfortingly. 'You've got a schoolgirl's complexion, you have. Not a tinky, winky wrinkle in sight'

'This isn't getting us anywhere. Where were we up to last time around on casting?'

'Well, we had planned to give AC2 Newley top billing'

'Is he still around?'

'Gone away, I believe, posted'

'So it's back to the superbitch, Greta Garbo. She's still around I suppose?'

'Oh yes, and as vile as ever they tell me'

'What else have we got as a star attraction?'

'How about using Ginger Harrison and his gormless mate as a comedy double act?'

'Oh well, I don't think that would cut the mustard. There's no call for Widow Twankey or Mrs McGillicuddy in a revue as swish as Extravaganza'

'We could put a few routines together, dress them up in funny suits, and see what comes out using Harrison as a stand-up'

'But didn't he say he couldn't tell jokes?'

'So he said, but he's a natural, an unconscious comedian'

'Well…'

*

'The answer is 'no'.' Ginger was quite emphatic. 'Anyhow, Sticky and me will be demobbed by the time you put on your show'

'When's your release date?' asked Bunny.

'Two months come next Thursday'

'Ample time,' said Stan confidently. 'We'll cut a few corners, pull everything forward, and stage it next month'

'No, I'm not interested' persisted Ginger.

Bunny switched to persuasive mode in a last ditch attempt to break Ginger's resolve. 'Look, do you still harbour longings for a career in show business?'

'Well, yeah, the money's good and it beats working for a living – but I'm not doing your show and that's final'

'What if I could fix you up with an agent?'

'How?'

'You'll have to trust me on that for now, but if you'll agree to appear in Extravaganza, I promise I'll move heaven and earth to get you a start in variety'

'Bunny's word is his bond,' added Stan. 'What he says he will do, he does'

'Well...'

'We've come up with an idea for a great double act,' enthused Bunny, moving in for the kill. 'It's a knockout and I'm arranging for someone very special to watch you on the first night'

Ginger considered the blackmail proposition and relented. 'Go on then, one more time but -'

'Right, good,' broke in Bunny, assuming control of the situation before there was a change of heart. 'As Stan said, we'll cut a few corners. The title stays but out goes sophistication and high comedy. We'll go for knockabout farce, fast moving sketches, and vulgarity'

'Nothing too near the bone mind,' cautioned Stan.

'We'll have to think of a name for the act'

'Tall and Short'

'Too commonplace'

'Muff and Jeff'

'Naff'

'How about Brylcreem and Brasso?' suggested Ginger, tongue in cheek.

'Brilliant!' said Bunny

'Inspirational,' echoed Stan

'I was only kidding,' protested Ginger.

'We're not. We're deadly serious' chided Bunny. 'I can see it now on the show bill. Brylcreem and Brasso writ large immediately beneath the Extravaganza logo'

'Top billing?' queried Ginger.

'I'll make your double act a byword on the variety circuit. See if I don't. And now to work: Stan, I want everyone connected with Extravaganza onstage in the camp theatre tonight. Artistes, chorus, scenery designers, wardrobe, music, sparks, chippies, stagehands....'

*

Thirty nights later came the opening performance of Extravaganza and as usual the first three rows of the stalls were reserved for officers, wives and dignitaries, with the remainder of the auditorium allocated to the hoi polloi.

After the overture and some high kicks from the chorus line, the double act made its debut. First on stage was Ginger in the guise of Brylcreem wearing a black and yellow suit in loud checks, luminous bow tie and pork pie hat.

He shaded his eyes against the footlights, picked out the toothy padre in the second row and began,

'Here's one for you vicar. Faith healer comes to town and the crowds flock to the local theatre. On the opening night he looks out at the audience and says, "I want the most afflicted of you to come up on the stage and I will perform my first miracle." A little cross-eyed guy at the back with a gammy leg and an enormous hump on his back starts moves forward – '

Just then Brasso dressed in a sailor suit walked across the stage carrying a suitcase. As he passed by, Brylcreem called out, 'Where are you going?'

'Ah'm taking me case to court'

'Any road up,' continued Brylcreem, 'as the little guy moved up the aisle, dragging his gammy leg behind him, he stopped every now and then, looked up at the ceiling and cried, "Why me God, why me?" '

Brasso walked back across the stage from the other direction, this time in his underpants and carrying an empty coat hanger.

Brylcreem watched him pass by and then enquired,

'What's happening now?'

'Ah lost me suit in court'

'So,' Brylcreem continued regardless, 'the little fellow keeps on doing it; stopping, looking up and repeating, "Why me God, why me?"

Brasso reappeared in a boiler suit holding a stepladder.

'What now?' said an exasperated Brylcreem.

'Ah'm taking me case to a higher court'

'Why me God, why me?' shouted Brylcreem as Brasso walked off. Then turning to the audience, he said, 'There was a blinding flash and God appeared onstage, brushed the faith healer aside, pointed a finger at the little man and said, "Because you get on my bleeding wick!"

The toothy padre was horrified but the audience seemed to like it.

'See,' said Stan to Bunny in the wings. 'I told you he could tell jokes in the right atmosphere'

'That one's got whiskers growing on it, but no matter, the audience is lapping up the act'

The stage suddenly darkened to be illuminated several seconds later with a barroom backdrop, some tables and chairs and a swarthy, balding barman. Onstage strolled a weary looking Greta Garbo who dropped her luggage on the floor, sat down at a table, lit up a cigarette and instructed the barkeep, 'Gif me a visky with ginger ale on the side and don't be stingy baby'

The stage darkened again and as Greta Garbo exited on the prompt side in total silence, she detected tittering from the back stalls and what sounded like, 'Bloody great hairy fairy'

The next act was a nervous Guy Mitchell impersonator who endured a series of catcalls for ten minutes or so as he rushed through his repertoire to the final number.

'She wears red feathers and a hula, hula skirt - '

'Geroff, ye're rubbish. Bring back Brylcreem and Brasso'

To enthusiastic applause Ginger waddled back on looking like a barrage balloon in a full length wedding dress and clutching an outsize bouquet. Sticky was centre stage at the microphone. He wore a dinner suit several sizes too small and his hair was slicked in a middle shed. He sang,

'Here comes the bride
Short, fat and wide
See how she wobbles
From side to side'

Ginger Rogers was whooshed onstage by an energetic young Fred Astaire. He was in black tie and tails and she wore a dress made of feathers

'You're treading on my toes Mr Astaire,' she grimaced through her wide smile.

'Blow it out your ass Miss Rogers,' whispered Fred.

Seconds later an inebriated Scrounger Harris was observed by one and all standing up on a seat in the out of bounds front row, cupping his hands together, and yelling, 'Get them off Gropey. Show us your bum'

Miss Rogers silenced the musicians in the orchestra pit with an urgent wave of the hand, and began to remonstrate with her oppressor.

'How dare you! I'm a professional artiste, I am. You are a drunken, uncouth lout who should never have been allowed admission. That's it, I quit'

Miss Rogers stormed offstage leaving her dancing partner stranded. Fred shrugged, put out his arms and announced to the audience just before the lights went out,

'That's show business'

As Miss Rogers' high heels went clickety-clack through the wings Bunny called after her,

'Come here you bitch and get yourself back on stage. No one behaves like that in one of my productions'

'Watch me,' retorted Miss Rogers.

'You'll have to go back on Ginger,' said Stan in exasperation.

'What, now?'

'Yes, now. That cow has ruined the sequence. We'll bring forward your taxi scene with the girl'

'You'd best get Sticky out there then, centre stage beside his lamppost'

'I will, I will,' said Stan, scurrying off.

Ginger clambered aboard the cutout taxi front followed by a voluptuous chorine, who muttered, 'What a bloody balls-up Ginger'

'You look divine Sid – but your mascara is smudged'

'Piss off'

The lights came back on just as they were being pushed onstage to arrive on cue at the bus stop situated centre stage. To thunderous applause, Ginger and the chorine were caught in a passionate embrace in the back seat.

'What were you doing in there with that young lady?' asked Sticky.

Ginger disembarked, casually brushed himself off and replied, 'Just seeing how far I could go in a taxi with no one driving'

*

Stan burst into the dressing room shared by Brylcreem and Brasso, Ginger Rogers and Fred Astaire. 'Charlie Fzackerley wants to see you Ginger,' he announced.

'Who, me?' enquired Ginger Rogers excitedly.

'No, bitch, not you; you are not *that* Ginger.' With hands on hips, Stan continued savagely. 'Charlie only deals with class acts, acts that don't go in for ructions on and off stage, acts that respect the authority of the management, acts that – '

'Charlie Who?' broke in the senior partner of the comedy double act.

'Charlie Fzackerley. He's a big wheel in the northern variety circuit, he is. Well, lower echelons, that is'

'Talk in English Stan'

'He's a booking agent for music hall speciality acts. He's the one who came to catch your act like Bunny promised'

'Why didn't you say so in the first place, show him in'

Thumbs in the corners of his vermilion waistcoat, Charlie Fzackerley entered the room, sat down in the only spare chair, lit up a huge cigar, and began, 'I don't book acts from camp shows as a rule but your act intrigues me. The material is rubbish but your delivery shows promise. With a bit of coaching, grooming, some decent clobber and a professional writer, I reckon I can make something out of you. I like the double act bit. Kind of sobered up Jimmy James and Eli'

'Who's Eli?' asked Ginger.

'You've heard of Jimmy James?'

'Oh aye, good he is'

'Eli is Jimmy's feed, straight man, foil, whatever you'd like to call it,' contributed Stan helpfully.

'Your mate looks like Eli Woods, talks like him, daft as him,' added Charlie.

'What do you have in mind then?'

'I think I'll start you off in the C circuit around the middens. Girlie shows'

'Girlie shows?'

'Nudes, you'd do a bit of MC'ing and have a twenty minute spot for the double act at the end'

'How much?'

'Start you off at one hundred pounds a week – for the act'

'Bloody Nora, hundred quid a week and free crumpet on tap,' acknowledged Ginger gleefully.

'How about me, how much do ah get paid?' asked Sticky who was bewildered by the proceedings but not so confused as to neglect making a stab at establishing his market value.

'Don't you worry Sticky lad,' replied Ginger, placing a brotherly arm around his partner. 'I'll look after you. We're partners, you and me. Fifty-fifty'

'How much is that then?'

'Twenty five quid a week'

'Thanks Ginge'

'After a trek around the provincial Cs,' continued

Charlie, I'll fix you up with a summer show in Llandudno followed by a panto in Skegness. They lap up your sort of crap in the sticks'

*

The last half-hour of the evening's entertainment was reserved for The Great Mysterio, an amateur magician and hypnotist whom Stan had imported from nearby RAF Kirby. In his floor length coat of many colours and pointed wizard's hat, the tall lean, bespectacled Mysterio performed a series of unusually clever close magic tricks during the first part of his act. It was in the second half that disaster struck. He called for a volunteer from the audience to be hypnotised. By previous arrangement, the volunteer was Sticky who walked up onstage from a seat in the stalls.

'It's a fix,' shouted an airman.

'Shut your gob or I'll thump you,' advised Ginger in his ear from the row behind.

'Have we ever met before? 'enquired The Great Mysterio.

'No Vince, we haven't'

The audience howled its appreciation at Sticky's gaff.

'Right then, do you have a favourite farmyard animal?'

'Hens,' replied the volunteer. 'Me mam keeps hens'

'Well, hens are not strictly animals, more like livestock, but that's okay. What I'm going to do now is to turn you into one of your mam's hens for a few minutes. Is that all right with you?'

'Oh aye'

The Great Mysterio lulled Sticky into a trance within seconds. 'Now, I want you to strut around the stage clucking like one of your mam's hens'

Sticky duly complied with the instruction to the delight of the audience, who were even more enchanted with his accompanying and intermittent cry of,

'Cluck, cluck'

The hypnotist snapped his fingers at which Sticky ceased his perambulations and stood rock still.

'Let's give him a big hand for being such a good sport – and finally, on behalf of the management, I'd like to thank you all for allowing us to entertain you tonight'

Generous applause followed before the final curtain descended and the audience prepared to leave the auditorium. During all of this Sticky remained rigid.

'Are you all right?' asked the hypnotist anxiously as he and his volunteer stood together centre stage behind the safety curtain.

'Cluck, cluck'

'Oh dear'

'What's to do?' called Ginger, emerging from the OP side.

'Cluck, cluck'

'I don't understand. This has never happened to me before —but your friend appears to be still in a trance'

'Cluck, cluck'

'Well, get him clucking out of it'

The hypnotist snapped his fingers.

'Cluck, cluck'

He snapped them again, louder this time, 'Cluck, cluck'

'Cluck, clucking cluck,' despaired Ginger.

Barry Emerson and Scrounger joined the group onstage.

'What's happening?' enquired Barry

'Cluck, cluck'

'He's still in a chuffing trance,' said Ginger.

'Cluck, cluck'

'I've got some budgie seed back at the billet. Maybe that would help,' suggested Scrounger.

'Bog off, you're pissed'

'Let me have a go,' said Barry.

'Doing what?' asked Ginger.

'This,' said Barry as he yelled in Sticky's left ear, 'CLUCK, CLUCK'

Sticky woke up at once, looked around and announced,

'Ah've been having a dream, ah dreamt ah was an 'en'

'You was,' replied Ginger, and looking hard at him, added, 'Are you okay now?'

'Oh aye, fine thanks'

'Good'

'Cluck, cluck'

Who shot the chef?

The main topic of conversation in the officers mess for some weeks had been the forthcoming banquet in honour of the ministerial visit of Sir Humphrey Alcock-Flakbottom, Secretary of State for Defence, responsibility for the co-ordination of which occasion the commanding officer had charged Squadron Leader Phartingail ffoulkes-Knight.

'I want an outstanding show here, Farty' the CO instructed, 'esprit de corps, that sort of crack'

'I have to say sir,' the squadron leader replied, 'I'm most awfully grateful at being selected to supervise the arrangements'

The commanding officer eyed him curiously. 'Got no alternative, have I? You're my next in command, senior man, what?'

Phartingail ffoulkes-Knight saluted and retired somewhat miffed.

*

'You will act as my major-domo for these arrangements,' Phartingail ffoulkes-Knight informed Sergeant Jordan.

'Eh?'

'Chief Steward'

'Yes sir, I'll soon get everyone whipped into shape'

'No Jordan,' corrected the squadron leader testily. 'There

will be no requirement to whip anyone into shape. Good God, man, this is to be a joyous occasion, not a ruddy field combat exercise'

'Sir'

'Our first task will be to select a chef. Any ideas?'

'Well sir, how about Sergeant Wetherby at the officers mess. I hear tell -'

'Out of the question, quite unsuitable; the fellow's a damn nancy boy who becomes over-demonstrative as the slightest criticism. We need someone with rather more steel, someone who can command the kitchen and produce a creative menu with the minimum of fuss and bother'

Jordan gave the matter further consideration and suggested, 'I reckon Slimy Jake could handle it sir'

'Whom did you say?'

'Slimy Jake up the other ranks canteen, sir. That's his nickname, he's actually Corporal Prodworthy'

'Indeed'

'I have most of my meals up there and on Tuesday nights he serves up for me and a few mates from the sergeants mess the finest Chateaubriand de froid gras I've ever stuck my choppers into. He's also handy with duck l'orange and he knows all about fine wines. He's wasted up the canteen and he beats the balls, begging your pardon sir, beats the socks off the tulip what cooks up our mess'

'Hmm, sounds promising; have him prepare dinner for me to be served in my quarters tonight and I'll let you know if I share your enthusiasm for his culinary skills'

'Sir'

'We'd have to change his name for the evening though to something like, Francois'

'Very good sir'

*

Ginger and Sticky were making their way to work when they espied a vehicle in trouble by the side of the road. It was clear from the incessant spluttering that the driver was having difficulty starting the engine.

'She'll do in the battery if she carries on like that,' observed Ginger.

'Who's she?'

'The commanding officer's wife, I'd best go help her'

'But you know nowt about cars'

'I do and all,' asserted Ginger. 'I worked as an apprentice mechanic for a while back home'

As they approached the stationery vehicle, the lady in question ceased her fruitless endeavours and wound down the window to greet them.

'Can we help ma'am?'

'Oh, I do hope so, I'm already late for luncheon at the officers' wives club and I'm the guest speaker today'

'Have no fear missus we'll have you going again in a couple of ticks'

Ginger opened the bonnet and within seconds located the source of the trouble. He borrowed her car keys, unlocked the boot, took out a can of petrol and a clean rag and returned to the bonnet. 'It's your spark plugs, you see, they just need a bit of a clean.' True to his word, he rapidly effected the required maintenance and switched on the engine, which started first time.

The CO's wife thanked Ginger profusely, took a note of their names and promised to commend both to her husband for diligence in her time of need.

*

'Ah, Farty, come in, come in old boy,' greeted the commanding officer amiably. 'Grab a pew and sit down'

'Thank you sir, most kind,' said Phartingail ffoulkes-Knight in anticipation of some good news.

'Yesterday evening Mrs CO informed me that two of your chaps came to her assistance when her car broke down on the way to luncheon. Extremely helpful and courteous they were'

'Indeed sir, that is most gratifying to hear. Did the good lady mention names?'

'She did indeed and I'm just coming to that, but first, what I want to know is why no one from the mechanical transport section offered to rescue her. That's what we employ the MT blighters for, isn't it'

'Indeed sir, I shall look into the oversight'

'Now, as to names, Airmen Harrison and Albright'

Phartingail ffoulkes-Knight felt uneasy and experienced a sense of foreboding about what was coming next.

'Most impressed Mrs CO was, so impressed in fact that she insists that Harrison and Albright act as serving orderlies at the banquet. Make a note of that, will you'

'Ah, sir, I feel obliged to point out that these two individuals would almost certainly prove unsatisfactory as participants at such a high hat affair; that they have in fact both appeared before me on several occasions-'

'Are you seriously questioning my wife's judgement?' asked the CO belligerently.

'Au contraire sir, not at all, I'd only like to -'

'Then see to it'

*

The commanding officer's done what, sir?' asked Jordan with popping eyes.

'I've just told you, man' replied the squadron leader abruptly. 'Issued me with instructions on the recommendation of his good lady that those two louts in your platoon be appointed as the serving orderlies for the banquet'

'But sir -'

'I know, I know, I know,' screamed Phartingail ffoulkes-Knight, 'but what can I do, hardly rescind his command, can I? I did attempt to remind him that they have been up before me on numerous occasions on a variety of misdemeanours but he refused to credit me'

'Sir'

'I strongly recommend that you be on constant vigil against the possibility of the fat one half-inching the cutlery or the dopier alternative falling into the soup urn - or worse'

'Sir'

'Oh, and by the way, the meal prepared for me last night by Francois was quite excellent'

*

The commanding officer was well pleased at how smoothly the banquet was progressing. He had been privately concerned that the Secretary of State for Defence might prove to be a stuffed shirt, but he was well wide of the mark in that assumption. The Right Honourable Humphrey Alcock-Flakbottom was in fact an amiable fellow who regaled the assembled guests with a stream of anecdotes on the goings-on at Westminster and Whitehall. The food too was excellent and chef's menu was a delight. 'My compliments to the chef,' the honoured guest had whispered in Ginger's ear. Talking of Ginger, the CO was most particularly impressed at how efficiently his wife's protegees were carrying out their duties at table.

But of course, it was all going far too well to last.

As Ginger was tempting Mrs CO to another portion of croquet potatoes, the joyous occasion was shattered by the crack of a pistol shot from the kitchen area. Ginger dropped his tureen on the table and rushed through the swing door to investigate. Francois was lying on the floor clutching his right knee and screaming, 'Oh fuck, the bastard's shot me,' as out of the corner of his eye Ginger saw a shadowy figure disappearing out of the back door.

*

Ginger returned to the billet after lights out and unravelled for one and all in total darkness the mystery behind who shot the chef.

'I know who did it,' he announced.

'Who?' cried out the residents in unison.

'Sergeant Wetherby'

'What? Just because they didn't make him chef?' speculated Scrounger Harris.

'No, it goes deeper than that. About an hour ago I was passing the education hut when I noticed that the lights were still on. I looked through the window and saw Stan comforting Bunny who was crying his eyes out. I went in and they told me the whole story. It seems that Slimy Jake nobbled Wetherby's girlfriend and that's why he took a pop at him'

'Girlfriend, what girlfriend?' asked Barry Emerson.

'Bunny'

'Have you reported it?'

'No, and if any other bugger does, I'll split him from tip to toe. Bunny's been good to me and I don't want him caused any embarrassment over that ponce Wetherby's act of revenge. Got it?'

'Oh aye,' said a lone voice.

'Thanks Sticky, mate, and now let me hear from the rest of you'

'Yes Ginger, we've got the message,' they chorused.

'Did they cancel dessert after Jake got shot?' asked Barry as an afterthought.

'No, one of the lads rustled them up plum duff and custard just like we have at the canteen on Fridays,' replied Ginger. 'The old government geyser loved it, said it reminded him of school dinners'

'Plum duff a la canteen, what sort of school did he go to?'

'Borstal, most likely'

Big night out

'That's settled then. Big night out before Flying Officer Beamish leaves us.' Squadron Leader Phartingail ffoulkes-Knight swung around in his armchair and called, 'Steward'

Senior mess steward Corporal Mellow materialised at the officer's side.

'Sir'

'Same again bar steward'

'Sir'

'Oh, and steward…'

'Sir?'

'What do you know of the Effingham Club in town?'

'Superior class of gentlemen's establishment, sir,' The normally colourless mess attendant became animated as he extended on his reference. 'Haute cuisine par excellence, silver service, cut glass crystal, pre-prandial cocktails of exceptional quality'

'Chosen well then, eh, what?' surmised the host, looking to his guests for confirmation.

'Ra-ther,' said Emery.

'Spiffing wheeze,' reckoned Ashford.

'Top hole,' added Beamish.

Corporal Mellow continued in a reverential whisper, 'His Royal Highness the Prince of Wales and Mrs Wallis Simpson dined there on one occasion'

'Good God. Well I'll be dashed. When was that?'

'1935, sir'

'Formal dress at the trough, I presume?'

'Oh yes, indeed sir. Formal dress at dinner always'

'Oh, I say,' broke in Pilot Officer Emery.

'Problem?' asked the host.

'Left the old fish and soup at mater's billet, no matter though, I'll have Greaves the butler drive up in the Bentley with it'

'Good man. Don't want to let the side down. Best bib and tucker on the night, eh, what?'

'Rather,' agreed Beamish who then posed another problem to his host. 'I say sir, might a chap invite two of his chums along to join in the festivities?'

'Of course, of course, old boy,' beamed Phartingail ffoulkes-Knight. 'Who did you have in mind, old school friends, that sort of crack?'

'As a matter of fact, no, two jolly fine types I've befriended during my time at Padgate'

'Ah, civilian wallahs'

'No sir.' Beamish hesitated before continuing, 'Airmen Harrison and Albright'

The squadron leader regarded him with astonishment, as did the other guests.

'Heavens above, Beamish,' he exploded. 'Have you taken leave of your senses? We can't possibly allow riff-raff of subterranean gutter level status to join our company at the Effingham. Bad form old boy, out of court, not done. Good Lord man, didn't you just hear the bar steward say the Prince of Wales once dined there?'

'Sorry sir,' apologised Beamish, who would have given much to be elsewhere. 'Dreadful clanger, don't know what came over me, sir'

'I should damn well think not. Now, where's Rawlings tonight?'

'Indisposed sir,' answered Pilot Officer Emery. 'Confined to bed with a chill'

'Not back on the sauce, is he?'

'Oh no, sir, he's been teetotal since – ah –'

'Being dried out,' supplied the squadron leader. 'Hopefully he'll stay that way. Don't want anyone letting the show down on the big night out, what?'

'Good grief no, sir' chorused the guests.

'Right, let's recap chaps. Drinks at the mess 1800 hours

Saturday evening, followed by dinner at the Effingham Club'

*

In much less salubrious surroundings one hundred yards away, another big night out was about to be planned at Hut 29. The inmates were clustered around ex Corporal Smudger Jacobi who was paying them a surprise visit.

'So, what are you up to these days Smudge?' enquired Ginger.

'Bit of this, bit of that, ducking and diving, bobbing and weaving'

'Yeah but what exactly do you do?'

Smudger fished around in the inside pocket of his expensive black Crombie overcoat, pulled out a business card and handed it to Ginger.

'Oh well, still in the old trade I see,' and then for the benefit of the others he read out the inscription on the card. '*Smudgers Surplus Stocks*. You name it, we've got it, and if we haven't, we'll find it". What are you doing back in Padgate then?'

'Got some business on'

'What, here in the camp?' asked Barry Emerson.

'Yeah, shtum though,' replied Smudger, looking around the faces for confirmation.

'Well, it can't be Flight Sergeant Bristow you used t'deal wi' at t'stores,' suggested Del. 'He's doin' three years in

Colchester for reset'

'No, his replacement, Harry Reeves'

'How long are you here for?'

'Until Sunday'

'Great,' enthused Ginger. 'We'll fix up a night out on the town come Saturday when we've all got brass. It'll be like old times. A few ales at the NAFFI, get boozed up in the Farmer's Arms, and then on to the Carlton Club for dancing and crumpet'

'Where are you staying Smudge?' asked Barry.

'I'll fix up a B&B in Warrington'

'You chuffing won't mate,' contradicted Ginger. 'You're staying right here with us.' He cast an eye over the billet residents, pointed to one of the newcomers and instructed, 'You, Davis, get your gubbins together and sling your hook next door; there's around eight spare beds in Hut 28'

'Get stuffed, I'm going nowhere'

'Do as I say or you're barred from the crappers for the next fortnight'

'But – '

'It's only for a few days Spike,' said Barry comfortingly.

*

On Saturday morning Greaves the butler drove the

Bentley through the camp gates and proceeded to the officers living quarters as instructed by the guardroom duty corporal.

He knocked on the young master's door but there was no reply. He knocked a second time and it opened to reveal Pilot Officer Emery in partial dress and a face full of shaving cream.

'Ah Greaves'

'Your dinner suit sir'

'Ah, good man'

'Thank you sir'

'Have any difficulty finding the base?'

'No sir. I arose at two thirty am and drove straight here from Wessex Towers using her ladyship's 1927 AA guide'

'Good man'

'Will that be all sir?'

'Look here Greaves, I'm just about to crack open a bottle of champers for breakfast. Would you care for a beer?'

'No thank you sir. Not with such a long journey back'

Emery took a coin from his trouser pocket.

'Take this and have a cup of tea on your way back'

'Thank you sir'

As he turned away to leave, Greaves looked at the shilling coin and muttered under his breath, 'Tight fisted little fucker'

'Did you say something Greaves?'

'Only, I'll get some tucker, sir'

'Good, capital. Carry on then'

*

It was half day working at the latrines on Saturdays and Ginger was anxious to have everything completed before noon so that he could take Smudger to a local football match in the afternoon before getting ready for the big night out.

'Get a frigging move on Sticky. Them's not the crown jewels you're polishing'

'Ah were only trying to get the brasses sparkly, the way Sergeant Jordan likes them'

'Bollocks to Bandy. Just rub them over quickly with your duster and let's be out of here'

'What about sploshin' out the cubicles?'

'I'll do that'

'Don't throw no water over the top yet,' yelled a voice. 'I'm in number seven'

'Well, get a jildy on Scrounger. Stop playing with yourself

and start a bowel motion. Your time's up'

*

In the officers mess at six thirty in the evening, Phartingail ffoulkes-Knight was holding court when Flight lieutenant Rawlings made a belated appearance.

'Ah, Rawlings, good you could join us. What will you have to drink?'

'Just an orange juice sir'

'Quite, of course, just the ticket, steward, one large orange juice if you please'

'Sir'

'Now then Rawlings old chap, looking forward to tonight's jollifications?'

'Indeed sir'

'Should be a splendid show, bar steward here was telling us all the other evening that the Prince of Wales and Wallis Simpson dined at the Effingham back in 1935'

'Yes, I knew that sir'

'Oh, you know?'

'The late Lord Effingham and my father were at Harrow together in their formative years. Great chums all their lives, don't you know.' Rawlings went on to explain, 'As a matter of fact, pater and Lord E enjoined HRH and Mrs WS at the very dinner of which you speak'

'Isn't that astonishing, well, well, well, this will be quite an occasion for you then Rawlings'

'Indeed sir'

'Now, young feller me lad,' continued Phartingail ffoulkes-Knight, addressing Flying Officer Beamish. 'Where is it again you're off to teach?'

'Charterhouse sir'

'Charterhouse, damn fine school, damn fine'

*

Around the same time, festivities were beginning to flourish at the Farmers Arms.

'I always reckoned you'd be in the nick by now Smudge,' announced Ginger over the Saturday night din.

'Could have been nicked a couple of times - once over a deal on naval rations'

'Went bad did they?'

'No, but the sod that sold them to me did. Got his collar felt and welshed on me to the filth'

'Talked your way out of it as usual, did you?'

'Something like that'

'Hey Sticky, go easy on the fizzy, else you'll get pissed again,' yelled Ginger. 'I'm not carrying you home on me back this time'

'Babycham is nobbut sugarelly waater,' protested Del. 'Nobody gets pissed on that'

'Sticky does,' replied Ginger.

*

The party of officers had been allocated the prestigious Satinwood private dining room for the big night out. It was small in size but elegant in décor and furnishings. A superior looking waiter passed menus around the table while the guests sipped their pre-prandial cocktails.

'Damn menu is in froggie,' complained Ashford. 'Never did manage to master that blighter at school. Can you follow the lingo Beamish?'

'Yes indeed. For starters we're having iced melon, followed by marinated shrimps accompanied by French toast, followed by duck a l'orange and all the trimmings - and, oh ah, crepe suzette for afters'

'Jolly good'

'Ra-ther,' added Emery appreciatively.

'Back to school for you then next week Beamish old boy, eh, what?' commented the host cheerfully.

'Yes sir, looking forward to it immensely'

'Cricket on the village green at weekends?'

'I dare say sir'

'God, how I envy you; I miss the thwack of leather on willow and the scent of a newly rolled crease'

The superior waiter made another appearance to enquire at what time the party would prefer dinner to be served.

'Leave it for an hour or so yet, there's a good chap'

And so the conversation continued, the merriment gathered momentum, and the claret flowed for all but Rawlings who was slouched back in his seat, nursing his orange juice and staring ahead in blank silence. Then all of a sudden he perked up and spoke out loudly.

'Of course, pater was rogering Wallis athletically on a regular basis'

'Did I hear you aright Rawlings?' asked the astonished Ashford.

'Couldn't keep their hands off each other, old boy; at it like the clappers whenever they got the glimpse of an opportunity. Oh yes'

'What?' exclaimed the host.

'My father and Wallis Simpson,' clarified Rawlings.

'Are you seriously suggesting that –'

'Well-known fact among the Dorsetshire county set; tried to keep the matter hush-hush of course but there you are, everyone knew'

'I should imagine Edward Prince of Wales, might have had something to say on the subject,' suggested Ashford snidely.

'Didn't know a damn thing about it don't you know.' Rawlings looked around the table and continued, 'Look here chaps, this party's as dull as ditch water. Let's liven things up a trifle'

There was an empty table butted onto theirs at right angles forming a t-junction, the purpose of which was presumably to act as a servery when the food arrived. Rawlings stood up and with a flourish whipped away the cover, climbed upon the hardwood top and began to dance in a soft-shoe shuffle. This in turn gave way to an energetic tap dance that soon increased in tempo and intensity.

'I say Rawlings,' said the host sternly, 'come down from there man. You're making an ass of yourself'

'Not to mention disturbing club members in the adjoining dining rooms,' added Beamish anxiously.

The door opened to admit the maitre d'hotel, the head waiter and two flunkies, all of whom viewed Rawlings' antics with extreme displeasure.

'Bit early in the evening for cabaret,' observed the head waiter solemnly.

'Gentlemen, this is outrageous,' thundered the maitre d'hotel.

'I say, I'm most awfully sorry,' apologised the host. 'Chap appears to have taken a turn'

'He's pissed as a newt,' was the theory advanced by one of the flunkies.

The maitre d'hotel motioned to the head waiter who moved in on Rawlings to drag him from the table but he was too late because the miscreant leapt onto the crystal chandelier, swung back and forth, beat his chest and emitted a Tarzan like scream.

The anchorage gave way, broke loose from the ceiling couplings and the chandelier dropped like a brick on top of the dining table with Rawlings still clinging to the remains.

'Out, out, out,' yelled the maitre d'hotel.

Before departing in shame, the host sniffed at Rawlings' diminished beaker of orange juice.

'Damn waiter was right. The bloody thing's mostly gin'

*

The crowded dance floor of the Carlton Club vibrated to the rhythm of the Harry Flaxman trio, and Harry, tinkling the ivories with gay abandon and a modicum of expertise, smiled widely at the patrons. Some would have it though that the smile was more of a leer directed in the main at the male element. Ginger, Smudge and Tiny Loftus stood among the spectators while Barry, Scrounger and Del were strutting their stuff on the floor to the strains of 'Bewitched, Bothered and Bewildered.' Sitting on the hard wooden bench situated flush against a sidewall was Sticky with his arms around two young ladies; Barbara on his left and Dorothy on his right.

'Look at him,' remarked Smudger. 'I didn't think he could pull nails never mind tasty crumpet'

'He only just knocked up both of them a few weeks past,' replied Ginger.

'Never'

'Straight up'

The dance ended and Barry rejoined the group.

'I'm off now. I've just pulled'

'Little black haired piece in the red dress?' enquired Ginger.

'Yeah'

'Nice one'

'I'm off too for a little while Ginge,' said Smudger. 'It's a bugger not being able to buy booze in this club. I'll have a few swigs in the bog from my half-bottle'

'I'll join you; my carry-in is finished'

About ten minutes or so later as they were coming out of the toilet, Ginger was shoved roughly from behind. It was Sergeant Jordan who was highly intoxicated.

'What were you two up to in the bog?'

'Having a nightcap,' replied Ginger.

'Nightcap my arse, you're a couple of shirt lifters'

'Look sarge, I don't want no truck with you. I'm with me mates on a night out, I'm getting demobbed in two weeks and I'm not looking for trouble. Okay?'

'You'll be back or you'll end up in the nick. There's no room in Civvy Street for skivers like you. You'll be back, you'll see'

'Don't hold your breath'

Jordan punched Ginger in the breadbasket at which he retaliated with a head butt on Jordan.

'You've busted my fucking nose'

'Good'

The club stewards moved in quickly and that was the end of the other big night out.

As the first party was being ushered out of the main door by the club stewards, Rawlings tripped, stumbled down the steps and ended up in a heap on the pavement. The incident was observed from across the road by a group of naval ratings accompanied by a Chief Petty Officer. They crossed over hooting and catcalling.

'Chucked out was you?' enquired the CPO gleefully as he stooped to peer at the spread-eagled Rawlings.

'Just push, will you,' said Phartingail ffoulkes-Knight.

'Push off yourself

'I give you fair warning, chief petty officer. I was a boxing blue at Cambridge'

'Oh yeah, and I'm Little Boy Blue from Battersea. Cop this

you toffee nosed twit'

He smashed a fist into the squadron leader's solar plexus and the victim slithered downwards on top of the recumbent Rawlings.

'Call the constabulary,' Beamish instructed the club stewards who quickly disappeared inside, slamming the door after them.

Just then the other party of ejected revellers spilled out onto the road from the Carlton Club situated directly opposite the Effingham.

'Look,' said Sticky, 'them sailors is knockin' seven bells out o' old Farty an' his mates'

'Gordon frigging Bennett,' shouted Ginger. 'They're being hammered. Right lads, let's get tore in'

'Here, hold on,' said Sergeant Jordan. 'That's that barstard CPO who called me a prick a few weeks ago'

'Good judge of character I reckon,' replied Ginger.

'I shall fucking have him, I shall'

'Go to it then'

They joined the melee. Jordan jumped on the CPO's back and pulled him to the ground while Ginger and the others put themselves about the ratings.

A black Wolseley with its siren blaring turned the corner at speed and halted abruptly in the middle of the road outside the Effingham Club. Uniformed constables emerged and one of them attempted to restrain Ginger who knocked his helmet to the ground.

'Shove off rozzer. This is a private party'

*

Just before he was due to be called before the magistrates on Monday morning, the helmet-toppling offender was visited in the court cells by Phartingail ffoulkes-Knight.

'I've been making some enquiries and I've discovered that the senior magistrate and I are old friends,' announced the squadron leader encouragingly. 'We belong to the same club'

Barry, who had arrived in the cells a few minutes earlier, leant over Ginger's shoulder and whispered, 'Madame Golightly's, no doubt'

Ginger's case was called. The magistrates listened attentively to the police evidence regarding the fracas and to the laments of the naval authorities on the brutal treatment inflicted on their ratings, after all of which a report was read out in court. It emanated from the management of the Effingham and it dwelt at some length on the deplorable behaviour occasioned in its club premises by a party of RAF officers prior to the incident leading to the arrests. The bench members conferred briefly after which the senior magistrate addressed the court.

'This court will not tolerate such unseemly goings-on in our beloved town centre, and most especially when members of His Majesty's Armed Forces stationed nearby in sufferance perpetrate the offences described here this morning. In the case of Chief Petty Officer Hardcastle, we find the accused guilty and sentence him to fourteen days imprisonment. In the case of Airman Harrison, we find the accused has no case to answer on the grounds of unpremeditated reaction in the heat of the moment'

*

Later in the afternoon Squadron Leader Phartingail ffoulkes-Knight took up his position as presiding officer at Ginger's second court appearance of the day.

'Airman second class Clarence Harrison, you are charged with causing an affray in the premises of the Carlton Club, Warrington, and aggravated assault on the person of Sergeant Wilberforce Jordan. How do you plead?'

Ginger and Jordan glanced at each other.

'Not guilty sir'

'Are you calling witnesses?'

'No sir'

'Think on airman. Lack of evidence might jeopardise the validity of your plea'

'Don't care sir. There are witnesses prepared to come forward in my defence but I'm not calling them. Some of them like myself are due for demob in a few weeks. I don't want to jeopardise their chances'

'I see. Sergeant Jordan, are you calling witnesses?'

'Yes sir, fourteen in all'

'Good God man; that is an unnecessary waste of court time. Anyway, it would be a fruitless exercise. I find the accused has no case to answer on the grounds of unpremeditated reaction in the heat of the moment. Case dismissed'

As escort, accused and prosecutor marched out of the room Jordan complained bitterly, 'You jammy fat barstard, I'll get you yet'

'Best crack on then sarge, I'm out of here in twelve days'

The flea that jumped the midden

Flight Lieutenant Ashford had just completed his final round of inspection prior to being posted as adjutant to the camp commander at RAF Kirby.

'My replacement will be calling upon you later this today to introduce himself,' he informed the assembled orderlies. 'His name is McFarquhar, Alisdair McFarquhar'

Jock Burns broke off from swabbing the tiled floor to enquire, 'Is he fae Glesca sir?'

'Glasgow, you mean?'

'Aye sir'

'I believe so, yes'

'Ah ken him'

*

'The ranks are starting to thin out,' reflected Ginger. 'First Beamish, now Ash; and soon Sticky and me will be on our way.' He looked over his shoulder towards Jock and continued,

'What makes you think you know the new bloke?'

'Oh, ah ken him alright'

'But how?'

'He lived up a wally close doon the road'

'Could you give us a translation Jock?' pleaded Ginger.

'Tenement tae you,' explained Jock. 'Only his hud tiles oan the wa's'

'I'm little the wiser'

'He's the flea that jumped the midden', decreed Jock.

'I give up,' said Ginger.

*

Standing six foot four inches tall with a back like a ramrod, Flight Lieutenant McFarquhar made an imposing entrance into Hut 29 at five o'clock that evening; he was accompanied by Sergeant Jordan, who barked,

'Officer present, stand by your beds'

There was a scuffling of boots as the residents departed the card table, took up their positions and stood rigidly to attention. The officer strutted leisurely down the passageway, glanced occasionally at his new charges and halted briefly at the card table. He moved on without comment and continued to the end of the hut where he turned to address the assembly.

'Before calling upon you, I had just completed my first appraisal of the latrines servicing Huts 1 to 29 and I have to report that the overall standard of hygiene is much below that which I would be prepared to accept'

He looked around for a reaction and got one in the shape of a raised hand. It was that of Ginger.

'Begging your pardon sir, but Flight Lieutenant Ashford

never had no complaints,' he commented.

'Shut your row Harrison or I'll -'

McFarquhar broke in on the sergeant's tirade.

'Airman Harrison is entitled to his observation. I always encourage discourse on matters relating to duty. However, I repeat, the standards are below my expectations, and looking around me, I see why. Can anyone offer an opinion as to why I say that?'

'Not using enough Vim, sir?' suggested Sticky, under Jordan's glare.

'Good try airman, but not Vim the product, vim as in vigour. You are all seriously unfit, and I will remedy that situation forthwith. It is my intention to implement an all-round programme of activity guaranteed to produce exponential results'

'You what, sir?' enquired a bewildered airman.

'I mean that I intend to raise overall fitness levels so that your daily duties will be carried out more efficiently and with the utmost dexterity; more rapidly, in other words. Sergeant Jordan will now post instructions on the prescribed fitness regime'

As Jordan made his way to the billet notice board, McFarquhar walked to where Jock Burns was still standing to attention.

'At ease, airman, do I know you?'

'Sir'

'Burns, isn't it?'

'Sir'

'How are your people?'

'Eh?'

'Your parents, how are they?'

'Ma faither still gets pished every night an' ma mither's still washin' doon wally closes'

'I see…carry on'

He turned to leave but stopped in his tracks to conclude, 'I won't be asking you to do anything that I myself am not prepared to undertake. I shall be taking personal charge of all the fitness routines'

*

'Chuffing Nora,' bleated Ginger as he read the notice. 'Physical jerks at five frigging thirty of a morning followed by a two mile run before breakfast'

'And over the assault course twice a week,' added Scrounger dolefully.

'And two kit inspections daily,' Tiny Loftus reminded them.

'Glad I'm excused,' said Barry.

'How come?' enquired Sticky.

'All this sadism only applies to latrine orderlies. It says so at the foot of the notice'

*

As he fondled the dregs of a pint pot in the saloon bar of the Farmers Arms, Ginger turned to Jock and asked, 'What did you mean when you described McFarquhar as 'the flea that jumped the wotsit'?'

'Midden'

'You what?'

Jock brooded for a moment before replying,

'Ally McWally, as we cried him, was brought up in a wally close by two aunties who idolised him. They spoiled him rotten - prep school, boardin' school, university. He wis the wan that didny huv tae get stoored up dumpin' ash inty the dust bins every mornin', thanks tae them auld biddies'

'But why is he so hooked on getting you lot fit?' enquired Barry out of academic interest.

'Because he's a fitness freak, champion runner, jumper, hurdler, swimmer - schoolboy rugby international -signed fur Queens Park at the fitba' when he wis only fourteen -'

'Bloody hell,' lamented Ginger.

*

Seven days on and McFarquhar's new fitness regime was already having a marked effect on the latrines servicing manpower, but not in the direction intended. Several of their number were in sick bay; one from a hamstring injury occasioned by the early morning runs, another with a broken leg sustained when he fell from a rope wall on the assault course, and three more suffering from general fatigue. Surprisingly perhaps, Ginger was holding up well. Although regularly finishing last, he was nevertheless the only one to complete all of the activities for seven consecutive days.

'First class show Harrison,' shouted the officer as he was energetically fording a stream monkey-style on a greased log. 'You are a shining example for the others to follow'

'Sir'

'It's not winning that matters; it's taking part'

'Falling apart more like,' muttered Ginger.

As the bedraggled troops trudged into the billet at teatime, Tiny Loftus complained, 'This is doing my head in. I'm thinking of going AWOL'

'He can't keep it up for much longer,' suggested someone hopefully. 'We're dropping off like flies'

'Aye, he can,' contradicted Jock. 'He's a bloody sadist. It comes fae a' the kickin's he used tae get as a boy dressed up like Little Lord fuckin' Fontleroy. He's getting' his ain back oan us'

'There must be something you can do,' said Barry. 'It's inhuman'

'Maybe there is a way,' replied Ginger. 'Look Jock, we know he's Mr Superfit, but he must have a weakness. Can you think of anything?'

'Aye, ah can'

'What?'

'Burds, big clatty scrubers an' the rougher the better'

'Don't see how that helps us'

'But it might,' said Barry, picking up the thread. 'Does anyone know what McWally gets up to of an evening?'

'I do,' said Tiny. 'He has a swift lime cordial in the mess after dinner and spends the rest of the night pumping iron in his quarters. He never goes anywhere'

'How do you know that?' asked Ginger.

'Because his batman told me'

Barry's master plan was beginning to take shape. 'Jock, you did say big and rough?'

'Aye'

'They don't come any bigger and rougher than Big Trixie up the NAFFI,' volunteered Scrounger, 'and she'd anything for five bob'

'Sticky,' continued Barry. 'Do you still have that camera your aunt gave you last Christmas?'

'Aye'

'Does it have a spool inside?'

'Oh aye'

'Then how's this for an idea. We catch McFarquhar on film, in his quarters, in a compromising situation with a female decoy'

'Hold up,' countered Scrounger,' when I said she'd do anything for five bob, it didn't include getting into the sack with that scroat'

'Would she do it for a fiver?'

'For a fiver, she'll get togged up in her belly dancer gear, strip him bollock naked - and every other bugger in camp as well'

*

At ten-thirty the following evening, the ingénue blackmailers were secreted behind a bush opposite Flight Lieutenant McFarquhar's self-contained quarters. They watched as Trixie gained admission at the second knock.

'Now, are you absolutely sure there's a spool in the camera?'

'Oh aye,' confirmed Sticky.

'Best have a check on it,' said Ginger, flicking open the retaining cap in the darkness. 'There is, and it's set at the start'

Some ten minutes later on the prescribed signal, a high pitched giggle from Trixie, Scrounger entered through the window conveniently left unlatched by Tiny's friend, the batman. He was wearing a black balaclava with matching slacks and pullover. His mission was over in a flash.

'Right,' said Ginger, removing the spool, 'I'll get this down to Mad Taffy. He'll have it developed overnight and the prints will be ready for uplifting at teatime tomorrow'

'What about Trixie?' asked Barry.

'What about her?' replied Scrounger.

'Will she be okay?'

'She'll be fine'

'What if he calls the SPs - or sets about her?'

'He won't be calling no SPs and if he laid a finger on Trixie, she'd flatten him. I wouldn't put tuppence on his chances of coming out best of three falls. She's a champion all-in wrestler - with cups and all to prove it'

*

'Look at these,' said Ginger in total dismay, 'They're all double images'

'You're a prat Sticky,' moaned Barry. 'The spool was used before'

'Aye, at me mam's on Boxing Day'

'Why didn't you tell us?'

'Ah didn't think it'd matter. Ah thought you used same spool all the time'

'That's it then,' concluded Ginger resignedly. 'We're lumbered'

'Dead lumbered,' growled Jock.

The door of the billet opened to admit Pilot Officer Dawkins and all eyes turned to look on him expectantly.

'At ease chaps,' he greeted them brightly. 'Thought you should be among the first to learn the news'

'What news sir?' asked Ginger, fearing the worst.

'You won't be seeing Flight Lieutenant McFarquhar again. He has just been posted'

'Already?'

'Yes, poor chap, got himself caught up in rather unseemly circumstances last night'

Now they all feared the worst.

'On an anonymous tip-off the local vice squad raided a certain club of ill repute around midnight and arrested Alisdair, among others. The CO took a dim view of the matter and thought it best to get the blighter out of the way, straightaway'

'Would that be Madame Golightly's club, sir?' enquired Scrounger.

'I believe so, yes'

'By the left,' observed Ginger when Dawkins had

departed, 'Ally McWally's proved to be a right raver. But how did he end up there?'

'Trixie took him,' answered Scrounger. 'She's on commission for introducing new punters to the club'

'But who tipped off the rozzers?'

'Trixie'

'What?'

'She's also a coppers nark'

'Whatever, she's well in pocket over this deal,' said Barry.

'Wonder if she'd refund our fiver?' speculated Ginger.

Brylcreem and Brasso

'Only seven more days as bog orderlies and we're out of here and free to do what we want with the rest of our lives,' said Ginger cheerfully as he scrubbed the porcelain basins with more enthusiasm than he'd shown in almost two years.

'Yeah,' agreed Sticky.

'No more kowtowing to old Bandy Jordan'

'Yeah'

'No more camp patrol duties'

'Yeah, an' no more skives'

Ginger eased off on his exertions for a moment and reflected, 'You're right mate. Hadn't reckoned to that, I'll miss the old skiving lark'

'Co-eee,' called a voice from outside.

'That's either Bunny or your mam's come to fetch you home early'

Bunny and Stan entered the latrine in a state of high excitement. 'Guess what?' blurted Stan.

'What?' asked Ginger.

'You'll never guess,' gushed Bunny.

'I know I won't, not if you two keep cackling on like a

couple of hens on heat'

'It's unbelievable'

'Let me have a try. They've found Hitler alive and well and working as a house painter in West Hartlepool'

'Nothing of the sort, you cheeky devil,' said Stan, nudging Ginger. 'Charlie's only managed to book B&B for a one-night stand at a Bradford working men's club'

'Who the chuff are B&B?'

'You, silly, Brylcreem and Brasso'

'Charlie Fazackerley telephoned me first thing this morning,' explained Bunny. 'One of his acts, the Kaye Brothers, have had to call off this evening's performance on account of Billy Kaye pulling a muscle in bed last night'

'Sure it wasn't a cockle?' suggested Ginger. 'He's a right little lothario, so they say'

'Anyway, Charlie's using B&B in their place'

'What do you think to that?' asked Stan.

'We can't do it,' replied Ginger.

'Why ever not?'

'Because it's lights out at midnight and we've got to be tucked up in bed by then or else Old Bandy gets very cross'

'No problemo, Bunny's already arranged for you to appear before your flight commander this afternoon on an application for one night's leave of absence'

'The application will be approved,' added Bunny knowingly. 'Madame Golightly will see to that'

'But what about material for the act?' protested Ginger vehemently.

'You'll repeat the stuff you did in *Final Curtain* – plus some new material that Charlie's dropping off to me later today'

'How do we get there?'

'By service lorry, it's already organised with the MT section. Stan will drive and I'll navigate. We'll stay overnight at a B&B in Bradford'

'Ooooh,' squealed Stan. 'You just made a funny, bunny'

'How much?' asked Ginger suspiciously.

'Three hundred pounds for the act'

'Bloody Nora!'

*

Ginger and Sticky sat in the reception area of the flight commander's office awaiting his arrival back from lunch at the officers mess.

'What if he says no, Ginge?'

'Then we go AWOL. I'll do jankers any day of the week

for three hundred quid'

Ginger got up and looked through the window.

'Here he comes and he's carrying a cargo. Can't keep a straight line – and that's a good sign'

The door opened and Squadron Leader Phartingail ffoulkes-Knight regarded the subjects of his first appointment of the afternoon.

'Waiting for me are you? Be with you in a jiffy'

As he staggered along the corridor Ginger observed, 'Gone for a Jimmy Riddle, he has'

*

'So, you're both bound for a career treading the boards, eh, what?'

'Yes sir,' replied B&B in unison.

'Had a distant relative in the profession once'

'Sir'

'Arthur Chesney. Heard of him, have you?'

'No sir'

'Good old Arthur, stage wallah all his life. Appeared in some films though, silents mainly, before your time. Oh, ah, just remembered. He was in *The Lodger* in 1926, Alfred Hitchcock's first film as director, dreadful piece of nonsense, but no matter.' The flight commander made as if to get up, decided against it and sat down again.

'So, you want one evening's leave of absence from camp?'

'Yes sir'

'Granted, wouldn't stand in the way of a couple of chaps trying to better themselves in Civvy Street'

'Thank you sir'

'Give my regards to old Arthur if you come across him'

'Oh yes sir, we will sir, thank you sir'

*

Stan was making heavy weather of driving the service lorry on the late afternoon journey to Bradford. He was okay while in top but when he had to change down a gear, he invariably slipped the clutch and ripped through the gearbox mesh.

'Have you ever driven one of these before?' questioned Ginger.

'Of course not,' replied Stan petulantly. 'Not a big butch long distance driver, am I?'

'Have you driven *anything* before?'

'Stan is a very accomplished operator on the roads,' chided Bunny, coming to the rescue of his friend. 'He's got a dinky little pink MG sports car that he drives back home'

'Wish he was in it right now,' said Ginger plaintively.

The troupe soldiered on at a steady twenty five miles an hour, above which Stan refused to budge, until they reached the beginnings of the Yorkshire moors. At the outset of the long ascent, Stan dropped to first gear, as did his speed to ten miles an hour. Midway up the slope Sticky announced from the rear container section, of which he was the sole occupant, 'Ah need to go to lav'

'What,' squeaked Stan horrified at the announcement. 'Didn't you go before we left camp?'

'Ah forgot, like'

'You bloody pillock,' chastised Ginger. 'You spend your national service working in the bogs and you forgot to use one before we left?'

'Well, we can't stop here,' decreed Bunny. 'If we did, Stan would never be able to get the lorry going again, up and over the hill'

'He'll just have to hold on to it then,' added Ginger.

'But ah can't,' bleated Sticky. 'Ah'm bursting'

The subject was dropped and they drove in silence for a few minutes until Stan sniffed around and enquired anxiously, 'What's that smell? It's not burning is it?'

'I do not believe this,' replied Bunny.

'He's only just crapped in the back,' said Ginger.

'Ah couldn't help it' protested Sticky remorsefully.

'Open the windows!' screamed Stan. 'You, in the back,

open the rear doors!'

'But Stan, we'll freeze'

'I don't care. I'll do most things I'm asked in the cause of art, but I refuse to be asphyxiated. Refuse point blank, I do'

'Told him he shouldn't have the special for his tea,' announced Ginger loudly. 'Curried eel, Gawd knows what chef puts in it. Cat droppings, by the stench'

*

It was a much-relieved band of thespians who disembarked from the lorry's cab onto the pavement outside the club premises.

'Best get that mess cleaned up good and proper before you come in,' Stan instructed Sticky as he clambered down from the rear backdrop. 'I'm not driving this vehicle back to camp tomorrow morning until it's spick and span'

'But where'll ah get a shovel?'

'That's your problem mate,' said Ginger, 'Go find one and get some stuff to fumigate the inside'

'But where?'

'Ask someone round at the front of the club and have a scrub down while you're there. You're not coming in the stage door with us. You stink'

Ginger looked around the entrance, winced, and remarked to Bunny, 'Bit on the rough side, isn't it?'

'Well, what do you expect; it's a working man's club'

'Looks more like a thieves den to me'

A silent, sepulchral steward escorted them along a damp and dingy basement corridor and nodded towards a tattered door. From behind another door at the far end they could hear snatches of enthusiastic applause.

'This it then, the dressing room like?' asked Ginger but the steward ignored his question and walked away.

They entered to find Charlie Fazackerley already in residence and reclining on a bedraggled sofa.

'Good journey lads?' Charlie enquired.

'Don't ask, 'said Bunny, shuddering.

On a table behind Charlie were stacked a number of cylindrical canisters labelled '*gas fluid – highly inflammable*'.

'What's that then, Charlie?' asked Ginger, indicating the cans.

'They belong to the geyser on right now'

'Going well, whoever he is,' observed Bunny.

'I've not heard such sustained applause in a long time,' confirmed Stan. 'Who is it anyway?'

'One of my acts; The Great Farto'

'You what?'

'The Great Farto'

'You'll be telling us next he does farting as an act'

'Very popular, very successful'

'And he uses these cans in the act?' continued Ginger incredulously.

'Those tins contain the gases for his hand-held blow torch. He holds it against his arse, switches on, farts, and hey presto, instantaneous combustion. He creates gas explosions, one after the other, time after time. Club audiences love it, can't get enough'

'Fucking hell, Brylcreem and Brasso will die on their feet,' predicted Ginger with some agitation. 'How can anyone follow a farting act?'

'Don't worry, I know what I'm doing,' replied Charlie confidently. 'The Great Farto is just warming them up for you'

There was a final round of muted but prolonged applause followed by the door opening to admit a panting visitor. Ginger took the diminutive, mustachioed elf of a man to be the act in question. He was clad only in all-over body stocking and dragged a flame encrusted blow torch across the floor.

'By the left, they're a wild bunch out there tonight,' gasped the visitor. 'They wouldn't let me go, thought I'd blow me rectum off

'What, with the blow torch?' asked Ginger.

'Nay lad, wi' the farting'

*

Ginger's prediction was coming to pass. The first part of the act using the *Final Curtain* material was greeted in total silence but it was during the second part that the trouble really started.

'What have you got in that paper bag?' enquired Brylcreem.

'Fruit,' answered Brasso.

'Give us a piece, yum, yum, I like a nice plum'

'They're olives'

'Then give them back to Olive. They're much too hard'

The hissing began at the back and permeated rapidly through the audience.

'Here's one,' continued Brylcreem bravely. 'Two bishops in a bed together, which one is wearing the nightdress?'

'Dunno'

'Mrs Bishop of course'

Now there were catcalls, booing, and pennies thrown on the stage.

'I say, I say, I say. I've got a date with a tall boy'

'But a tallboy's a big thing with drawers on, isn't it?'

'I know...'

The booing was by this time universal and some wag shouted, 'Gerroff, ye're crap. Bring the farter back'

Ginger decided to take them on and started with the heckler, 'Where do you come from pal?'

'Leeds, and proud of it'

'Best be off then. There's a bus leaving in ten minutes. Make sure you're under it'

And so Ginger prevailed against the abuse for some time before walking off the stage to a smattering of applause. Sticky loped after him disconsolately.

*

In the pub across the road after the show, Charlie handed over a bundle of notes in large denominations. Ginger counted them rapidly.

'What's this?' Ginger flared. 'It's short, and after all that we bollocking we had to put up with'

'No it's not short lad. That's your agreed fee less thirty per cent. My standard commission is fifteen but I had expenses to cover on account of the late booking'

'Like what?'

'Travelling to Bradford to set things up for the act'

'Set us up, you mean'

'Now then'

'They hated us. The only setting up you did was to shove us on after your farting act'

'If they hated you, why am I sitting on a contract for six more appearances at the same money?'

'What?'

'Look lad, when working men's club audiences watch an act for the first time they always give it the bird, but when the act heckles them back, they love it. Brylcreem and Brasso are in on the club circuit'

'So,' said Ginger, brightening up, 'That means next time we get…'

'In hand, two hundred and fifty five quid a performance for the act, how long would it take you to knock up that kind of money on a building site?

*

As Ginger and Sticky donned their pajamas in the tiny attic room of the overnight digs, Sticky had a thought.

'Shouldn't we give Bunny and Stan summat?'

'I've already seen to it, gave them thirty quid apiece. They're knocked out'

'Nice place here Ginge'

'Aye, soft mattress and all'

'Beats the hard biscuits we have to lie on in camp'

'Just like home, eh?'

'Better 'n that. Ah don't have to put up with me brothers making rude noises' all night'

'Think yourself lucky then you're sleeping with me and not the Great Farto'

*

Next morning as the lorry was shaking off the dust of Bradford and making its way out of town towards the A62, Bunny let out a shriek.

'Oh, look Stan! They've named a theatre after us'

'Ooooooh, yes'

Ginger looked backwards over his shoulder to ascertain the source of the excitement and his gaze fell upon the outline of an unkempt old edifice with the word QUEENS screaming out in large garish letters from an equally unkempt vintage sign.

'Chuffing stroll on,' he muttered.

Halfway up the ascent on the moors a voice called from the back.

'Ah'll have to go'

Stan pulled over to the side, switched off the engine, lay his head on the steering wheel and wept.

Discharged

'With a blow torch, I don't believe it,' said Scrounger.

'Straight up, he walks out on stage, farts, lights up, and whoosh!'

Ginger was regaling the residents of Hut 29 with the happenings of the previous evening in Bradford, but at Sticky's insistence he omitted to inform them of the unfortunate incidents that occurred in the back of the lorry. He'd save that until later.

'Wi' that kind of money for a night's work,' remarked Del with a tinge of jealousy, 'you two will like as not be rich in a few months'

'Maybe aye, maybe no, if it works out all right, fine. If it doesn't, Sticky and me will set up as jobbing builders with whatever brass we manage to save'

'At any rate,' added Tiny Loftus, 'it'll be a good start for you, better than anything the rest of us can look forward to'

'Where's Barry?' asked Ginger.

'Off up the NAFFI to phone his bird'

'Getting serious then?'

'He's been out with her ten nights in a row'

'Jeez! Hope he takes time off for me demob party'

'And mine,' said Sticky significantly.

'And yours pal. So folks, it's tonight, and the drinks are all on Sticky and me'

'Glad to hear that. I'm skint'

'Scrounger,' replied Ginger, 'you've been skint since you got here eighteen months ago'

'Farmers Arms then?' enquired Tiny for confirmation.

'Yes, six o' clock until chucking out time'

Just then Barry entered the billet, looking pleased with himself.

'Hey up Barry,' said Ginger. 'All set for the piss-up tonight?'

'Sorry Ginge, I can't make it'

Ginger made no reply but looked crestfallen.

'I've got some news for you'

'What?'

'I've just become engaged'

'Chuffing hell,' said Ginger in astonishment.

'Got her up the duff already, have you?' said Scrounger maliciously.

'Of course he hasn't,' snapped Ginger. 'It's only pricks

like you that get caught out.' He paused, and then continued gently, 'You haven't, have you Barry?'

'No, hardly, I've only known her for a fortnight. Anyway, it's love, true love. Hazel and I are being married soon. We think it's pointless to wait, the way we feel about each other'

'Too right son,' said Ginger encouragingly, 'you always know what's best Barry'

'I've got another piece of news'

'Bloody Nora, there's more?'

'I'm signing on for three years so I can be near Hazel'

'But Barry mate,' cautioned Ginger, 'it don't always work out that way. What if you get a new posting?'

'I thought about that and made it a condition before signing on as a regular that they keep me at Padgate for at least two years'

'Well, that's okay then'

'And I get made up to corporal – plus the bounty money after three years'

'You're quids in'

'Ginge?'

'Yeah'

'Will you be my best man?'

'It'd be my pleasure. I'll give you me my home address and you can tip me the wink when it's happening. We can have us our own private piss-up then'

'What about me?' protested Sticky.

'You're invited too,' replied Barry.

'You can be best maid,' said Ginger dryly.

*

Ginger consigned his bucket, mop, wet cloths and dusters to the stockroom cupboard for the final time.

'That's it Sticky, last bulling session ever in here'

'Aye'

'Just think. A couple of sprogs straight out of square bashing will be taking over tomorrow morning from where we left off; that were us two years ago'

'Aye, it were'

As they were about to lock up and leave Sergeant Jordan made an appearance.

'Stand easy!' he barked, proceeding thereafter to make a tour of inspection. He examined the wash basins, the cubicles, and cast a searching eye over the walls. 'Cleanest I've ever seen. Good work'

The departing orderlies glanced at one another in amazement at this unprecedented compliment.

Jordan's stern face regarded each of them in turn.

'You've been nothing but a pain in the arse since you first arrived here, but – I've known worse'

'Sarge,' replied Ginger at a complete loss to say more.

Jordan marched off but turned around again at the exit. 'Going on the stage are you?'

'Yes sarge'

'You should do well'

'Thank you sarge'

'You're bloody barstard clowns, the pair of you, and you always will be'

*

The newest candidates for demobilisation welcomed their guests in the snug room of the Farmers Arms where they had laid on an abundance of filled sandwiches as well as free drinks until closing time.

'Why did you invite them two?' said Del to Sticky, pointing to Barbara and Dorothy who were sitting together at a corner table. 'Demob piss-ups is for mates only'

'They are me mates'

'How can they be? You knocked up both of them a few months back. You don't tub your mates, now do you?'

'Ah do'

Standing at the bar just behind them Ginger was holding court with Scrounger and Tiny in attendance.

'Ah'll have to go, he says, and then he crapped in the back of the lorry'

'Never'

'Not only that but he nearly did it again on the way home'

'You promised you'd say nowt about it,' said Sticky accusingly.

'Ah, but that were in the billet. I didn't make no promises about not telling them in the pub'

Sticky walked away in a huff to join the company of his lady friends.

*

Ginger and Sticky boarded the train for Gloucester and their final port of call as national servicemen. They found an empty compartment and took up seats facing each other by the door.

'By heck, I'm fair parched,' said Ginger.

Pulling the window down he hailed a passing refreshments trolley.

'What have you got to drink mate?'

'Lemonade, orange squash, lime cordial – '

'Any beer?'

'Fowlers Wee Heavy, OBJ – '

'Anything softer, I don't want to be pissed when we reach Gloucester'

'Pale ale'

'That'll do. Give us just a round dozen of your screw tops and have one yourself'

The next morning they attended the last pay parade and collected their discharge certificates from the demobilisation centre.

'Well, that's it then Sticky mate. We're civilians again'

'Ah'll miss the lads,' replied Sticky mournfully.

'Never mind, we'll go back for a visit and we'll have brass in our pockets to treat them'

'That'll be nice'

'But think on. Someday soon they'll be gone too. Even Bandy Jordan and old Farty Night will have to go sometime'

'Sad, isn't it?'

'Sad be bolloxed,' Ginger disagreed. 'Nothing lasts forever. You have to keep moving on to survive'

'Aye, well...'

'Cheer up. You know what Bunny and Stan would say. The show must go on'

'Happen they're right'

Printed by Amazon Italia Logistica S.r.l.
Torrazza Piemonte (TO), Italy

11746118R00216